WANTED:
Dead or Alive

**Center Point
Large Print**

**This Large Print Book carries the
Seal of Approval of N.A.V.H.**

WANTED: Dead or Alive

A Western Duo

RAY HOGAN

CENTER POINT LARGE PRINT
THORNDIKE, MAINE

This Circle Ⓥ Western is published by
Center Point Large Print in 2015 in co-operation with
Golden West Literary Agency.

First Edition
March 2015

Printed in the United States of America
on permanent paper.
Set in 16-point Times New Roman type.

ISBN: 978-1-62899-489-6 (hardcover)
ISBN: 978-1-62899-494-0 (paperback)

Library of Congress Cataloging-in-Publication Data

Hogan, Ray, 1908–1998.
[Novels. Selections]
Wanted : dead or alive : a western duo / Ray Hogan. — Center Point
Large Print edition.
pages cm
Summary: "In two western stories, two lone travelers have their plans
change unexpectedly when they happen upon people in need of help"
—Provided by publisher.
ISBN 978-1-62899-489-6 (hardcover : alk. paper)
ISBN 978-1-62899-494-0 (pbk. : alk. paper)
1. Large type books. I. Title.
PS3558.O3473A6 2015
813′.54—dc23
                                                          2014046961

Table of Contents

Between Life and Death

I

Dade Lockett drew the big chestnut gelding he was riding to a quick halt in the deep brush. The muted thud of horses walking nearby had come to him through the darkening hush arousing instantly the quick caution that countless days and nights on remote and lonely trails instills in all men. Silent, broad hand resting lightly on the worn butt of the pistol on his hip, he waited, listened. Somewhere ahead in the valley he was entering, a cow lowed mournfully, and high above it a limp, ragged column of crows winging westward etched themselves blackly against the gray sky.

He heard the sound again, this time more distinct and accompanied by the dry swish of displaced branches whipping back into place. Fingers tightening about the handle of his weapon, he fixed his eyes on a dense stand of oak brush off to his right where the noise seemed to originate. He froze as a voice cut through the stillness.

"Forget it, mister!"

Lockett allowed his hand to slide away, hang at his side. There were two of them, and they had come in on him from opposite points that indicated they had spotted him before he had become aware of their presence. He settled back gently, swore; both were wearing flour sacks over their heads in which holes had been cut for eyes and mouths—night riders.

The pair closed in, one to the left, the other to his right. The sacks, bleached bone white in the failing light, had a draw string that held them snugly about the neck and allowed the lower portion, slashed at the sides, to spread over the shoulders. These were no spur-of-the-moment, makeshift masks, Dade realized; undoubtedly they were being used regularly. Their horses, ordinary-looking bays, were unbranded, as could be expected. He studied the riders briefly, shrugged.

"Well, what's on your mind?"

The man on his offside leaned forward, rested a forearm on the horn of his saddle. "Don't go getting wise with us or we'll mighty quick show you," he said in a hard voice. "Now, what're you doing here?"

"Riding through."

"To where?"

Lockett shook his head. He was on open range as far as he knew, and unless somebody'd got around to changing the custom, a man had the right to travel across such land as long as he did no damage and caused no trouble. "Don't see as it's any put-in of yours where I'm . . ."

"Making it my put-in!" the masked rider snapped, and reached for the coil of rope hanging from his saddle.

Dade Lockett smiled bleakly. "Now, if you're thinking about using that on me, best you change your mind," he drawled, his voice low, almost kind.

The man hesitated, glanced at his partner. "There's two of us, only one of you," he said. "You figure you can handle them odds?"

"I reckon. One thing for sure, when you get done making your move there'll only be one of us left and it'll be me or your friend there. Sure won't be you."

"Leave off the rope," the rider on the right said. His voice sounded deeper, more muffled. "Ain't no call for it near as I can see. Says he's riding through, maybe that's what he's doing."

"Then why's he so god-damn' jumpy about answering questions?"

"Expect it's them flour sacks," Lockett said mildly. "Always had me a sort of a thing about talking to somebody I couldn't see. Now, were you to pull them off . . ."

"Nope, guess not," the second man said. "This here place you're riding through to . . . it around close?"

"Place I'm heading for ain't so close, it being Tucson. Where I'm going right this minute I ain't sure."

"Could it be to some folks named Raker?"

"Raker? Never heard of them. I was told there was a town called Mule Springs, however."

Silence greeted that. Finally the man with the rope said: "What're you going there for? You got yourself a job of some kind lined up?"

Dade grinned, wagged his head. "You sure got the knack for asking questions that ain't none of your business."

"I'm making it my business."

"Then I suppose we'd just better figure on going 'round and 'round. Who'll open the ball, you or me?"

"Never mind," the other rider cut in wearily. "Ain't no call for this . . . and it's getting late. We've got something else better to do. Mister, you say you're just plain riding through, that go for Mule Springs, too?"

"Far as I'm concerned."

"Then move on. We ain't going to give you no trouble long as you keep going."

"Well, I sure thank you. It's mighty seemly," Lockett said dryly. "Yes, sir, it purely is."

The rider to his left swore angrily. "You looky here, saddle bum! If you . . ."

"Easy," Dade said, raising his hands in mock protest. "Just showing how much I appreciate what you fellows are doing for me. Were I you, however, I'd get on about that business your partner was mentioning. I've got me a funny feeling that if we're together much longer, things are going to start happening and I sure don't want to be responsible for that."

12

The rider cursed again, spurred forward. "By God, I ain't . . ."

"Aw, come on, let's get going," his partner said, quickly riding in between the two. "Rest of the boys're probably waiting on us."

The masked man swung off, muttering oaths. His friend cut in beside him, looked back to Dade. "Mule Springs is about a dozen miles straight south. Head out."

Lockett made no reply, simply watched the pair fade off into the brush. Somebody was due for trouble, he reckoned, remembering what had been said; visits from hooded night riders were never sociable affairs. After a moment he glanced to the sky. A while yet until full dark, and the man had said it was around twelve miles to the town where he'd intended to rent himself a room in a hotel, spend a night in a real bed, under a ceiling for a change. He guessed he could still make it if he pushed right along.

Gauging his directions by the flare hanging in the west, he moved on, thoughts again shifting to the masked men. Everybody had trouble, it seemed—including him. His had begun three years ago and centered on a man named Pete Dillard. He'd been just past twenty then, and Dillard around double that. But Pete had had a way about him that wiped out the age difference, and being wise and smooth and expert in many things, he had drawn Dade Lockett to him. They had knocked about together for a time and then the opportunity had come to hit it big—to get rich. A stagecoach carrying close to $50,000 was making a run from one of the Colorado mining towns to Denver. There'd been no hold-ups in the area for years, Dillard had learned, and the coach would have no extra guards. Relieving it of all the gold would be a lead-pipe cinch.

They'd laid plans, or rather Pete Dillard, the expert, had, and the stagecoach was duly stopped and robbed. The only thing wrong was that there was nearer $2,000 in gold coin in the strongbox, than $50,000, and then afterward, during the escape from a posse quickly formed, Dade caught a bullet that knocked him off the saddle while another killed his horse. Dillard had not paused to give the help he could so easily have rendered, had instead hurried on with the gold and left Lockett to the posse, and to a judge who, a month or so later, sentenced him to a two-year term in the territorial prison. Bitter, disillusioned, his hatred for Pete Dillard had increased with each passing day spent behind the high, grim walls of the reformatory, and when his time was finally finished and he was once again a free man, he set out to right the wrong he felt had been done him.

Working his way down into New Mexico, he found himself a job on a Río Arriba cattle ranch, built up his tack as well as his poke. Then, ready at last, he bought the horse he was riding from the rancher for whom he rode and started on the search for Pete Dillard. His so-called friend and partner was somewhere in Arizona Territory, according to a rumor he had picked up. Likely he would be found in the Tucson area; he had spoken of the town, had a yen someday to have himself a ranch close by. It was a long shot, Dade realized, but it was all he had to go on, and, bearing that in mind, he took pains to make inquiries for Dillard in all of the settlements and at the ranches he encountered along the way. It would take time, perhaps years, for during the three that had elapsed since the stagecoach robbery, Pete Dillard could have moved about considerably.

It didn't matter to Dade; one thing he had learned in prison was a bitter sort of patience of a kind that caused him to look upon the world and all who populated it with hard, sardonic humor. Someday he'd find Pete, and when he did, he'd collect his half of the stolen gold for which he had paid with two years of his life—and then he'd kill Pete Dillard for leaving him behind to die when he could so easily have helped him escape. He had it all worked out. Pete would die but it would be in a manner that would not cause him again to face prison. While waiting for the day to come, he had spent time and effort in honing his already considerable abilities with a six-gun; it would simply be a matter of calling out Dillard, forcing him to draw, and shooting him down.

That way the law would let it pass, it having been a fair contest with the faster man the winner. But that would come only after he had collected his share of the gold.

Lockett drew the gelding to a halt once more. A light, soft and yellowish, was ahead through the trees—a ranch, or some squatter. He'd stop there, ask a few questions concerning Dillard, and move on if the answers were the same as all those received before when he'd paused along the way to inquire . . . A few more minutes reaching Mule Springs would make no big difference.

Lockett moved on through the brush, almost a solid wall of mock-orange, doveweed, and briar bush at that point, broke finally into the open. With the chestnut tossing his head and snorting from the clawing branches, Dade again drew to a stop. The valley now lay before him, a broad, sweeping expanse rimmed by fairly high ridges to the east and west, limitless plains to the south and north. The amber light of day's end lay upon it all in a gentle glow, but in the washes and other hollows darkness was now beginning to build. Lockett sat motionlessly for a time, drinking in the scene while the long, deep loneliness that occasionally touched him came, placed its stillness within him, and then as his eyes drifted on to settle upon the small ranch house just ahead, the remoteness that gripped him became more pronounced.

He had never known the warmth and love of a home such as this represented. That it was small, appeared in gross disrepair, and presented only the poorest of aspects, did not matter; it by far surpassed the string of orphanages he had known as a boy, struggling to grow up in one of the larger Eastern cities. And looking at it now, seeing the peaceful, friendly glow of lamplight in the windows, smelling the good smell of wood smoke curling up into the gathering night sky, he was moved as always to think of what he had missed in life—of what might have been. But such thoughts were without rancor; there was no one to blame, that had simply been his lot and he accepted it now as he had done while a boy. But there had always been hope and for such he had looked when he grew large enough to escape the sooted, cold buildings and brick streets of his birthplace and make his way west to the frontier where there was excitement, adventure, and fortunes to be had.

It was a different world, he discovered, but one that posed the identical problem he'd faced before—that of survival. In this the raw, new West was no different from the cold, bloodless East; it was a matter of holding your own against all comers or be ground under, and this Dade Lockett did, filling his swiftly passing young years with time in the gambling halls, the wild trail towns, the roaring gold camps, the noisy saloons. And then one day he'd met Pete Dillard. Lockett shook off his dark thoughts. Tipping back his head, he sniffed the still, warm air. Coffee boiling on a stove. Fresh bread. Frying meat. At once he roweled the chestnut. Maybe he could wangle an invitation to a good supper, or, if necessary, buy himself a seat at the rancher's table. In either instance the answer could be no worse than a flat no, and a man telling him that'd sure get no . . . A spatter of gunshots ripped through the hush. Lockett hauled up short as half a dozen riders, white cloths over their heads showing up ghost-like in the gloom, burst from the line of brush to the east of the yard, firing as they came.

Dade swore, settled back to watch. This was the unlucky rancher the night riders had planned to visit. Evidently the two he'd run into were scouting the area prior to the actual raid. They probably thought he was someone, a hired gun perhaps, the rancher had hired on to help him fight. The raiders surged toward the house in a fairly straight line, triggering their pistols at whatever struck them as targets. A sudden splash of light fell across the yard as the door to the house was flung open. A man, young, possibly even a boy from his bearing, ran into view, a rifle in his hands. He dropped to one knee on the hardpan, began firing at the masked riders. They broke formation at once, and swung apart into several directions.

Another figure came through the doorway. A girl. She looked to be about the same age as the boy. She had what appeared to be a single-barreled shotgun, and, bracing it against her shoulder, she released a blast at the nearest raider. It was a clean miss, for the man at whom the load of shot was aimed gave no indication of having been hit, but continued on. Yells sounded from the rear of the house. A third person, an old man with bowed legs, white hair shining in the weak light, was crossing the yard at a shambling run. He evidently had been in the bunkhouse when the attack started, and was trying now to join with the other members of the family. A hooded rider, sweeping around the corner of the low-roofed structure, swerved in his course, spurring his mount directly for the oldster. The horse, instinctively striving to avoid hitting the man, shied wildly but his rider savagely jerked him back on course. He struck the old man a glancing blow, knocked him into a pile of split wood near the back door of the house.

Lockett frowned, turned his attention back to the front. The boy was down, sprawled in the dust. The girl had snatched up the rifle, was frantically attempting to lever a fresh cartridge into its chamber. The mechanism had jammed and she was having no luck—nor would she, Dade knew;

19

the particular weapon involved was well known for its tendency to falter. The night riders began to shout back and forth among themselves, laughing, making jokes. The one who had downed the old man cut back to rejoin his companions, now closing in on the girl in a half circle.

"Get a torch, somebody!" a voice shouted. "Might as well do this up right."

"There's burning wood 'round back."

"Get some!" the first voice directed. "We'll be corralling the gal."

The girl threw the useless rifle aside, began to back toward the house. Two of the riders spurred toward her.

"Whoa-up, lady!" the one to her left shouted, laughing. "Ain't no cause for you being scared!"

"No, ma'am!" the other added. "We're just aiming to have us a little fun with you. You sure won't mind that none, will you?"

The girl stumbled over the old shotgun. She stooped, grabbed it by the barrel, prepared to swing it as a club. "Stay back!" she warned.

The two men halted before her, laughing. Other riders in the yard had paused to watch. "There ain't no use you acting that way," one called. "It's all coming out the same in the end, anyways!"

Dade Lockett, a man not inclined ever to horn in on another's affairs, scrubbed angrily at the stubble on his jaw. Getting himself mixed up in a quarrel like this was the last thing he wanted. He

20

had his own plans, his own problems, and they certainly didn't include bucking up against a bunch of hooded night riders. Still, having spent all of his cognizant life with the short end of the string as his lot, he had a natural affinity for the underdog, and, too, the odds were all wrong. The two men on the place were both down and now the band of raiders were moving in to grab the girl, carry her off to somewhere for their amusement. It was pretty hard to look the other way, and he reckoned he'd best break his rule this one time and see if he couldn't put a stop to at least what was about to happen to the girl. Then he could ride on.

Coming to a decision, Dade drew his pistol and, jamming spurs into the gelding's flanks, spurted from the brush into the open. The quick thudding of the gelding's driving hoofs brought attention to him immediately. He saw the pair near the girl pause, look toward him. Leveling the .45, he sent a bullet at the one to his right. The rider jerked away, wheeled his horse about. The others, taking their cue from him, cut in beside him, began to move toward Lockett uncertainly.

Dade threw two more shots directly at them. A yell of pain went up and a man near the center of the party clawed at his arm. Lockett grinned, triggered another bullet as he continued straight on. The line of night riders wavered. Their horses began to shy and mill nervously, making it difficult for the men astride them to get set and make use of their weapons with any effectiveness. Another cry of pain sounded, followed by a string of deep, harsh oaths. Immediately the party split, half lining out for the brush to the east while those remaining whirled, hammered for the corner of the house where they apparently hoped to make a stand.

Lockett veered sharply as a burst of bullets whipped by him. He felt one pluck at his sleeve, another at his hat, and he grinned bleakly. Bending lower over the saddle, he emptied his pistol at the cluster of raiders, jammed the weapon back into its holster, and jerked the Henry repeater from the boot. Levering the rifle with one hand, he brought it up level and fired. At the blast of the heavier weapon the last of the riders pulled away, curved off into the closing darkness, and raced for the band of brush into which their friends had disappeared.

Lockett brought the chestnut to a halt, his lean, hard-cut face turning toward the ragged growth beyond the yard where the night riders had sought safety. He was no man to fool himself; there were half a dozen of them, only one of him—and surprise had been on his side. This would become apparent to them shortly, and the chances were better than good they would take steps to rectify their poor showing. Best be ready.

III

At once Lockett raked the chestnut with his spurs and, pivoting, doubled back across the yard to where the girl crouched over the wounded rancher. Throwing himself from the saddle, he kneeled beside her.

"Inside . . . we're making mighty good targets out here," he said, sliding his arms under the man's body.

The girl turned her strained, taut face to him. She would be no more than eighteen, he guessed, and badly frightened. Lips tight, she nodded and, coming to her feet, started for the house. Lockett, rising, glanced at the man in his arms as he followed. About the same age as the girl, possibly a year or two older. *Husband and wife—or brother and sister?* Dade wondered as he stepped into the usual combination kitchen, dining, and living room area of the ranch house. Kicking the door shut with a heel, he glanced inquiringly at the girl.

"In there," she replied, and pointed into an adjoining room.

Dade carried the boy into the area, laid him on the bed banked against the rear wall. He seemed barely conscious although his injury appeared to be no more than a bad flesh wound in the leg.

"There's another one out back," Lockett said then, moving toward the door.

The girl's features stiffened. "Renzo! Did they kill . . . ?"

"Don't know. One of them rode him down. Could be he just got a bad bumping. I'll fetch him," Dade said, and then paused, made a motion at the windows. "Draw the shades. Got to block off the light."

Continuing then, he crossed the room to the rear door, pulled it open, and stepped out onto the narrow landing. The old man was sitting up near the woodpile dazedly rubbing his head. Dade took him by the arm, pulled him upright.

"Let's be getting inside," he said and, hanging the slight figure over his shoulder, carried him into the house and deposited him in a worn, leather rocking chair standing in the center of the room.

"The little gal . . . the boy . . . they all right?"

At the oldster's mumbled question Lockett stepped back, nodded. "Boy's hurt some. Girl's fine."

He eyed the man critically. Renzo, she had called him. He was a small, wiry cowhand with a sharp, veined face, stringy gray mustache and beard, a cap of snow-white hair. He would be well up in his sixties, but despite his years, he seemed to be suffering from no more than the hard jolt given him by the night rider's horse. Given a few more minutes he should be all right. Lockett started to ask about the raiders, decided it was not the time, and, turning about, glanced around the house. The girl had not bothered to pull the oilcloth shades that hung above the windows, had instead closed the wooden shutters. Her better judgment pleased Dade, and, moving up to the nearest, he opened it a narrow crack and looked out.

The yard, its hard-packed surface shining in the moonlight, was empty. It could mean the hooded raiders had pulled off, did not plan to make a second attack. If such had been their intention, it was only logical to think they would have struck before then, not held off and permitted those inside the house to get prepared. He hoped that was the case; he could then be on his way.

Closing the wooden panel, Dade locked it and crossed the room to the bedroom where the girl was working over the wounded man. A pan of steaming water, a bottle of some sort of antiseptic, and a stack of clean, white cloths were on a table nearby. She glanced around as he filled the doorway.

"Renzo . . . is he . . . ?"

"Doing fine. Horse just knocked him flat. Probably could use a drink of whiskey more'n anything else. How's your husband?"

She turned back to the chore of completing the bandage on the boy's leg. "He's my brother Clint," she said. "My name's Roxanne. We're the

Rakers." She hesitated, added: "I'm . . . we're grateful to you, Mister . . . Mister . . . ?"

"Name's Dade Lockett. You don't owe me no thanks. Kind of odds you were up against called for help from anybody around. Just happened I was close by."

The girl nodded, continued with the bandage. Lockett considered her with interest. She had a quiet, refined way of speaking that assured him she had come from some other part of the country—the East undoubtedly—and her name—Roxanne—that was a new one on him. He'd never heard it before. Roxanne Raker—it sure had a fine ring to it.

She looked up at him suddenly as if remembering something. "The whiskey," she said, pointing toward the shelving in the far corner of the kitchen. "It's up there."

Lockett retraced his steps into the adjoining room and made his way to the specified corner behind the stove. Searching about in the mason jars of preserved fruit and vegetables, he finally located a pint bottle of liquor. It had never been opened, he noticed, and, pulling the cork, he returned to where Renzo was slumped in the leather rocker. The old man nodded as Dade halted before him.

"Ain't sure where you come from, friend, but I'm mighty thankful you showed up when you did."

"Forget it," Lockett said, and handed the bottle to him. "Take a swig at this. It'll fix you up good."

Renzo accepted the whiskey, downed a healthy swallow, and smiled. "Just the kind of medicine I was needing. Clint . . . you said he was some hurt."

"Caught himself a slug in the leg. Be laid up for a spell. Nothing worse than that."

Renzo heaved a sigh. "Real pleased to hear that. With him gone I just don't know what the little gal would do. What about them jaspers? They still hanging around?"

"Maybe. No sign of them. Could be lying back in the brush, getting set to try again. You some kin to the Rakers?"

"Nope, just sort of a hired hand doing whatever's needful."

"You all the help they got?"

"Yep, just me."

Lockett shook his head. A boy barely a man, a young girl clearly out of the world she ordinarily could be found in, and a stove-up old cowhand trying to run a ranch, small wonder they were having little if any success. He turned as the girl came into the room, carrying the pan of water and other medical items, stopped in front of Renzo, and peered anxiously at him.

"Don't fret none," the old man said quickly. "Ain't nothing wrong with me. I been hurt worse shaving myself."

Roxanne smiled, breaking the taut lines of her face. She was dark-haired, had light blue eyes, and a dusky skin. The dress she was wearing, a plain, cotton print, set off a good, well-proportioned figure.

"Your brother doing all right?" Lockett asked.

"He's in pain but there's nothing serious. The wound was a clean one. The bullet went straight through." The girl hesitated, faced Lockett. "I'm grateful to you for what you've done. I'm telling you so again because I really am. If you hadn't come along . . . if we hadn't got Clint inside, there's no telling what those men would have done."

"Ain't hard to figure," Renzo said grimly. "And it ain't over yet."

Lockett wheeled, crossed to the window. Again opening the shutter slightly, he studied the open ground fronting the ranch house and the line of brush fringing its far edge. There was no one to be seen. He turned, met the girl's anxious gaze. "Think maybe they've given it up," he said.

Her shoulders went down with relief, and, nodding, she moved on into the kitchen area. Renzo scratched at his jaw thoughtfully.

"Expect they're gone for the night, but it sure ain't over. Thing is they wasn't looking for somebody like our friend here."

"Folks call me Dade . . . Dade Lockett."

The old cowpuncher extended his hand. "I'm Renzo Clark. Mighty pleased to know you."

"Same here."

"Like I said it sort've caught them flat-footed, and they ain't sure what to do."

Roxanne, emptying the pan of water out the back door, hung it on a nail in the wall, moved up to the stove. "They'll know . . . and they'll be back. Grosinger isn't one to quit until he has what he wants." The girl's voice was low, laced with despair.

Renzo nodded solemnly. "That's for certain, but I'm betting that bunch of his'll be a mite careful next time they come a faunching in here. I didn't see nothing, me getting knocked slantwise by that horse, but I could sure hear the shooting. You nick any of them, Dade?"

"A couple," Lockett replied. "Not bad but they won't be comfortable for a spell. You mind telling me what the ruckus is all about? And who's Grosinger?"

Roxanne, in the act of setting plates, knives, forks, and other such items on the table, shrugged. "It's a long story. Began when my father was killed . . . murdered," she said. "We can talk about it after supper, that is, if you'll stay and eat with us?"

Lockett smiled. "Sure wouldn't want to put you out none."

"You won't be. There's plenty and it's all ready except for dishing it up."

"Got me a whiff of it while I was out in the brush."

"Then you'll stay?" the girl pressed eagerly.

"Yes, ma'am," Lockett said. "And I can tell right now it's going to be a real treat."

IV

Lockett and Renzo Clark took chairs at the table. Roxanne, after a quick glance at her brother to assure herself he required no attention, began to place the food before them—fried meat, warm light bread, several vegetables, fresh butter and honey, hot apple pie, and coffee. For Dade, a solitary man most often on the trail eating his own cooking, it was a meal he would not soon forget. Finished, he leaned back, sighed comfortably. "Sure can't thank you enough," he said to the girl. "For somebody like me that kind of supper comes along maybe once in a lifetime."

Roxanne smiled, her wide-set eyes glowing from the compliment. Renzo gulped the last bit of his pie, sloshed it down with a swallow of coffee, and brushed at his mouth with the back of a hand. "Them's the kind of vittles we get around here regular," he said, reaching for his pipe and tobacco. Looking up through his shaggy brows at the girl, he added: "One of the real good things that comes from working for the Rakers."

Lockett made no comment, dug into his pocket for the makings, and began to roll himself a cigarette. Across the table Roxanne took up the granite coffee pot and refilled the cups.

"You was asking about our trouble," Clark said, striking a match to his charred bowled old briar.

"Was just wondering," Dade said, "but I reckon I already know what it's all about. Always the same, seems . . . big man trying to take over the little one."

"That's just what's happening," the girl said. "There are several ranchers who would like to have our place. It's at the head of the valley."

"Was we of the notion," Renzo pointed out, "we could close off the range, keep everybody from going through."

"Which is something we never intend to do," Roxanne continued. "My father assured John Grosinger, and all the others in the valley, that it would never happen. That there will always be a trail to the north across our land. Clint and I have repeated that promise but they don't want to accept our word."

"Reckon you're meaning *he* . . . not they. It's John Grosinger we're talking about," Renzo growled. "Ain't nobody else giving us trouble."

Lockett nodded. "Wants the land himself so's he'll not only be sure the trail will never be closed but so's he can close it himself if ever he wants.

Who is this John Grosinger? Has he got the biggest spread around here?"

"Yes, the Diamond G, he calls it," the girl replied. "When my father came here about three years ago, this ranch was owned by a man named Fedderman. He wasn't doing much with it and my father bought him out. He started fixing up the place and brought in some cattle . . ."

"That's when Grosinger and a few of the others began flirting their ears and taking notice," Renzo broke in. "Long as nobody was doing anything special with the place, they didn't pay it no mind. But soon as Charley Raker started making a real ranch out of it, then that there was a different pair of boots we was talking about."

"Grosinger the only big outfit in the valley?"

"Well, no, there's Ed Cushman," the girl said. "He's to the south of us. He's almost big as Grosinger, but the two men aren't anything alike. Mister Cushman's an old family friend."

"Offered to buy you out same as Grosinger," Clark said.

"I know, but only if we finally decide to sell. He says it's up to us, strictly, but that if we do, he's asking for first chance to make a deal."

"And if he gets the place," Renzo said, "it'll make his C-Bar-C a bigger layout than Grosinger's."

"I can understand why John Grosinger's anxious to take over," Lockett said. "Those night riders, are they working for him?"

"Who else?" Roxanne answered with a small twitch of her shoulders. "Mister Cushman would never stoop to that . . . and he was always a friend of my father's."

Dade studied the tip of his dead cigarette thoughtfully. The story was not a new one—and certainly none of his business. He had his own problem—that of tracking down Pete Dillard and settling with him. But conversation was welcome after so many empty days and nights on the move, the company pleasant, and the coffee good. "Has this been going on ever since your pa took over the ranch?"

"Just about. Actually, Renzo can tell you more about that. He went to work for Father when he bought out Fedderman. Clint and I didn't come until about a year later. You see, after Mother died, my father left us with an aunt . . . back in Indiana. The town was called Frenchman's Crossing. He came West and the plan was to send for us when he had a place for us to settle down and make a home. It took ten years but he finally did."

"Weren't much trouble to start with," Clark said. "Reckon they figured Charley was just like Fedderman and wouldn't last no longer'n a June bug in a chicken pen. But Charley fooled them. Rebuilt this shack into a house like it is now, got a garden to growing, brung in some livestock, and put some cows to grazing right fast. By the end of that first year he was going good. Then . . ."

The old man paused, shrugged. Lockett nodded and said: "That's when things started happening."

"Just about. First off, howsomever, he sent for Roxie and Clint. Was right after they got here that trouble busted loose. First there was some fires. Part of the range was burned off. Then one night a shed caught on fire."

"Masked men, like those calling on you this evening?"

"We never knew," the girl said. "Nobody ever saw who did it. It just happened. We lost some cattle, too, about fifty head. That's when my father was murdered. He set out to follow the steers. We didn't know he was going to do it, and when he failed to come home that night and the next morning, we got worried and began to search for him."

"Found him in a dry wash," Renzo completed as she looked down. "Danged bushwhackers'd got him from behind. Had a bullet in his back."

"You call in the law?"

Roxanne nodded. "Reported it to the marshal at Mule Springs. He tried to run down whoever did it but failed."

"What about the steers? They ever show up?"

"They wouldn't," Renzo said bluntly. "Whoever it was took them, used hisself a running iron and changed the brand. Like as not they're wearing a Diamond G now."

"Probably. Just can't see a man big as this

Grosinger bothering to rustle fifty cows, however."

"Could be he just let the bunch that bushwhacked Charley have them as sort of extra reward."

"Makes more sense. It's been you three running the place ever since, I take it?"

"We've tried," the girl said. "It's been terribly hard and now we're getting down to where matters are critical. We've only about three hundred steers left and we need to sell off at least fifty of them to pay our bill at the general store and buy other things we must have. Our plan was to drive the stock over to the Box-B, that's Bern Pogue's ranch this week."

"You're selling your beef to another rancher?"

Roxanne's lips tightened into a small smile. "Only choice we have. Mounting a drive to the railhead is out of the question . . . we haven't the crew and chances are the night riders would never let us get out of the valley. Pogue's ranch is only a couple of days away and most of the time we'll be on our own range."

"Who'd be moving the cattle for you?"

"Just Clint and I. Renzo can look after the place."

Lockett frowned. "Now, with your brother laid up . . . ?"

"I'm not sure what we can do. I'll try to figure out something else . . . another way."

If it was not a hard drive, why couldn't Renzo

Clark handle it? Dade wondered, but kept the question to himself. There evidently was a good reason. "How much does Pogue give you for your beef?"

"Ten dollars a head."

"Ten! The market's paying seventeen . . . maybe even eighteen by now for prime stock."

"I know, but that's for cattle driven to the shipping point. We can't do it that way . . . and ten dollars is better than nothing at all."

Clark stirred wearily. "And I'm wondering now if we'll even get the chance to deal with Pogue, seeing as how them masked critters are hanging around."

"This the first time they've hit you?"

"Not the first time . . . just the first time lately. Been about three months since they rode in, called out Roxie and Clint, and give them a warning."

"Told us that we had better move on or we'd find ourselves in a lot of trouble," Roxie put in.

"Didn't they tell you who you had to sell out to?"

"No, just that we'd better go, and hinted if we didn't, we'd end up like Father did."

"Roxie . . . !"

At her brother's call the girl rose hurriedly, crossed to the bedroom, and disappeared into its dark interior. Renzo Clark watched her with doleful eyes. "Sure is too bad," he murmured. "Them two youngsters have worked mighty hard to keep this place going. It's all they got in the world and it'll be a powerful shame if they lose it."

"They'd have a pretty fair shake if they sold out to this Grosinger or one of the others, wouldn't they?"

"Now, I don't figure any of them wanting it will pay much. They'll try to steal it, and if the Rakers are put down tight in a bind, they'll be able to. But I'm suspecting that's the way it'll end up, no matter what. With them flour-sack-wearing skunks moving in like they've done, and meaning business for sure this time . . . and with nobody to drive them cows over to Pogue's so's they can raise a little cash, I reckon they're done for."

"No . . . maybe not," Roxie said, coming from the bedroom. She was smiling and there was a brightness in her eyes. "Clint was listening to us talk and came up with an idea."

The old cowpuncher scowled, heaved himself half out of his chair. "Now, missy, you ain't thinking of doing it your . . . ?"

"No . . . someone else. Instead of selling only fifty head to Bern Pogue, we'll sell him fifty-five and give the extra fifty dollars to Dade for driving them for us."

V

Renzo, grinning broadly, turned to Lockett. "Now, that's right good thinking! And good pay . . . fifty dollars for a couple of days' work."

Dade felt Roxie's eyes upon him, anxious, imploring. He shook his head. "Hate saying this but I've got to be riding on."

There was a long moment of silence broken finally by Clark. "You must be in a powerful lot of hurry."

"Just what I am."

Roxanne settled into her chair. "Would two or three days make such a difference in where you're going?"

"Could. Been hunting a fellow for quite a spell. Got word he was around Tucson. I fool away time getting there he just might be gone."

"I see," she murmured dispiritedly.

Lockett rolled another cigarette. He would like to help the Rakers—and help was something they really needed. But even before he started the quest for Pete Dillard—while he was still behind prison walls in fact—he had made a vow to himself that he would let nothing interfere in the search, once begun, and so far he had not broken that promise. Nor would he now, even for a girl like Roxanne Raker. It would be his kind of luck that, should he delay a couple of days, he'd reach Tucson and discover that Dillard had been there but pulled out for parts unknown only the night before.

"I guess that leaves us with only one answer," Roxie said. "I'll drive the stock to Pogue's myself. We have to get that money."

Clark wagged his head violently. "You ain't doing no such a thing! You know them raiders'd love to catch you out there alone."

"Maybe they won't notice."

"Way they been eagle-eyeing this place? They'd know and plenty quick." Renzo paused, slapped at his legs. "Sure wish't my riding days wasn't done . . . I'd run them cows over to Pogue's for you sooner'n soon. Can't set a saddle no more," he added, shifting his glance to Dade. "Bronc' busted me up something fierce a couple of years back. Ain't been much account since."

That answered a question that had puzzled Lockett earlier. He nodded his understanding. "One thing I can do, when I get to Mule Springs, I'll hire a 'puncher for you, send him right back."

"Not much chance of that," the girl said. "We've tried before to get help but men are afraid to work for us."

"Was one, last year, that figured he wasn't going to get scared out by the night riders," Renzo recalled. "He changed his mind, I reckon. Went out on the range that first morning, never did come back. Heard later he stopped in town long enough to wet his whistle at the Muleshoe Saloon, then lit out. Didn't even wait around to collect his day's pay."

Lockett stirred impatiently. Nothing seemed to work for the Rakers—they were hard luck plagued, it seemed. "What about the law . . . the sheriff of the county, I mean, not a town marshal. You ever go see him, tell him what's going on?"

"Sure did," Clark replied. "Me and Clint made a trip over in the buckboard to the county seat once. About all we got out of it was the ride. Said unless he could catch them red-handed a-doing it, masks and all, wasn't anything he could do about it."

"If he'd come around and spend a little time here with you, or maybe send a deputy . . . ?"

"We can't blame him," Roxie said, rising. "He has to look after a lot of territory and . . ."

"Rats!" Renzo snorted. "He's been told to keep his nose out of it, that's what, and being a big politicker that's what he'll do."

The girl said no more, began to collect the dishes, carry them to the work table near the stove, and place them in a deep pan. After a bit she turned to Dade. "I'm sorry we've burdened you with our trouble. We had no right . . . and we are grateful for what you've done. Are you riding on tonight?"

Lockett got to his feet, gave it some thought. "No big need. Can stay till morning in case those night riders pay you another call."

"I've thought of that and, if you would stay, I'd appreciate it. There's plenty of room in the bunkhouse."

"I'm the one that's obliged. Sleeping under a roof'll be a pleasure. Expect I'd best be seeing to my horse first, however."

She nodded, forced another small smile. "You'll find feed in the barn. Renzo will show you. Good night."

" 'Night," Lockett said, and moved toward the door with Clark shambling off ahead of him.

The chestnut was standing patiently where he had been ground reined. Taking up the leathers, Dade waited patiently while Renzo collected the abandoned rifle and shotgun, and then, following the old cowhand, he led the gelding around the house and across the cleared yard to the bulky structure at its lower end. Halting in the doorway, he delayed until Clark had struck a match to the wick of a lantern hanging just inside, and then stabled the horse in the first empty stall. While he stripped his gear, Renzo forked fresh hay into the manger and dumped a quart can of grain into the side box.

"Reckon that'll hold him until morning," the old man said, stepping back and watching Dade untie his blanket roll from its place on the saddle.

"Be needing watering later."

"Bucket out there at the well. Just help yourself," Clark said, and, returning to the doorway, crossed to the small log hut Charley Raker had built for cowhands he was never able to hire.

Firing a match, Renzo lit a wall lamp placed just inside the entrance, another on a table in the center of the room.

"It ain't much, but it's home," the oldster said, grinning as he made a sweeping motion with his hand.

There were several bunks built against the walls and besides the one table, there were two chairs and a washstand above which was suspended a square of mirror.

"Anybody ever use this but you?" Dade asked.

"Been a couple others . . . a time ago. Just pick yourself a bed anywheres . . . excepting that one next to the window. It's mine. Gets a mite hot here, come July and August and a man has to sleep close to fresh air."

Lockett tossed his blanket onto the one on the opposite side of the dusty glass, swore quietly. "Just too bad things are working out wrong for the Rakers. Mighty hard on them, too, 'specially the girl."

"For sure," Renzo said, settling onto his bunk. "Little gal was used to lots more . . . nice quiet home, gentle folks, church socials, things like that. Clint was, too, but it ain't so tough on him, being a man."

"No, wouldn't be. That name of hers . . .

Roxanne, it sure is a fancy one. Don't much fit this part of the country. Where'd she ever get it?"

"Was her ma's idea, I heard tell. Seems she was a book-reading woman. Got the name from a story about a fellow with a long nose."

Lockett stared at the older man. "Long nose?"

Renzo shrugged. "What I heard. You'd best ask her about it if you want to know more. Anyway, hardly anybody 'cepting her pa ever called her Roxanne. Most folks just say Roxie."

"That's a lot better-sounding," Dade said. Far off in the distance a coyote yapped into the clear moonlight. He listened until the bark died, eyes reaching through the open window into the night. "This Charley Raker picked a fine place," he said absently. "Could be made into a real fine ranch."

"For certain!" Renzo declared quickly. "All them two youngsters are needing is a little help from somebody with enough sand to stand by them and buck Grosinger and his bunch. You dead sure there ain't no chance of you hanging around for maybe a week or so?"

Dade nodded. "Not even for a day."

Clark leaned back, disappointment sagging his cheeks, dulling his faded eyes. "Must be something mighty important if it'll keep you from helping them youngsters get tromped under by the likes of Gros—"

"It is to me," Lockett interrupted coolly. "Man I'm about to catch up with owes me plenty. Has

43

for three years now, and I aim to collect. Nothing's going to keep me from it."

Renzo studied Dade thoughtfully in the yellow glow of the lamps, not missing the grim set of his jaw, the hard, unrelenting planes of his face. "I'm sort've getting the idea," he said slowly. "It ain't only money you're meaning to collect."

Dade Lockett shrugged, got to his feet. "Takes more than cash to pay a man for two years of his life," he said, and began to unroll his blanket.

Roxanne, without conscious thought, lifted the kettle of steaming water from the stove and poured its contents into the pan of supper dishes. Outside, she could hear Dade Lockett and Renzo moving about in the yard, their boot heels beating a hollow tattoo on the hard ground. After a few moments that sound died and she guessed they were on their way to the barn. It was hot inside the house with everything closed, and, crossing to the nearest window, she opened the shutter and raised the sash. Breathing in the cool, fresh air, she stood there looking out into the silver-shot night. As if touched by magic all things had changed; the harshness of the day was gone and in the pale glow the land and all upon it now appeared soft-edged and gentle, and friendly. But reality was still there, and the world was her enemy in daylight or dark. She leaned forward, rested her head upon the window's frame. For her—she who had once possessed such fine dreams, who had hoped for so much—there was no escape. She was doomed to a slavish existence, a drudge in a savage creation that broke women before their prime, and brutalized men beyond all belief. Worse, hers was a dual rôle for she was both woman and man in a household with none of the advantages of each and all the burdens of both.

Dade Lockett had offered the first good possibilities she'd known since the day of her father's death and she had been compelled to shoulder the responsibilities of the ranch, but he had turned out to be like all the others, so totally wrapped up in his own troubles that he had no room for others. But that was natural, and human, she supposed. This was far different from the way it was back home. There, if a person needed help, he got it almost without asking. Of course, their way of life was not the same; things were not so vitally important and it was simply a matter of living graciously rather than waging a constant battle for survival. And poor, bewildered Clint, it had been too much for him from the start. Lying in there now with a bullet wound in his leg, he would have reached the end of his wits. He hadn't wanted to move West when their father had sent for them, had, in fact, done everything possible to get out of it. But he had been only fifteen at the time, and so had been given no choice other than to make the journey with her to join their father on the ranch.

Ranch. Roxie's nose wrinkled slightly at the word. Ranch, indeed! It had been a total disappointment, far, far less than they had been led to expect from their father's letters. Why, she knew sharecroppers back home who lived better and in more comfortable surroundings than this! Abruptly it came to her; it wasn't worth fighting for. She didn't know why she hadn't realized that before; why had it taken a bullet in Clint's leg and the flat refusal to help of a tall, hard-visaged stranger called Lockett to make her see it? But, no matter, that was it. She was finished, done. Clint would agree, would welcome the idea. Renzo, of course, would object, but after all what Renzo wanted or didn't want wasn't important. It was their life—hers and Clint's that mattered.

Tomorrow she would ride over and talk to John Grosinger, find out what he would pay to get them to pack up and leave, turn everything over to him. His men wouldn't stop her once they knew the nature of her errand. After she knew what he would pay, she'd talk with Ed Cushman, get his offer. And then she'd take the best. Men did things that way, played one against the other. There was no good reason why she couldn't do as they did.

VI

Breakfast that morning was a quiet, polite affair. Roxie had little to say and Renzo Clark's words were gruff and to the point. In reply to Dade's inquiry concerning her brother, the girl said only that he was doing all right.

Finished, Lockett expressed his thanks for the meal, went immediately to the barn, and began to saddle and bridle the chestnut. He would have liked to pay for the food he had eaten as well as for the gelding's keep but knew that despite the Rakers' reduced circumstances, to have offered would have been taken as an insult.

"You ain't changed your mind none, have you?"

At Renzo's question, Lockett glanced around. The old cowpuncher was standing in the doorway, chewing on a match.

Dade shook his head. "Can't do it. Maybe I'd like to, but what I've got to do for myself is more important to me than anything else."

Clark spat the sliver of wood aside. "Didn't figure you had but reckoned I ought to ask. You still aiming to go by Mule Springs?"

Lockett nodded.

"And you're still planning on trying to hire us a hand?"

"Going to do what I can."

"Well, I'm obliged but I ain't putting much hopes in it. Mighty hard to find a man around here that can't be scared off."

Lockett said—"Seems so."—and ignored the possibility that the old cowhand was referring obliquely to him and such was the basis for his refusal of the job. The chestnut ready, he led him into the yard, started to mount, paused. It was only good manners to thank the girl again. Continuing on, he circled the house to the front, aware that Renzo was following silently.

Stepping up to the door, Dade knocked lightly. It opened at once and Roxie faced him. A flare of hope brightened her eyes, and then faded as quickly.

"Just want to say thanks again for the meals and the bed. Was right nice of you."

The girl nodded woodenly. Her lips parted to speak, closed as the quick beat of a running horse sounded across the morning's quiet. Lockett turned swiftly, hand dropping to the weapon on his hip.

"It's only Cushman," he heard Renzo Clark mutter.

The rancher rode in close, nodded curtly to the old cowhand, gave Lockett a quick, suspicious raking with his small eyes, and placed his attention on Roxie. He was a stockily built man with a head of brick red hair that hung well below the wide-brimmed hat he was wearing. "Heard what happened here last night," he said. "A shame . . . a mighty big shame! They do any big harm?"

"Clint was shot in the leg but he'll be all right. We were lucky that Mister Lockett happened by at just the right time and drove them off."

Cushman again gave Dade close scrutiny. "I'm obliged to you," he said. "Would grieve me sorely was anything bad to come to these young folks. Sort of look upon them as my own kin. You going to be around for a while?"

"He's riding out now," Roxanne said before Dade could answer. "We offered him a job but he has important business elsewhere . . . business that can't wait."

"Too bad," the rancher said, and frowned. "Was the same bunch, I expect."

"Far as we could tell."

"You didn't recognize any of them?"

"No. They were wearing those masks, same as before."

Cushman stirred angrily. "Well, there's no doubt in my mind who they are. Can't be anybody but Grosinger's men."

Lockett, arms folded across his chest, considered the rancher narrowly. "How'd you hear about the raid?"

"One of my hands," Cushman said promptly. "He was hunting strays south of here. Heard the shooting and rode over to see what it was all about, but by the time he got here the raiders was gone."

"A little sooner he could've done some helping," Renzo observed dryly.

"What I told him . . . that he should've pitched in, done what he could anyway. Instead, he turns around and busts a gut getting back to my place to tell me about it. Was too late then to do anything. There anything you're needing, Roxie? Anything I can do for you?"

"She can use a man for a couple of days," Renzo said quickly.

"That so?"

"I need someone to drive fifty head of cattle over to Bern Pogue's place," the girl explained. "He's agreed to buy them from us. It would be a big favor."

Cushman was wagging his head slowly, regretfully even before she had finished speaking. "That's probably the only thing I can't do . . . spare a man. Roundup's just finishing and branding's going full blast. Every man I've got's tied up."

"It would only be for two days . . . at the most."

"I realize that. Now, was it any other time of the year . . ."

"Of course," Roxanne said indifferently. "I understand."

Ed Cushman wasn't quite as good a family friend as some believed, Lockett thought. Sparing one cowpuncher for so short a time would hardly create a hardship. Dade shrugged, a wry realization coming to him; he had taken the same position as the rancher, feeling that he could not afford to give up any of his time to help the girl either. But there was a difference, he assured himself; he was merely a passing stranger, Ed Cushman was a friend of some standing, professed to be greatly interested in the welfare of the son and daughter of an old acquaintance.

"Well, expect I'd best be getting back to business. Cowhands are all alike. Unless you keep right at them they start dogging the job." Reaching up, he touched the brim of his hat with two fingers. "I'll look in on you again later. You need anything, just let me know."

Roxie nodded to the rancher as he wheeled about, set spurs to his horse, and hammered out of the yard.

Renzo Clark spat in disgust. "Yeah, you just let him know . . . only don't figure on nothing! He's the kind that's always willing to give you the shirt offen his back . . . only he just never gets around to giving it."

"Now, Renzo . . ."

"It's the truth! Been promising to give you and Clint a hand right along, but I ain't ever seen him doing it."

"He has a big ranch to look after and has plenty of problems of his own. We can't expect him to neglect his own place for us."

"Loaning us one hired hand . . . I sure don't figure that'd be doing any neglecting."

The girl sighed. "Perhaps not, but there's nothing we can do about it and we'll manage. We have before and we will again."

"One stinking cowpuncher . . . he'd never be missed."

"We don't know that, and it is his busy time. Mister Cushman brought in a lot of new stock, and the calf crop was good, I hear. There'd be a lot of extra work."

Lockett, inclined to agree with Clark, made no comment. He could offer nothing but words and Roxie was getting plenty of those. Turning to the chestnut, he swung onto the saddle. "Hope your brother does fine," he said. "I won't be forgetting to stop in town to see if I can hire you some help."

"Thank you," the girl said soberly. "Good bye."

"So long," Dade answered, and, ducking his head at Renzo, struck out across the yard for the road.

VII

The air was cool and an early morning haze hung over the land as Dade Lockett turned onto the road that led south. He followed the not-too-well-defined tracks for a short distance, his glance appreciatively taking in the long sweeps of grassy flats and low, rolling hills, and then forsaking them, cutting directly for the cone-shaped mountain in the distance where Renzo Clark had said the town of Mule Springs lay. The road would take him there, also, he knew, but it would pursue a more roundabout route, one suited to wagons and other vehicles; he could save time and enjoy a pleasant ride by angling across country to reach the settlement.

Sitting easy in the saddle, allowing his body to flow with the motion of the chestnut, he swept the valley with a lingering gaze. Far to the right were the Peloncillo Mountains, and beyond them Arizona—and Tucson. To his left reared the Pyramid Hills, below them the range called the Animas beyond which was Mexico. He tried to recall the name of the taller mountains to the east, failed. When he had looked over the map of the area that was on the wall of a saloon in Willow Gap, up in Colorado, he had concentrated his attention on that part that would get him in Tucson by the shortest course, thus he had paid little attention to the fringe portions.

Topping out on a fairly good hill, he dropped down its opposite slope and crossed a small, fast-running creek in the cleavage between it and its neighbor. Patches of yellow and purple flowers edged its banks and in a wider section where the water flattened out to form a marsh, sunflowers and crownbeard, still in the budding stage, grew thickly. It was a fine land, Lockett thought, one a man could find easy to settle in, start a life of his own. Cattle would do well; there was ample water, a wealth of grass, and this far south the winters should not be too severe. It was not hard to understand why Grosinger and Cushman, and others like them, craved more of the land—and why the Rakers stubbornly held on against such odds to the piece that was theirs; it was prime country well worth fighting for. At least, where the Rakers were concerned, that was how it had seemed the night before. Now he was not so sure. There seemed a change in Roxie this morning, a coolness in her determination. She had said nothing that would indicate a difference in her thinking, yet he sensed that she no longer . . .

"You . . . hold it!"

At the harsh command Lockett jerked the gelding to a halt, hand going quickly to the pistol on his hip in the same instant.

"Never mind that," the voice warned. "Be a damn' good way to get your head blowed off!"

Dade hung motionlessly, eyes on the two men who sat their horses in a slight coulée a dozen paces away. Deep in thought he had ridden straight into them without noticing their presence. One appeared to be an ordinary cowhand, but the other, the one doing the talking, was a large, powerfully built, dark-faced individual with hard eyes and a slash for a mouth. The white-stockinged bay he rode bore a Diamond with a G suspended in its center on its hip; Dade knew at once that the rider could be no one else but John Grosinger.

"What the hell you doing here?"

Lockett settled back, sighed quietly. With matters the way they were he should have expected this, stuck to the trail. "Just riding," he said laconically.

"Where to?" Grosinger snapped.

Dade ducked his head in the direction of a cone-shaped mountain. "Mule Springs."

"There's a road going there. Why ain't you on it?"

"Figured to take a short cut."

"Across my range. Know who I am?"

Lockett nodded, unwilling to give the rancher the satisfaction of speaking his name. Grosinger was a tough one, it was easy to see that, and he'd be a hard man to beat at anything. Temper began to stir within Dade. What sort of a chance did folks like the Rakers stand against the self-made kings such as John Grosinger? None at all.

"I'm going easy on you," the rancher said in a patronizing tone. "I'm telling myself you just made a mistake. But it ends there. Turn that horse around and start backtracking. I want you off my range."

"Seems you want a lot," Dade said mildly. "Like the Raker place, for one."

Grosinger scowled. "What about the Raker place?"

"I know you're out to get it."

"Sure. I can use the grass. Anyway, the country's better off without them little two-bit, starved-out spreads." The rancher's eyes narrowed. "What's it to you?"

"Happened to be there last night when your sack-wearing boys rode in and shot up the place. Think maybe I winged a couple of them for you."

Grosinger shook his head. "Wasn't none of my outfit."

Lockett smiled bleakly. "Didn't much figure you'd own up to it. I can tell you you'll just about get your way now. Clint Raker got shot and I think the girl's about ready to give in. Sure can't handle the ranch by herself."

"They shouldn't have ever started trying. They're not cut out to do ranching."

"Expect they could've made it if their pa hadn't got himself bushwhacked. You don't know anything about that, either, I reckon."

"Heard about it. Hardly knew the man myself."

Dade shrugged. "Somebody knew him," he said pointedly.

The cowpuncher with Grosinger stirred. The rancher's jaw tightened. "Sounds like you're calling me a liar, mister."

"Take it how you like," Dade replied coolly. "I figure if the hat fits, you'll put it on."

"Well, it don't, and I ain't listening to that kind of talk. By rights I ought to turn you over to some of my boys, let them drag you off my land."

"The same flour-sack-wearing gents you've got ragging the Rakers, I'll bet."

Grosinger swore softly, considered Lockett angrily for a long moment. Then his big shoulders lifted, fell. "I've got too much on my mind to let myself get all worked up by you, cowboy. But I ain't long on patience, so best thing you can do is turn around, get back on the road. You keep cutting across my range and I won't be responsible for what'll happen to you."

Abruptly the rancher wheeled the bay around and, using his spurs, struck out across the flat to a second scatter of hills to the east. The rider with him remained unmoving, his glance on Dade. "Was you smart, you'd do like he says."

"Was I smart," Lockett said dryly, "I'd be the President of the United States."

The cowpuncher's expression didn't change. After a bit he glanced over his shoulder at Grosinger, now well in the distance—and beyond range of a pistol, Dade realized. "Reckon you can go now," he said. "I can't shoot him in the back from here."

The rider roweled his horse out of the coulée and loped off in the wake of the rancher. Lockett, eyes on the pair, now dropping down into a deep swale, waited until they had vanished, and then, twisting half about on the saddle, hooked a leg on the horn, took out his sack of tobacco and fold of papers, and rolled a cigarette. Grosinger was just about as he had figured the man would be—big, arrogant, and cold as a rattlesnake. He already had a world of land, still wanted more. And once he got it, he'd still be unsatisfied. They were all alike, the Grosingers, never content, always out to get bigger and bigger regardless of actual need or who they hurt or what it cost. When the time came, when the hour was right, John Grosinger would ride roughshod over Roxie and Clint Raker and take what he wanted, regardless. That was the way men like him accomplished their end—wear down the opposition, reduce it to shreds, then move in and take over. And more the shame and sorrow, he'd get away with it because there was never anyone around to take a stand with the little people like the Rakers; they always had to go it alone—even the law, too often influenced by the politicians, usually turned its back on them.

Dade Lockett straightened himself slowly on the saddle. By God, this was one time the song was going to be different, he decided, flipping the cold cigarette into the grass. He'd gamble a few days just for the sake of seeing John Grosinger fail in his efforts to grind the Rakers underfoot. Cutting about, he doubled back over his tracks at a steady lope.

VIII

He was a fool, a voice within him kept warning, a fool to deviate from his avowed purpose of tracking down Pete Dillard and calling him to account, a fool for mixing into something that was none of his concern. To turn away now when he was so near Tucson, take a hand in a range-grabbing affair that could end only one way, with the big man grinding the little one under, was utter foolishness. He should forget the Rakers, the night riders, and greedy men like John Grosinger; he should stick to his own need, find Dillard, and ease the fires of vengeance and hate searing through his guts. The inner voice pushed at him relentlessly, reminding him over and over again of his original determination to right the wrong Dillard had done him, but it did not slow or turn him back, something stronger than his own hunger holding him steadfast. In his own mind he was not sure why he was doing it. Perhaps it was an outgrowth of his own early struggle against over-whelming odds, the weak against the strong, the David and Goliath story in 19th-Century dress, or possibly it simply sprang from the innate goodness of men always present in one form or another. He didn't know and he was a man who dwelt little on cause and effect and did what he felt he must do.

An hour later he broke out of the tree-studded hills and came onto the long flat that formed the floor of the valley. At once he came to sharp attention. Far ahead a smudge of dirty gray was mounting into the sky. Lockett frowned as he studied it. The Raker place lay in that direction. Could it be the raiders had struck again, or was it just a range fire? He wasted no time puzzling over it but immediately roweled the chestnut into a fast lope for the ugly mass rapidly growing in size and darkening in color as it hung over the land.

Dade swore deeply. John Grosinger, at the very time they were holding their conversation, and who had taken such pains to deny any connection with the hooded riders, had been aware that his men were probably moving in on the Raker place at that moment! He was a cold-blooded one all right, and everything old Renzo Clark figured him to be. The chestnut raced on and with each passing mile the anxiety within Dade Lockett increased. He was certain now it was not a range fire; the source of the smoke was too concentrated and not spreading as it could be expected to do. Judging from the size of the blackening cloud, he would guess that the raiders had fired all of the buildings on the ranch; likely their orders had been to leave nothing standing, and faced with this Roxie and Clint would have no choice but to give in. Again, he swore. He should never have ridden out that morning! He should have stayed there, then he could have been of some help to the Rakers. Now maybe it was too late.

Cresting the last rise on the vast plain, he saw the ranch on ahead. Flames were shooting into the sky and smoke was a great, boiling cloud surging upward. He could see Roxanne and Clark running back and forth in the yard behind the house, which had not yet caught fire, realized most of the ominous cloud was arising from the hay stored in the barn.

Reaching the gate he swung onto the hardpack, thundered across the intervening space, and pulled up short. Leaping from the saddle, he hurried to join the girl and the old cowhand. Roxie glanced up, fear blanking her eyes, and then they filled with relief when she saw he was not one of the raiders. Seizing one of the buckets, Lockett dipped it into the water trough, hurried to where Renzo was sloshing his container full against one of the small sheds. The barn was lost, burning furiously out of all possible control; the need now was to save the nearby sheds.

Clark bobbed to him as he rushed up, moved on by on a return trip to the trough. Dade tossed his bucketful against the steaming tool shed, assessed its probabilities and that of other nearby structures in a quick glance, and wheeled to refill his container.

Roxie, breathing heavily, was resting against the side of the pump housing. Renzo, too, had paused, and was sucking hard for wind. Taking up the bucket being used by the girl, Lockett filled it along with his own and for several more minutes continued to soak the walls of the structures that faced the doomed barn until danger of their breaking out into flames had passed.

"Reckon we done it," Renzo said wearily, mopping at his sooty face with a bandanna. "Sure glad you come along when you did."

Dade squatted on his heels, glanced around. Only the barn had been consumed by the fire. "The horses?" he asked.

"Got them out in time," Roxie replied. Her features, too, were streaked with black and there were several burned places in her shirtwaist and dress where live sparks had fallen. "All we lost was the barn . . . and the things stored in it."

"The same bunch of raiders?"

"Far as we could tell."

Lockett could feel the girl's eyes on him, studying him closely. "I was talking to Grosinger. Must've been about the time they hit you."

"That'd be him, all right!" Renzo declared angrily. "Ain't taking no chance hisself . . . just sets off to the side and lets them sidewinders do the dirty work for him."

"He claimed the raiders don't work for him."

"You figure he'd say they did?"

"No. I expected him to deny like he did. Clint all right?"

Roxie nodded, said quietly: "Why did you come back?"

Lockett shrugged. "Ain't real sure. Guess it was running into Grosinger. The way he acted stirred me up some. That job you offered still open?"

The girl stirred indifferently. "Oh, I don't know. Not sure I want to stay now. I'm tired of . . . of all this," she said, motioning at the charred, smoking remains of the barn.

Renzo Clark drew himself up in surprise. "I ain't hearing you right, am I? You thinking on quitting right when you got a chance to beat Grosinger?"

Roxie gave that several moments' consideration. She faced Dade. "You believe we can?"

"Ain't nothing in this world that's a cinch, but we can sure give it a mighty good try."

"But with the men he's got . . . and there's only three of us . . . maybe four if Clint gets better . . . how can we . . . ?"

"First thing to do is fort up, be ready for them when they come back."

Renzo was nodding vigorously. "That's the kind of talk I been wanting to hear. We can do it if we just set our minds to it."

Roxie gave the older man a quick, sidelong look, then smiled tiredly. "What do we do first?"

"Start getting set. I'll plan on driving those steers over to Pogue's in the morning. You said it'd take a couple of days or so . . . and that's the part that's bothering me. Don't like leaving you here alone."

"It might be best to forget it."

"No, that'd be backing down to Grosinger and we don't want him thinking that. Besides, you said you needed the money bad."

"We do."

"Then we go ahead. Only thing, while I'm gone you're both to stay close to the house."

"Got chores to do," Renzo said doubtfully.

"Have to let them ride until I'm back. We'll spend the rest of the day getting things lined up just in case. Are there plenty of cartridges for those guns I saw you using?"

"I guess so," Roxie replied.

"See about it. I want all the weapons you've got, along with all the ammunition put there on that table in the front room where they'll be handy. I aim to work that rifle over, too, see if I can keep it from jamming. Renzo, I'd like for you to take a close look at the doors and windows, be sure they can be locked tight and there's no chance of busting them in."

"You bet," the old cowhand said, grinning. "That bunch shows up again they're going to be bucking for the graveyard."

"I'm hoping it won't come down to that but we'd best plan on it just the same. Anyway, if nothing happens while I'm gone, it's sure to come later and we want to be ready."

64

"We?" Roxie repeated. "Does that mean you're going to stay even after you've driven the cattle to Pogue's?"

"Yeah, figured I'd stick around for a spell, keep the odds sort of evened up until things are settled one way or another. That is, if that's what you're wanting."

The girl was silent for a long minute. Then: "It is. I had my doubts after you rode off this morning. Actually I was about ready to make a deal with anybody who would give me a good price for the place. But now, if you're willing to help, I can see things differently."

"Ain't no guarantees how we'll come out."

"I know that and it doesn't matter. The fact that you are giving up whatever that important business was that you had in mind to stand by us made me realize how necessary it was that I . . . we . . . hang onto what is ours. I'm ready now to fight John Grosinger, and everybody else to a finish."

"Win, lose, or draw," Renzo Clark added soberly.

Roxie nodded. "Win, lose, or draw."

IX

By sundown all was in order. The window shutters had been examined and strengthened where necessary. Doors both front and rear were reinforced with crossbars. An extra supply of water and stove wood was on hand and the arsenal, consisting of two rifles, the single-barreled shotgun, and an old converted Colt pistol, was ready. There was ammunition enough for two dozen or so rounds each.

"These were all the bullets I could find," Roxie said later when Lockett was going through the supply.

"Reckon we can hold them off sure enough," Renzo stated confidently, hefting one of the long guns.

"We will," Clint Raker said.

Dade turned in surprise with the others. Raker, clad only in pants and undershirt, supporting himself by leaning on the back of a chair, faced them from the doorway of the bedroom.

Roxanne frowned disapprovingly at him. "You know you shouldn't be up."

Clint shook his head, his features pale and drawn. "I'm not a baby, and I want you to stop treating me like one."

Dade smiled at the younger man. It was his first

good look at him—a tall, lean youngster with a thick shock of blond hair capping his head. He had the same blue eyes as his sister. "Best you save up your strength," he said. "Could be needing it tomorrow or the next day."

"Intend to," Clint replied, "but I wanted you to know we're obliged to you for your help."

Dade Lockett's shoulders stirred indifferently.

"Like Roxie told you, if we can get those steers to Pogue and collect, then we've got a chance to make it." Clint paused, glanced through a rear window. Smoke was still rising from the embers of the barn. "Assuming, of course, that we can keep them from burning us out completely."

"It'll be different if they try it again," Renzo said. "They caught us flat-footed this morning. Next time we'll be ready."

"And we'll have to keep on being ready," Roxie added quietly. "At least until we can convince Grosinger that we're willing to fight to hold what's ours."

Dade Lockett made no comment. The Rakers were in for a tough go and his being there wasn't going to make all that much difference in the odds. He could only expect to even things up a bit.

"You've got to get back in bed . . ."

"All right, all right, but first there's something I got to ask Lockett."

Dade nodded to the boy. "Fire away."

"I'd like to know why you changed your mind

about coming back to help us. There some special reason?"

Lockett stiffened slightly at Raker's tone. He glanced at Roxie. She was staring at her brother, a deep frown on her face. "Is it important that I have one?"

"Far as I'm concerned it is," Clint snapped. "I don't figure anybody's going to be doing us favors unless they're getting something back."

"Well, I don't see it that way," Roxie said in a clipped voice. "Dade will get paid, of course, for driving the herd to Pogue's just as we promised. I don't think he expects anything else."

"And you figure he's going to put his life on the line for what we offered to pay him? I don't! He's got something more working."

Lockett brushed aside the temper rising within him, turned, dropped back to the table in the center of the room, and began pawing through the ammunition piled on it.

"There'll be no more of that kind of talk," he heard Roxie say firmly. "You get in that bed . . . and you stay there. If I need you, I'll call you."

Clint mumbled a reply of some sort, the words inaudible to Dade, but he wheeled about and with the girl's assistance retreated into the adjoining room.

"You've got to 'scuse the boy," Renzo said, moving up to Lockett's side. "Feeling poorly like he is, he just ain't thinking straight."

"Means nothing to me. I'm not sure why I did come back, but it wasn't because I figured to get something out of doing it."

"I know that, and so does the little gal . . . and that's who counts, her. She's the one running this outfit. Has been ever since Charley got hisself killed. A lot like him she is . . . plenty of sand and smart, too. Maybe it don't show much but it's there."

Lockett shifted his attention to the adjoining bedroom. He could hear Roxie talking to Clint in a low, stern voice. Whatever the subject, she was making her point in no uncertain terms. Dade nodded to the old cowhand. "Beginning to realize that," he said. "Makes me feel some better about things around here."

By midmorning the next day Lockett had cut out fifty head from the Rakers' small herd and was moving west with them. It was a two-day drive, he'd been told, and he should encounter no problems; there was ample grass and water for the beef, and since Pogue's Box-B Ranch lay in an opposite direction to the holdings of John Grosinger, it was doubtful the Diamond G owner would even know the drive was under way. For a time the herd moved steadily along over a grassy plain, and then, late in the afternoon, they reached short hill country. It was not so easy from there on as the steers kept striking off in singles and doubles into the numerous draws taxing Dade's patience and the quickness of the chestnut. But eventually he got the cattle through the brushy hogback and was again in a broad valley.

At dark he halted in a swale where a spring formed a fairly good pond. The steers settled, he built a small fire for coffee, and digging into his saddlebags for the sack of lunch Roxie had prepared, he ate a hurried meal. By that time the following day, he calculated, he should be at Pogue's with the herd. He'd not wait for the succeeding morning to begin the return trip, would instead pull out for the Raker place as soon as he had the cash in hand. Leaving them, despite the precautions he had taken, weighed heavily on his mind.

He wished now he could have held off on the drive until the danger of another raid by Grosinger's men had passed. But there was no way of knowing just when the masked riders would come again—that day, perhaps, or possibly not for a week, and delaying could have been a waste of time. Too, holding off could have cost Roxie and her brother the sale of the cattle to Bern Pogue since he wanted them on hand before he began his annual drive to the railhead, and getting the cash for the beef was of the utmost importance to the Rakers. He guessed, when you came right down to it, there really had been no choice. But he worried about it, nevertheless. Despite the fact the three of them, forted up inside the house and well-armed, could undoubtedly give a good account of themselves should an attack come, he still had fears. None of them knew how to cope with men such as rode for Grosinger and who, safe behind masks, would not hesitate to kill to accomplish the job they had been hired to do. And fire—that was his chief worry. The raiders had employed it once; unquestionably they would make use of it again—this time on the ranch house itself. He had taken care to warn Roxie and Renzo Clark to keep a sharp watch from the windows if the raiders did strike again, to be certain that none of them was allowed to get near. Since there were three of them, assuming Clint could take his place in the defense, it should be possible to maintain a close watch on all four sides of the house except at night under the cover of darkness.

Disturbed, Lockett rose, stored away the remainder of his food supply, and mounting the chestnut, circled the herd restlessly. The cattle were content, and after a time he cut back over the route he had covered, rode to the crest of a fair-size hill, and for a while kept his eyes turned to the northeast, the direction in which the Raker Ranch lay. Later he began to doze fitfully, rousing now and then to scan the sky for any telltale glow that would indicate fire, and when morning finally came after a night that had aroused no alarm, he heaved a sigh of relief, and, stepping again into the saddle, dropped back to the herd. The Rakers had apparently gotten through the dark hours with no trouble.

Taking time only to make coffee, Dade soon had the cattle once more on the move, pointed due west across a vast flat. The grass was thinner here, had a burned, gray look rather than the rich green of the valley, but the steers drove well regardless, and by noon he had the herd well across the seemingly endless expanse. He should be seeing signs of Pogue's cattle or perhaps a rider or two, he thought, and then remembering that it was the time of year when stock was being gathered for a trail drive, reckoned that all hands were likely busy at that task.

Around midafternoon, as the herd moved slowly down a deep-cut arroyo under a sun that had warmed greatly, Dade caught sight of several riders. Box-B men, he supposed, and settled back in satisfaction and relief. Evidently he was near Pogue's ranch house. Moving on ahead of the herd, he rode up onto the left bank of the wash where he could be seen. At once the riders pushed forward. Apparently they had been waiting for him.

That was good. He could use the help. Dropping back down into the wash, now that his presence had been established, Lockett resumed his position at the side and slightly behind the herd where the dust was at a minimum. It shouldn't take long now to complete the delivery to Bern Pogue, collect the money promised, and head back to the Rakers. He had made better time than expected, and with luck and riding straight through he should reach the ranch by midnight, or shortly afterward.

Then what? It had been in his mind to hang around the Raker place for a few days, see if he could help some in forcing John Grosinger to back off, forget about taking over the Raker property. But matters had changed a bit. Clint, plainly, was suspicious of him and his intentions, and while this bothered him not at all, he felt he would as soon not be a party in a family quarrel between Roxie and her brother that could erupt because of him. As Renzo had said . . .

The sharp, decisive crack of a rifle cut through Dade Lockett's thoughts. Startled, he reached for his pistol and spurred ahead. The riders he'd assumed were Pogue's were rushing in on him from both sides of the arroyo. He cursed savagely. They weren't cowhands—all were now wearing flour sacks over their heads. *Raiders!* Whipping up his pistol, Dade fired at the nearest, twisted, threw a shot at the one on the opposite side. The sandy cut rocked with the blast of his weapon and of those being used by the hooded riders. Suddenly the cattle were all about him, running hard. He jammed his pistol into its holster, began to work the nervously plunging chestnut toward the edge of the flowing mass of clicking horns, colored hides, and wildly rolling eyes.

The gelding reached the fringe, broke clear of the now thoroughly stampeded herd. Lockett brought out his gun, turned again to face the men who had caused it. He'd been lucky; had the chestnut been more to the center of the arroyo when the run started the chances were he'd not have gotten out so quickly—if at all. Abruptly a rider loomed up through the dust ahead of him. Another wheeled into view a stride beyond him. Lockett fired twice, saw one flinch but the other was a clean miss. He triggered again, now aware of a third man racing along the bank of the wash above him. He twisted about, steadied his weapon on his left forearm. The chestnut, pounding hard over the uneven ground was making it almost impossible to get in an accurate shot—and with a half a dozen men closing in on him, he had to make every bullet count. He pressed off the shot, saw the rider jerk back, and then consciousness was torn from him as a shocking blow smashed into the side of his head, knocking him from the saddle.

X

Lockett stirred, feeling the heat of the sun driving into his body. Opening his eyes, instinctively moving no other part of his body, he looked around. He was alone, or appeared to be, lying flat on his back in the loose sand of the arroyo bed. There was a stickiness on one side of his face and down his neck, a dull pain in his head, a steady burning along his left arm.

For a long minute he remained motionless, listening intently. There was only silence. Cautiously he raised himself on his elbows. Sickening pain rushed through him in a sudden gust. He paused, chin sunk into his chest, allowed it to subside. When it was over, he continued to draw himself into a sitting position. He saw his pistol half buried in the sand nearby. Reaching out, he retrieved it, knocked it against the heel of his boot, slid it into its holster. He did it without conscious effort. There was a haziness in his mind and a dullness that made it difficult for him to collect his senses, piece together what had happened. Raiders. They had jumped him, made off with the herd. He'd thought them Bern Pogue's men. Instead, they had pulled on masks and opened fire on him, some of them scoring. Gingerly he ran his fingertips over the numbed side of his head. A bullet had grazed him, knocked him cold. He glanced down at his arm, saw the smear of crusted blood there where a slug had sliced a groove across the flesh. He flexed the limb. It seemed no worse for the wound, only slightly stiff and stinging smartly.

They'd nailed him twice, he realized grimly. Both wounds had bled considerably, the one on his head especially. That had probably saved his life, judging from the number of hoof prints on the sand nearby. The outlaws had ridden in for a close look at him, saw the large amount of blood, and figuring him for dead had ridden on. He grinned tightly, picked up his hat, and, getting a grip on his strength, drew himself upright. The endeavor left him spraddle-legged, head down and swaying weakly, but he fought it off, and after a few moments he steadied, glanced around. He saw the chestnut a hundred yards or so up the arroyo, and breathed a sigh of relief. At least he wasn't set afoot. Slowly, knees uncertain and threatening to buckle, he moved toward the big gelding.

His head had cleared and considerable strength had returned by the time he reached the animal and managed to climb onto the saddle. That effort was more than he'd bargained for and once again he gave in to pain, sat hunched limply while the universe swirled sickeningly about him. Finally that, too, ceased, and reaching for his canteen, he took a long swallow and then poured a quantity of the water over his head. That brought an immediate stinging to the wound but he did begin to feel better. He completed his ministrations then by taking his bandanna, ripping it into strips, and using it as a bandage.

Raising his eyes he looked out across the flat. There was no sign of the cattle. He wondered how long he had been unconscious, glanced at the sun. It was low. He had lain there on the sand for at least two hours, he reckoned, perhaps a bit more. The raiders would have a good start on him—but it wouldn't matter, trailing the herd would be easy. Roweling the gelding, Dade moved forward, following the definite tracks of the steers as they continued on down the arroyo. The marks in the sand were deep, giving proof the cattle were running at a headlong pace.

A quarter mile later the herd had swung up out of the wash. The raiders had evidently turned them at that point, pointed them into a southeasterly direction across the plain. Lockett, no anger thrashing at him but possessed only with a grim determination, drew the chestnut to a halt. Raising himself in the stirrups, he studied the sky ahead. There was no haze of dust, not in this section of the country or in any other; it could mean only that the raiders had halted for the night.

They could not have gone far, he reasoned, and touching the chestnut with his spurs, moved on, now keeping to the low ground as much as possible but always with the trail of hoof marks left by the steers in sight nearby.

He became aware of the raiders' whereabouts before he saw them. As he rode quietly along through the fold of hills, the smell of cigarette smoke came suddenly to him. Halting instantly, he slipped from the saddle. Gun in hand, he worked his way through the gullies and across a series of slopes to a slight rise on his left. The pungent odor was stronger now, and with it came the rank smell of cattle. Immediately he dropped to his belly and, hat off, wormed to the top of the grassy ridge. A grunt of satisfaction slipped from his lips.

Before him was another arroyo, one narrower but much deeper than the one where the attack had occurred. The steers were bunched in a natural corral a short distance away. Two of the outlaws were squatting, backs against the sandy wall of the wash while they enjoyed their smokes, off to his right. Dade gave that thought. There had been half a dozen or so in the raid; where were the others? After a time he dropped back, circled to a position a few paces lower where a better view of the arroyo was possible. He located the raiders' horses. There were only two. The others had ridden on, leaving the steers in the care of two of their party.

Again Lockett pulled back, considered his best course. It would be no big chore to show himself and recover the herd from the pair below. But night was at hand and it would not be possible to move the stock any distance before darkness set in. To wait until daylight to act, however, would be a mistake; the remainder of the gang likely would return and his chances for regaining possession of the cattle, and hanging onto them against such odds, would be much reduced. He would have to act now. It was better to gamble on being able to move the herd far enough to where, in the darkness, it would be reasonably safe should the raiders return soon. Too, being a distance from the arroyo would afford him a good start on the way to Pogue's when daylight came if the outlaws didn't put in an appearance until then.

Cutting back to the chestnut, he mounted, spent a moment or two testing the action of his pistol to make sure sand had not fouled its mechanism, and then with the weapon in hand circled to where he entered the arroyo above the two men. Allowing the gelding to walk slowly in the soft sand, he made a quiet approach.

The raiders did not see him until he was no more than a dozen yards away. Both stared, lunged to their feet. The younger of the two made a stabbing grab for his gun. Lockett calmly shot him before he could clear leather with his weapon. His partner, a dark-faced Mexican *vaquero*, abandoned a similar notion, raised his hands hastily. Lockett, eyes on the cattle that were aroused and stirring restlessly from the gunshot, rode in nearer to the man who continued to stare.

"I . . . I think you dead, *señor*."

"Not yet," Dade said coldly as he swung off the gelding. "Make one wrong move and you will be."

Stepping forward, Dade lifted the outlaw's pistol from its holster. That he was undoubtedly a fearful sight with smeared, dried blood plastering his head, face, and neck, as well as an arm, had not occurred to him until that moment. And the water he'd poured over himself as an aid to conscious-ness had likely given him even a more sanguinary appearance. But there'd been no time to clean up back in the arroyo; he'd do it later. The important thing now was to get the herd started in the proper direction for Pogue's.

"We're moving the steers out," he said. "You're helping . . . or I'll kill you. Take your choice."

The *vaquero* blinked, his dark eyes like two burning coals. "*Seguro*," he murmured.

"Get your horse," Lockett ordered, putting no trust in the man. "You try something and . . ."

"No, *señor*," the outlaw replied, nodding hurriedly. "You are the boss."

Dade went back onto the saddle, moved slowly toward the nervous herd. The *vaquero* mounted, began to circle in from the opposite side.

"It is soon dark. These cows they will not go."

Lockett shook his head at the man. "We'll drive them far as we can. Don't aim to be here in the morning when your friends come back."

The *vaquero* shrugged, removed his broad, soft-

80

brimmed hat, began to wave it at the steers. "Friends, *señor?*" he said as the cattle started slowly off down the arroyo. "I do not know them. It is only they hire me to drive the animals."

"Sure, sure," Lockett said, sliding his pistol into its holster. He was looking farther along, searching for a break in the wall of the arroyo that would permit the steers to climb out onto the flat above. There appeared to be an opening not too distant.

"*Es verdad* . . . the truth."

Lockett ignored the statement, pointed to the lowering in the side of the wash. "We'll head them up through there, get them on the flat. Then we'll talk about who you are and why you bushwhacked me and rustled my herd."

"I am Cuchillo," the Mexican said, bowing his head slightly, and then smiling, he veered off toward the opposite side of the arroyo to take his position at the rear of the sluggishly moving steers.

"All right, Cuchillo, if you only . . ."

The words froze on Dade's lips. He saw the quick motion of the *vaquero's* arm as it came up, fingers reaching for the back of his collar. In almost the same instant the last of the yellowing sunlight flickered brightly on the blade of a knife. Lockett drew and fired in a single flow of motion. The bullet caught the *vaquero* in the chest. The narrow bladed knife, plucked from its neck scabbard and poised for hurling, dropped from his long fingers as he slammed sideways, and fell from the saddle. Dade wasted no second glance on him. The gunshot was all the cattle needed to start them down the arroyo at a hard run.

Roxie, sitting in her father's old leather chair in the open doorway, eyes on the alert for signs of the raiders, brushed back a stray lock of dark hair and sighed quietly. She had been there, off and on, for almost the entire day, and vigilance was becoming boring. But she would not neglect the task. Dade Lockett had impressed her with the importance of not being caught unaware, an effort on his part that was totally unnecessary. She guessed she should be making some plans, now that she had fully made up her mind—"crossed her Rubicon," as old Miss Gayley, one of her girl-school teachers had the habit of saying. Miss Gayley was great on such things, always had some sort of a Latin quotation to fit the occasion.

Dade would be returning sometime tomorrow night with the $500 he'd get from Bern Pogue for the steers. She could depend on it, she was certain; likely Dade would have no trouble on the short drive, but if he did he'd be able to handle it. He was that kind, thus the money was as good as in her hands. What he would do then was problematical; he might stay with the thought of helping them or he might decide that taking the cattle to Pogue was enough of a favor, and ride on to complete this all-important business he had in mind. That should be her first step, she decided—talking him out of that, keeping him here. Offering herself to him she supposed was the most effective means, becoming his woman, his wife if need be. It wouldn't matter—it was whichever suited him. Then she would have him with her permanently and the rebuilding of the place should be no great chore. With a man like Dade on the premises the work would go fast and John Grosinger would undoubtedly give up all thought of taking over the place. Then, in a few years, she'd really have something in the way of a cattle ranch—a spread her father could be proud of were he alive. It was best she get rid of Clint. He hated the life, always would. He simply wasn't cut out for ranching and unlike her wasn't interested enough in making an effort to change. Possession was no part of his make-up and he could care less about owning anything. He preferred to be no more than a city dweller, enjoying the products and offerings of such civilization with no plans or hopes for the future. She had been that way, too—at the start. But a metamorphosis had occurred, one brought about she supposed by John Grosinger and his night riders and their attempts to wrest from her something that was hers. Dade Lockett, too, could have had something to do with it.

Regardless, the best thing was to get Clint out of

the way; he would only be a hindrance in the future. She would take some of the money Dade would be bringing back, give a part of it to her brother—enough to buy passage on a stagecoach to Indiana or Kentucky, whichever he preferred, with some left over to keep him until he found himself a job. Later, when the ranch began to do well, she would send him more. All that would have to wait, of course, until he was able to travel, but that shouldn't be more than a week or two. Renzo could stay on. He wasn't of much use, being all crippled up the way he was, but he was handy to have around, and he was loyal. Dade liked him, too, so she should have no problems persuading him to keep the old man on when they began hiring regular hands to work the ranch, which could be soon once things were settled with Grosinger and they could get down to working the ranch. Meanwhile—until Dade got back— there was nothing to do but wait and watch and see that nothing more happened to her property.

XI

Raking the chestnut hard, Lockett surged alongside the racing herd. If he could draw abreast the leaders, he might be able to turn them into the break in the arroyo wall and up onto the flat. The rest of the steers would follow. Pistol ready, he veered the gelding toward the big wall-eyed dun that was slightly ahead of the others. Pointing the weapon down, he triggered two quick shots. The blast, so near the straining animal, caused him to swerve against the steer at his flank. The opening in the bank of the wash lay a dozen strides farther on. Without hesitation the rangy old dun headed into it, buck-jumped his way through the low brush, and clambered out onto the level ground above. The remainder of the herd, in a crowding, heaving mass of noise and color, poured in behind him.

Lockett holstered his gun and pulled to a halt a short distance away. When the last steer had made it to the higher ground, he rode up onto the flat and, putting the chestnut to a good lope, set out after the cattle. They would not run for long in the closing darkness; it was immaterial anyway since they were bearing west.

A half hour later he caught up with the steers. They had stopped in a swale deep in the pocket of a cluster of low hills. Having run themselves out, they were now ready to settle down for the night. Lockett glanced over his shoulder. It would have been better if he could have put more distance between the herd and the arroyo where the outlaws had corralled them. He had what could hardly be called a generous lead should they decide to follow and make an effort to recover the herd.

He swung his eyes then to the west, wondering

just where and how far away Bern Pogue's ranch was. He had been thrown off course by the outlaws and now had no idea whether he was far south or well north of the spread. It would be foolish, of course, to double back to the arroyo where the raid had occurred and head out from there. That would only be a waste of time. He could do nothing but continue on westward, he decided, and rode on in close to the herd. Some of the steers had already bedded down but the majority was still on their feet, heads low and swinging back and forth, tails whipping nervously. They had gone all that day without water and their natural thirst had been further heightened by two short, if fast, stampedes; he could expect to find them hard to handle, but it had to be done.

Working the chestnut into the herd, he began to swing his folded rope as a whip, got several of the steers into motion again. Despite the bright moonlight that was now flooding the land, they were reluctant to move, but he kept at them, fighting the stubborn ones that held back, hurrying to cut off the would-be strays that spurted from the main body in the hope of escaping into a brushy draw. Near exhaustion, sweat blanketing his body despite the coolness that had closed in, Dade continued the drive for a good hour and then, when they dropped into a deep sink, waterless but with a good stand of grass, he let the herd come to a halt.

By daylight he was up and had the cattle on the trail once again, following the same westward course. As he rode, he maintained a watch to the east. Late in the morning such care paid off. Four riders appeared in the distance, coming abreast over the tracks left by the herd. At once Dade began to urge the cattle to a faster gait.

Strangely the riders did not close in, simply maintained their position, neither gaining nor losing ground. And then abruptly, a short time later, they disappeared. Lockett puzzled over their behavior. He was certain they were the remaining members of the gang that had jumped him and taken the herd, yet they made no effort to recover the steers, or seek revenge for their two lost partners. He was at a loss as to what it was all about.

The answer came minutes later. The herd, crossing a rolling plateau sparsely covered with bunchgrass, snakeweed, and clumps of prickly-pear cactus, topped out the last rise and started down a long slope into a wide, green valley. A scatter of ranch buildings lay at its upper end, and strung out for miles below were cattle, bunched and ready for the drive to the shipping point. Riders drifted slowly about the fringes of the herd, keeping it closely knit.

Lockett grinned bleakly, brushed at his sweaty face. He had reached Pogue's. The outlaws had backed off, fearing to attack since gunshots would have been heard by the men working the cattle. He'd made it.

Riding to the front of the herd, Dade hazed the old dun leader into the general direction of the house. He supposed he could drive the cattle directly downgrade and turn them over to Pogue's cowhands, but it seemed best to report in to the rancher himself first. As he came off the slope and quartered into the yard, two cowpunchers rode out to meet him, their dusty faces registering surprise and wonder when they drew near.

"Steers from the Rakers," Dade said, waving at the herd now crowding up to one of the watering ponds. "Fifty head. Be obliged if you'll count them."

One of the riders, a slim, elderly man wearing scarred leather chaps and a hat that had lost half its brim, bobbed. "Sure thing, mister. You have yourself a spot of trouble?"

"Some," Lockett admitted. "Where'll I find Pogue?"

The cowpuncher pointed to a small, white-washed cabin set a short distance from the main house. "That there's his office. Reckon it's where he'll be."

Dade nodded his thanks, rode across the hard-pan, and halted at the rack fronting the rancher's business quarters. Dismounting, he stood for a minute looking off down the valley while the ache in his relieved muscles ebbed, and, then turning, strode to the entrance of Pogue's office, noting only casually the strained features of several women peering at him from nearby windows. The rancher was sitting at a roll-top desk. Several piles of coins, mostly gold, were stacked before him along with a considerable amount of paper money. Evidently he was paying off some of his help and preparing for the trail drive. He glanced up as Dade entered, drew back sharply, his small, dark eyes registering shock.

"Who the hell are . . . ?"

"Name's Lockett," Dade answered the half-finished question. "Drove in those fifty steers you bought from the Rakers."

Pogue, a gray, nervous sort of man, ran a hand over his balding head, frowned. Only then did Lockett realize that it was his appearance, blood-crusted, dusty, and haggard, that was creating a stir. "Sorry I ain't much to look at," he said. "Never had a chance to clean myself up. Be obliged if you'll ask my pardon to your women-folk. Reckon I gave them quite a start."

The rancher nodded. "Rustlers?"

"Good a name as any for them," Dade replied, and half turned as the old cowpuncher with the ragged hat clomped noisily into the office. He raked Lockett again with a curious look, shifted his attention to Pogue.

"Fifty head's what he brung, boss. All prime stuff. You want me to . . . ?"

"Deal's off," the rancher said in a low voice. "I ain't buying them."

Lockett drew himself up stiffly. The cowpuncher stared, pushed his hat to the back of his head. "Ain't buying? I remember you saying . . ."

"Forget it, Joe. Deal's off, like I said."

Dade stepped closer to the desk. Anger was sweeping through him in a hot wave. "Why?"

"Got my reasons," Pogue said doggedly.

"Well, that ain't no reason far as I'm concerned," Lockett snarled. "You made a bargain with the Rakers. The beef's here . . . in time and in good shape. I'm holding you to your word."

Bern Pogue squirmed in his chair. "It ain't that I wouldn't like to. It's only, well, I mean . . ."

Dade's eyes narrowed. "What you mean is that somebody told you not to buy them, that it?"

"Not saying that," the rancher protested, brushing at the sweat gathering on his forehead. "It's only . . . I . . ."

"Only that somebody put a bug in your ear about the Rakers, and sold you on the idea of helping drive them out!" Lockett's voice had risen to a harsh shout.

"Now hold on here. I . . ."

"It's you that'd best hold on, mister," Dade snapped. Jerking out his pistol, he dug the bill of sale for the cattle from a shirt pocket with his free hand, threw it onto the desk in front of Pogue. "There's your paper. Now count me out five hundred dollars." The elderly cowpuncher began to ease toward the door. Lockett made a quick gesture to him. "Far enough. Get yourself back here alongside your boss. I don't want to have to shoot you. Start counting, Pogue."

The rancher hesitated briefly, shrugged, and then began to form stacks of double-eagles. When he had set out the necessary number of gold coins, he leaned back, folded his arms. A slyness covered his features. "There's five hundred dollars. I expect you know I could have you jugged for a hold-up."

Dade smile tightly. "Maybe, but you've got the steers and a bill of sale . . . and one of your hired hands is a witness to what's happening. He knows you agreed to a deal with the Rakers, too." Pogue said nothing, only watched as Dade gathered up the coins, dropped them into a leather poke, and thrust it inside his shirt. He centered his attention on the rancher. "Reckon you know you're getting more'n your money's worth in this. The steers are worth half again what you've paid for them, but the Rakers ain't bellyaching about it. You and the rest of the big ranchers around here've got them by the short hair and they're having to do the best they can."

"No fault of mine."

"Nobody's saying it is and I guess it's only human nature for some folks to take advantage of others when they get the chance. Now, am I going to have trouble riding out of here?"

Bern Pogue glanced at Joe, pursed his lips.

"You can make it hard or you can make it easy," Lockett continued. "Whichever, you'd best know here and now I'll still wind up leaving and you'll be doing some burying."

The rancher shrugged. "Ain't nobody going to bother you," he said.

The hard set to Dade Lockett's jaw relented slightly. "I'm a mite tired so I'm obliged to you for that much," he said, and turned for the door.

XII

It could only have been John Grosinger who'd put pressure on Pogue to back out on his arrangement with the Rakers, Lockett thought as he mounted the chestnut and pointed east out of the yard. By queering the deal he hoped to ring down the curtain on the final, desperate effort of Roxie and Clint to keep their ranch alive. He doubted Bern Pogue would have ever thought of going back on his given word to purchase the steers himself; he was getting a bargain at $10 a head, and from the overall look of his spread, he was too good a businessman to pass up such a bargain. But there had to be some reason why he would knuckle under to Grosinger—a heavy obligation, perhaps, or a long-standing favor finally called in. Dade grinned. Bern would have a fine time explaining why he had completed the purchase of the beef after being told not to—but that was his worry.

Lockett glanced toward the sun. Shortly past noon and a good half-day's ride lay ahead of him before he reached the valley and the Raker place. He'd be lucky if he could make it by dark—and that possibility was dimmed by the fact he would soon have to stop, eat, and rest the chestnut. He rode on, holding the big horse to a steady if not fast gait. An hour or so later he halted in a small coulée where a cluster of cottonwoods grew in the sink of a dry spring. Loosening the gelding's gear, Dade picketed him on a patch of grass, and then, building a fire, brewed himself a lard tin of coffee. Bolstering the strong, black liquid with more of the lunch Roxie had prepared, he ate and took it easy for a reasonable length of time.

He would have preferred to press on without any break in the journey, but to halt was necessary for the sake of the chestnut. It was far wiser to sacrifice a few minutes than push him beyond his limit and break him down; a man on foot in this vast, treacherous country was quickly in serious trouble. Finally satisfied the gelding was again ready to travel, Lockett soaked a rag with water from his canteen and squeezed it dry into the horse's mouth to ease his thirst. That should relieve the animal for a while—at least until they reached a stream or live spring. Then, tightening the saddle girth, Dade mounted and rode on.

Late in the afternoon after a hot, sweaty crossing of a broad flat, he came to a fair-size creek flowing through the short hills from a mountain range to the west. He allowed the gelding to slake his thirst while he refilled the canteen, going about it hurriedly, reluctant to lose any more time than necessary. But as he hunched over the quietly moving water, he caught a blurred reflection of himself, recalled the effect of his appearance on Bern Pogue and others at the Box-B Ranch. Rising, he stripped off his clothing and stepped into the stream, gave himself a thorough scrubbing, employing, however, considerable gentleness when it came to his head. The track left along the side of it by the outlaw's bullet had swelled, felt raw, and smarted sharply at contact with the cold water, as did the welt across his arm. Neither was serious in his estimation; he'd been hurt much worse many times before in his life, but he could expect Roxie to insist upon applying some of the antiseptic she'd used on Clint, as well as doing a proper bandaging of the wounds once he was back at the ranch.

He was still thinking of the girl when, a time later, he was again in the saddle and riding steadily eastward. She would be happy when he handed over the bag of gold coins to her, for in them she would see the solution to their problems—at least the immediate ones. Her eyes would sparkle in that bright, happy way of hers and a smile would part her lips to show twin rows of even, white teeth. He kept remembering how she had looked at him when he had returned—how the relief and hope and happiness he'd seen there had all blended to make him feel as if for once, and perhaps the first time in his life, he was doing something worthwhile for someone. It pleased him that she was happy, that he was part of making her so. And he realized that a change had been brought about in him although he wasn't sure just what it was, but there was a lightness, a sort of freedom stemming possibly from a recognition that matters that once seemed important no longer were, while things that had meant nothing had assumed an opposite aspect.

He'd stay with the Rakers for a few more days, see them safely settled again, and then ride on to Tucson. When his affair with Pete Dillard was straightened out, he'd return. With Clint laid up and Renzo Clark too old to be of much use, Roxie would need a man around the place. He'd talk it all out with her when he got there, explain to her why he had to finish what he had started out to do. She'd understand, he was certain, and he hoped she'd welcome his plan to return.

Well out in the valley now, Lockett paused to breathe the tiring chestnut, let his glance sweep the country behind him. Several times he had taken the precaution of checking closely his back trail; the raiders, frustrated in their attempt to steal the herd, could now be hoping to ambush him, take the gold, assuming they were aware that a cash deal with Pogue had been made. He fell to wondering about the would-be rustlers; if it had been Grosinger who warned Bern Pogue not to buy the Raker cattle, was it logical to think it was his men who had attempted to rustle them? It was possible, he supposed. The rancher could have simply been playing it safe, trying to make doubly sure no deal would be made by having the stock hijacked before it could be delivered. Too, the masked riders could have been acting on their own, endeavoring to pick up a few extra dollars on the side. Regardless, it was John Grosinger he held responsible for the whole affair—for both the attempted rustling and Pogue's try at backing out on the purchase—and one day he'd call the rancher to account for it.

His continuing glances about revealed no raiders. A small bunch of cattle, only dark colored blots in the far distance, grazed near a grove of trees to the south. Overhead in the clean sky an eagle dipped and soared on broad wings as he rode the air currents, while a solitary quail called forlornly from a slope covered with false sage. Other than those ordinary items he was alone in a warm and silent world. Dade looked ahead, feeling a strange sort of anxiety come to life within him. He could recognize no familiar landmarks that would indicate he was drawing near that part of the country where the Raker Ranch lay. He was still too far south and maybe a bit west, he reckoned, but then he could not be positive. He had passed this way only once and that was with the cattle he was driving to Pogue's. At the time he'd taken only casual note of his surroundings, being far too busy keeping the steers bunched and moving. But he should be drawing near. He had been traveling steadily, with only one stop of any length since leaving the Box-B, and the sun was now dropping lower in the west. Again he felt a strong urgency to hurry, and, reaching down, he patted the big gelding on the neck and spurred him lightly. The horse responded with a longer stride.

Once more Lockett swept the country with his eyes in a search for riders, the possible source of the uneasiness that now filled him. And again he saw no one. The miles slipped by with the chestnut slowing as time and weariness took their toll of his strength, but the horse did not give up, gamely responding to Dade's every demand. Finally, with the sun not far above the mass of clouds piled upon the western horizon, Lockett rode off the crest of the last hill and looked down into the neck of the valley where the Raker place lay. Alarm rose instantly within him. Where once had been the ranch house and its scatter of sheds, there was now only blackened remains. The night riders had struck again, this time burning everything to the ground. Unmindful of the fagged chestnut's condition, Lockett dug his spurs into the horse's flanks and rushed down the slope.

XIII

Dade Lockett raced into the yard, pulled the gelding to a sliding halt, and leaped from the saddle. Clint lay stretched out on a pallet of quilts, his eyes closed as if sleeping. Roxie, now clad in a coarse shirt and an old pair of her brother's pants, was hunched beside him. Seemingly she was far off and wholly detached from the devastation that surrounded her. A dozen strides to her left was a blanket-covered figure. As Lockett hurried to her, the girl rose, turned to him. She stared at him in a sort of shocked wonderment, her eyes deeply remote, and then as if his appearance triggered a release to her locked-in emotions, she suddenly threw her arms about him and began to sob brokenly.

He held her close, soothing her as best he could while his gaze drifted about the confusion that had been the Raker Ranch. All but two of the horses had been shot, along with the Jersey cow. Chickens lay here and there, victims of target shooters, only a few escaping into the weeds where they soon would become prey for coyotes, hawks, and other animals. The yard was littered with clothing, boxes of personal belongings, several trunks of family possessions. All appeared to have been tossed from the house with little thought as to damage or care, but the fact that such had been removed from the building before the torch was applied indicated at least a small measure of consideration for Roxie and her brother.

Dade felt the girl stir, pull away from him. She had ceased weeping, and, brushing at her eyes, she looked out over the valley. "That's the last time I'll ever cry," she said in a low voice.

He looked at her closely, aware of the firmness in her tone. "I'm hoping you won't ever have to again," he said. "You all right?"

She nodded, again brushed at her eyes. "Renzo's dead. Clint's bad hurt."

"Shot?"

"No, one of them clubbed him with a rifle. I had a hard time bringing him to. I think he's sleeping now."

With the first moments of alarm and fear behind him, anger began to glow within Dade Lockett. He glanced at Clint and shook his head. "Ought to get him to a doctor. When did the raiders hit?"

"This morning, early," Roxie replied. She had regained her composure fully and now was in complete command of herself. "It wasn't even light yet . . . and we weren't watching. We . . . Renzo and I . . . had been up until after midnight and I guess we were tired . . . and careless." The girl paused, peered closely at him. "You've been hurt!" she exclaimed. "Was there trouble . . . ?"

"Didn't amount to much," he said, pushing her hand away. Reaching into his shirt, he obtained the pouch of gold coins, passed it to her. "Money for the steers. You get a look at any of the raiders?"

Roxie cupped the money in her hands. "No, like before, they wore masks . . . sacks . . . over their heads." Her fingers tightened about the gold. "Now I've something to fight with."

Dade smiled. With Renzo dead, her brother in bad shape, the buildings of the ranch in ashes, and the yard livestock slaughtered, she was not giving up. This was a different Roxanne than the one he'd met earlier.

"I've still got the land and a herd," she continued. "With this money I can start rebuilding . . . put up a small house of some kind, just enough to get by. And I'm through selling stock to Pogue or anybody else at a bottom price. Next year I'll make my own drive."

"You've still got Grosinger to deal with," Lockett broke in quietly. "His bunch'll be back."

"I know they will but this time I'll . . . we'll . . . be ready for them. I know we said that before but now I mean it. This is *my* land . . . *my* property. Nobody is going to take it away from me."

Lockett was looking about at the scatter of household goods. "They move all this stuff out before they set the place on fire, or was that you and Renzo?"

"It was them," she replied. "Why?"

"Saw they left two horses alive, and by them saving your belongings for you it means they're expecting you to pack up and move on fast. I had an idea that was what they had in mind."

"Well, I'm not doing it. They'll be back, I know, and I'll still be here."

"Could be I can change their thinking a little on that," Lockett said. "I figure it's about time I had another talk with Grosinger, sort of set him straight on a couple of things."

"You mean you're going to see him . . . warn him?"

"Only way I know to back him off. You think he might have been with that bunch this morning?"

"I don't know. Like I said, it all happened so early. They were breaking down the front door before we even knew they were here. Then Renzo grabbed one of the rifles and tried to stop them, but one of them shot him. That's when Clint got hurt. He started in shooting. Hit one of them, I think, but two of them started beating him with their rifles. I drove one of them off, and then when I looked again, Clint was being dragged out into the yard. He was senseless and bleeding. I don't remember much after that. I

101

was busy trying to help Clint, keep him from losing so much blood and bring him to. All that time they were throwing our things out into the yard and setting fire to the sheds, and then to the house. They started it burning last of all. Dade, it'll be too dangerous for you to go see Grosinger. You'd never leave his place alive. I won't let . . ."

"Sometimes it's the best way to handle a jasper like him . . . show plenty of brass and have a gun in your hand all the time you're talking. I'm pretty sure it was his bunch that laid this bullet track across my skull and nicked me in the arm yesterday. I don't like much getting shot at. I aim to tell him."

"You were attacked?"

"Rode right into an ambush. Figured them for Pogue's cowhands, turned out they weren't. They got the herd away from me but I got it back. Something else we can chalk up to Grosinger's credit, too. Pogue wanted to back out of the deal he'd made with you when I got there."

Roxie frowned. "Why?"

"Grosinger'd got to him, I reckon. Told him not to buy your stock. We did a bit of yammering and he saw it my way. Grosinger's doing everything he can to bust you, drive you out."

"But he's failed," the girl said. "That's going to make a difference in what he thinks. Your making Pogue go ahead with the deal and our staying here regardless of all he's done is proof that we won't quit."

"I expect it is," Lockett said, "but I figure it'll take a little more than that."

"You're paying a visit to him, is that it?"

"It is," Lockett said, turning and moving off into the scatter of boxes, trunks, and other articles. "And this time we're going to play it safe. You figure your friend Cushman would put you and Clint up for a few days?"

"I expect so."

"I'd like it to be that way until I get done what I'm thinking I ought to do." Reaching down, he righted one of the trunks, began to collect its spilled contents. "It'd be a good idea to get all this stuff together, stack it over there in the brush somewhere."

"You think Grosinger's men will come back tonight?" Roxie asked, crossing to where he was and adding her efforts to his.

"More'n likely," Dade said, picking up a tintype photograph that had slipped from its place between the pages of a leather-bound Bible. "If they find the place clean, it'll sort of make them ease off and . . ." Lockett's voice trailed off. His eyes were fixed on the tintype, on the likenesses of a man and woman portrayed there while a deep frown corrugated his brow.

Roxie, aware of the break in his words, glanced up, smiled. "That's a picture of my folks. It was made not long before my mother died."

A coldness had spread through Dade Lockett, tightening his body, bringing a grimness to his lips. There was no mistaking the man in the tintype—that faintly derisive grin, the solid line of thick, overhanging brows, the squared-off chin—it was Pete Dillard. The truth was instantly apparent. Dillard and Charley Raker were one and the same.

XIV

Stunned, angered, Lockett stared fixedly at the picture. Dillard, the partner who had deserted him, left him to die, cheated him, and who he'd vowed to find and kill, was the father of Roxie and Clint. A wryness pulled at his mouth. Dillard's kids—and here he was risking his neck for them. What the hell kind of a turnabout was that—fighting to save the son and daughter, and the ranch of the sneaking, crooked bastard who'd dealt him a hand from the bottom of the deck? He even had it in mind to call out the biggest rancher in the valley and swap lead with him if need be for their sake. And the Dillard Ranch? Hell, it actually was half his. Pete, or Charley Raker as it seemed his real name was, had blown into that part of the country and bought up the place about three years ago, so Renzo Clark had said. That was not long after the stagecoach robbery and just about the time

Lockett was on his way to the pen. It added up one way; Raker had fled West after the hold-up, probably with Tucson as his goal. *En route* he had come upon this ranch, the Fedderman place, found it for sale and to his liking, and bought it. Bought it—using his half of the money they had taken in the robbery and for which Lockett had paid with two years of his life. Dade swore silently, bitterly. Maybe the money wasn't really his just because he'd spent time inside the walls for taking it, but, by God, he had as much claim to it as Charley Raker.

"They were so happy then," Roxie mused. "I only wish Mother could have lived long enough to see the ranch the way it was when my father first brought us here. She would have been so proud of him . . . all he had done, buying this place, building it up."

Lockett looked off toward the lowering sun. The family wouldn't be so proud of Charley Raker, who also called himself Pete Dillard, if they knew the truth. His glance shifted to Clint, moved on to touch briefly the girl. Suddenly he was at a loss, facing a crossroads, uncertain of what to do. He couldn't very well state his claim on the ranch. That would call for a full explanation to Roxie and he didn't have it in him to destroy the one thing that she had left in life—a strong pride and belief in her father. And there was no taking back the things he'd done for the Rakers. Like words spoken, they were beyond recall. But he could call it quits right here and now; he could forget Roxie and Clint, and the dead Renzo Clark, and ride on. He'd already done enough for the children of the man who'd cheated him—too much, in fact.

From the tail of his eye he saw the girl bend down, pick up a flowered scarf, wrap it carefully about the tintype, and lay it back in the trunk. Methodically she then began to retrieve other articles, restore them to the domed, metal-bound box. Lockett stood silently, caught between two fires, unsure of himself and of his own mind. If he rode on, the Rakers would be at the mercy of John Grosinger—and if Roxie pursued her determination to resist, death would be the result. The rancher had undoubtedly played his last card insofar as being patient was concerned. His men had rendered them homeless and to him they would have but one recourse—give in, take what pittance he elected to give them for the property, and move on. That would be the sensible thing for them to do, take what they could get and run. Returning to Indiana, or wherever it was they had come from, was only logical. There they could resume the sort of life they were accustomed to and probably preferred despite Roxie's declaration to hang onto the ranch at all costs. He doubted she really knew what that sort of a statement actually meant, doubted, too, that she had what it took to fight, or kill a man when it became necessary.

Dade shook off his thoughts, vaguely irritated at himself and the position he was finding himself in. What the hell was he letting himself get all worked up for? It was Dillard's kids' problem—let them handle it. Let them get out of it the best way they could.

"What is it, Dade?"

At Roxie's voice he glanced up. She was watching him closely, a puzzled look in her eyes. Again he considered telling her the truth about her father, of his connection with him—and again he turned from doing so.

"Is it something about me . . . something that I ought to know?"

"Reckon it is. I've been running all this through my head and I figure you and your brother'd be better off if you'd take Grosinger's offer and pull out . . . go back where you come from."

Roxie's features stiffened. "I don't think so," she said quietly.

"You're going to get hurt . . . hurt bad."

"It's possible, but I'm not afraid, not any more. Does this mean you'll be riding on?"

He gave that thought. Perhaps, if she believed that he was, that he would not be there to help, she would change her mind and do what was best. "That's what I was aiming to do."

The girl's shoulders stirred slightly. "I'd hoped that we . . . ," she began, and abruptly broke off, lowered her eyes. In the last rays of golden sunlight her hair took on a reddish-brown glow. "I see."

"Maybe you don't," Lockett said, and paused as the drum of running horses sounded in the late hush. He wheeled, tense, alarm rushing through him as he glanced toward the gate. The tautness faded. Two riders. Ed Cushman and one of his hired hands.

XV

The rancher rode into the yard, aghast at the havoc the night riders had visited upon the Rakers. Halting in front of Roxie and Lockett, he dismounted.

"Them raiders again?"

The girl nodded dispiritedly. "This time they killed Renzo. And Clint's badly injured."

Cushman wagged his head. "It's a damned shame. Something sure ought to be done about it," he said, and turned to look at Clint, now sitting up. "You feeling better, boy?"

"Guess so," Raker replied woodenly.

"What you're needing is a doctor, and some good caring for in a decent house," the rancher continued. He hesitated, stroked his chin thoughtfully, and turned to Roxie. "Have you made any plans for what you'll be doing now . . . after this?" he asked, making a sweeping gesture at the blackened ruins of the ranch buildings. "Sure ain't nothing left here worth staying around for."

"It's all we have," Roxie murmured.

"I know, but it's worth nothing now . . . and you can't stay here. Best you and Clint come over to my place where you'll be comfortable. Then we can talk about what you ought to do."

"I know what I'm going to do," the girl said.

Cushman frowned. "That so? What?"

"Rebuild the ranch, keep it going."

"The hell you say!" Cushman said explosively. He brushed his hat to the back of his head, scratched at his red hair, and glared at Lockett. "This some of your doings, putting an idea like that in her mind?"

"No, it happens he's against it, too," Roxie said before Dade could reply.

"It's only good, common sense, girl," the rancher declared, recovering himself. "How can you even think about doing something like that? Place's been burned to the ground . . . and you're flat broke. I meant to say earlier I was sorry your deal with Bern Pogue fell through."

Lockett came slowly to attention. How did Cushman know that Pogue intended to back out on his promise to purchase the Raker cattle? How could he unless *he* had been the one to put pressure on Pogue? He saw Roxie give him a frowning glance. He shook his head. Facing the rancher, he asked quietly: "What makes you think he did?"

Cushman's features were a blank. "Well, that's what he did, didn't he?"

"Nope, not at all," Dade said coolly, and then added: "Pogue crossed you, Cushman."

The rancher drew himself up, flung a side glance at the rider, a lean, wiry man with close-set eyes, who was standing with the two horses. "You're talking loco, mister. I don't know what you mean."

"The hell you don't," Lockett snarled, gambling on being right in what had quickly taken shape in his mind. "It's been you behind the trouble the Rakers have had all along."

"Now just you hold on there."

"It's you wanting the place . . . not John Grosinger. Laying the blame on him was just a way to cover your tracks."

"That's a lie! I've been the only friend these folks've had in this whole valley. It's been me trying to help."

"Been you *offering,* you mean," Dade corrected. "From what I hear the only thing you ever parted with was a lot of talk."

Cushman's ruddy face darkened. He glanced once more at the man he'd brought with him. Lockett gave the rider a look, also, one that was swift, complete, and calculating, and then let his arms sink, hang loosely at his sides.

"That what you think, girl?" Cushman demanded, shifting his attention to Roxie.

The soft contour of her face had hardened,

seemingly freezing the beauty there rather than destroying it. A directness had come into her eyes. "Yes, every bit of it," she said in a firm, solid voice. "I can see now that all this time you haven't been helping us, you've just been making it sound that way while all the time you were gnawing away at us . . . at Clint and me, like . . . like some kind of animal, doing everything you could to pull us down, put us where we'd have to sell out to you."

Dade felt a current of pride sweep through him. Roxie was far more a woman than he'd thought. She was standing up to Cushman, man to man, and, he suspected, were he not there, she'd still do it.

"I'm not denying I offered to buy you out."

"Those night riders . . . are you going to deny they work for you?" she pressed.

Cushman shook his head impatiently. "I don't know nothing about them."

"I'll bet you don't," Lockett cut in. "Same as you don't know who it was that bushwhacked Charley Raker."

It was a shot in the dark, Dade gambling again on what he didn't actually know but suspected.

The rancher's eyes flared. "You can't prove . . . !" he shouted, and then, realizing the words were little less than an admission, broke off. He stared at Lockett for a long moment, whirled suddenly to face the rider behind him. "Shut him up, Abe!"

The gunman's arm moved slightly. Anticipating

it, Lockett rocked to one side, drew, triggered a shot. Abe's weapon blasted in almost the identical fraction of time.

Roxie jumped at the deafening sound of the dual explosions. She spun to Lockett, naked fear tearing at her features. A half dozen paces beyond her, Clint had again come to a sitting position, and was looking on in a dazed sort of way. The girl's voice was anxious, filled with dread. "Oh, Dade . . . are you . . . ?"

Lockett, poised, eyes on Cushman, waved her back. The rancher was wearing a pistol, but he seemed of no mind to use it. Instead, he was looking down at Abe, sprawled full length in the dust, as if unable to believe the gunman had failed. "He's dead, Cushman."

The rancher pivoted slowly, carefully, keeping his hands well away from the weapon hanging at his hip. "I can see that," he said harshly. "And if this is the way you want it . . ."

"It's the way we want it," Lockett echoed scornfully. "It's the way you've made it. First Charley Raker, then Renzo Clark laying over there under that blanket. It was only luck that Clint's not beside him. And a couple of days ago you tried your best to add me to the list."

"You'll make it," Cushman said in a tight, promising voice. "Every damned one of you."

"No point in waiting," Lockett said softly. "Might as well get it done now."

The rancher shook his head, forced a half grin. "No, you ain't suckering me into a shoot-out. That's what I hire men like Abe for." Still facing Dade, he backed slowly to his horse, thrust a foot into a stirrup, and swung onto the saddle, doing it all in careful, deliberate moves. "I'll handle this my way."

"Seems your way's caught up with you," Lockett said dryly. "Best thing you can do now is back off, forget about the Raker place."

"Nope, not about to." The rancher looked directly at Roxie. "This here's your last chance, girl. Load up what you're wanting to keep and go into town. I'll meet you there, pay you what I figure the place is worth . . . cattle and all."

"The answer's still no."

Cushman nodded briskly. "All right, it's you who's called the turn," he said, spurring his horse about. "I'll be back."

"Come ready to die," Roxie said coldly.

XVI

Lockett studied the girl, a mixture of surprise and admiration again running through him. The words she had spoken to Cushman had been hard-edged and to the point; they seemed unlikely to have come from her, yet they had. The flat warning had startled the rancher, too; he had paused in his departure, given her a puzzled, wondering look, and then ridden on, Abe's riderless horse trotting along in his wake. She came around slowly, features still set, lips in a firm, straight line. Her eyes touched Dade Lockett briefly, moved on to halt upon her brother, sitting up on his pallet and watching her. She crossed to him at once.

"Did you hear it all, Clint? It wasn't Grosinger who's been hounding us but Ed Cushman!"

Raker stirred. "He was our friend . . ."

"That's what we thought but he's been against us all the time. He's gone to get his night riders. Intends to drive us off our land . . . kill us if he has to."

Clint nodded woodenly. "It's all right. I'm not afraid to die . . . not any more."

Dade looked more closely at the boy. He evidently had shaken off the stupor induced by the beating he had taken, and was now thinking normally.

Roxie kneeled before him. "I told Cushman we wouldn't leave, that we'd fight, but for your sake we can . . ."

"We're staying here," Clint said. "We can't leave, you know that. Once we're off the place, Cushman and his bunch will take over and we'll never root them out."

The girl lowered her head. "I guess I've been wrong about you. I wasn't sure the ranch mattered enough to you to really fight for it."

"Maybe it didn't before. Things are different now." Clint shifted about on the pallet, seeking comfort. "I'm not going to be a help to you, but I won't be a hindrance, either," he said, and lay back. "I need a gun. If you'll hand me that belt and pistol of Abe's . . ."

Lockett stepped over to the dead gunman, procured the desired items, and carried them to Raker. Roxie was considering her brother carefully, realizing as Lockett did, that he was far from strong enough to be of much aid to her.

"Obliged," Clint said to Lockett in a worn voice. "Got to do my part. Can't let Roxie face Cushman alone."

"She won't," Dade said.

The girl wheeled slowly to Lockett. She was frowning, and there was doubt in her eyes. "You don't have to stay. We'll manage."

"Happens I want to," he replied. "Maybe you're forgetting I've got a score to settle with Cushman, too. I thought it was Grosinger and was about to take it up with him, but it turns out I was climbing the wrong tree."

Roxie smiled faintly. "Thank you."

"No need. The way it is we're sort of lined up on the same side against the same man. Only one thing I want to ask . . . you sure you want it this way?"

"Meaning what?"

"Clint ought to be getting to a doctor. We've got three horses. I could head for town . . ."

"No!" Raker said with unexpected vehemence. "I won't stand for that. If we leave . . . we lose everything."

Dade waited for Roxie to reply. She was looking out across the valley, her features intent. He wondered if she realized just how slim their chances of surviving the oncoming raid by Cushman and his hired guns really were.

"That would be best," she said finally, her voice pitched low. "But I'm wondering if he could stand the trip."

"It would be a hard one for sure. Maybe we could bring the doc here."

"Just what I was thinking, and that's what we'll plan. After it's all over and if we're still here and able, I'll ride in and get Doctor Hale. If we're not . . . well, it won't matter. I know Clint would agree to that."

"Fine . . . it's settled," Lockett said, and glanced to the west. "Not much daylight left. We've got to get ready and be waiting for them."

"You think they'll come before morning?" Roxie asked, her attention again on Clint. He appeared to be sleeping.

"My guess is they won't, but we'll play it smart, get set anyway. We need to fix us up a kind of a fort," he said, looking about.

"Not much left to use," Roxie said in a rueful voice. "They burned 'most everything."

"Saw some strips of tin back there in the yard."

"They're from the roof of the feed shed. We were having trouble keeping it dry inside."

"We can use them. I'll scout around to see what else I can scrape up." Dade paused, then added: "Right here'll be as good a place as any to make a stand. Puts what's left of the house to our backs. You and Clint eat today?"

Roxie shrugged. "Just never thought about it."

"Then you ought to throw something together now while there's time. We'll be needing it later."

The girl's shoulders twitched indifferently, but she turned, began to paw about in one of the boxes that contained odds and ends of food. Lockett circled the still smoking remainder of the main building to the area where the barn and sheds had been located. Seeking out the two sheets of thick, corrugated roofing, blackened by the flames but otherwise serviceable, he dragged them to the front yard. He remembered Abe at that moment and, crossing to where the body lay, transferred it to the edge of the hardpan where it would not be in the way. Turning then to Renzo Clark, he carried the old cowhand over and placed him beside the gunman, covering them both with the same blanket. Burial would have to wait until the following day.

Backtracking to the charred square of the barn, Dade hunted about in its remains, searching for anything that could be of use in building the fortification they must have. He managed to turn up several partly burned timbers, a section of a wagon bed and another strip of metal roofing, shorter than the two he had but equally useful. He lugged them all through the now full darkness to the chosen site, began to assemble them into a small square. While he worked he was aware of Roxie moving about a small fire that she'd built and of the good smell of frying meat and simmering coffee being prepared for a meal. At once it aroused the hunger within him, reminded him he'd gone for some time without food, and when she called to him, he abandoned his labor at once.

"There's not much," she said, taking a plate of her preparations and a cup of coffee to Clint. "Most of our supplies were left in the house."

"This'll do fine," Lockett assured her, helping himself. "We can stock up when we go to town tomorrow."

She came about slowly, her eyes meeting his. "If there is a tomorrow," she said quietly.

He took a swallow of the coffee. It was strong, bitter, like a shot of raw whiskey. "Yeah, if there is," he agreed.

She sat down on a box opposite him, poured herself a cup of the steaming liquid. "You don't think much of our chances, do you?"

"I've seen times when the odds were better."

Roxie sipped slowly at her cup. "I don't want

you to stay, Dade. This is my fight . . . and Clint's. You've no reason to lose your life in it."

There wasn't. He knew that—actually he had less reason to help them because of what their father had done to him than if they'd been total strangers, but that now was something that had receded into the inner recesses of his mind and no longer seemed of importance while standing by them—by Roxie—was. "Reckon I'll still hang around," he said, and rising, chunks of bread and fried meat in his hand, he continued to look about the yard for suitable items with which to build the barricade.

A pile of rocks, barely visible in the half dark of the moonlight, caught his attention briefly. He discarded them as not being worth the labor involved in moving them. There were several small trees at the south end of the yard. Cut to proper length, the trunks and larger limbs could be made to serve. He forsook that thought, also; there was no axe available, it having been lost in the fire. Bolting down the last of the food and topping it off with a third cup of coffee, Lockett retraced his steps to the back yard and resumed the quest. Shortly he turned up a partly destroyed wine keg, probably once used by the Rakers for water and a section of a door, its thick planking fairly intact, and half a dozen boards that had once been flooring.

Thus heartened, he worked steadily in the

increasing glow of the moon at collecting and assembling his finds, and by midnight he had completed a fairly solid bulwark. Within it, he then arranged the trunks and boxes, placing the larger ones about at strategic points. That done, he moved Clint and his pallet into the confined area, paused then, and glanced around to see if anything had been overlooked. Weapons . . . It occurred to him that he had not seen the rifles and pistols, and the old shotgun the Rakers owned. He turned to Roxie.

"Your guns . . . where are they?"

"The raiders threw them into the fire," she replied. "I thought you knew."

Lockett shook his head, swore silently. That really put them in a bind; they had two pistols, his rifle, and perhaps twenty or thirty rounds of ammunition to go against half a dozen or more well-armed men. With the weapons the Rakers possessed, by being conservative with their supply of cartridges, and keeping low in the barricade, the odds might be somewhere near even.

"That makes it bad, doesn't it?" Roxie said heavily, adding a handful of wood to the fire and settling down beside it.

"Not so good, for sure. We'll have to make every shot count."

"We will. Clint and I both learned to shoot."

Dade glanced to where the boy lay. "I doubt if

we can figure much on him. You do your best shooting with a rifle or a pistol?"

"Rifle."

"I'll give you mine. That'll leave the two pistols for me."

The girl sighed, her eyes lost in the fire. "It's hard to believe that everything has changed so quickly," she murmured. "In just a few days our lives have become so different."

"That's the way it works sometimes. You never know what's just around the next bend in the road."

"And Ed Cushman . . . that he was the one behind all of our trouble was hard to believe, too. But it's easy to see now. It explains a lot of things that happened."

"Reckon he's fooled about everybody around here excepting the gunhands he's got working for him. When this is all over, there'll be some of them that'll talk, and what they'll say will likely clear up plenty of things folks didn't understand. It's about time we were getting some shut-eye."

Roxie made no reply, just rose, took several blankets from a stack she had arranged, and began to set two beds on the ground at opposite sides of the fire. "No need of that for me," Lockett said. "I'll do my sleeping sitting up."

The girl handed him a pair of the woolen covers, wordlessly continued to prepare her own pallet. That she was near exhaustion after the long, terrible day was evident in her every move.

Getting to his feet Dade crossed to her, gently forced her to lie down, and then drew the covers over her. "Tomorrow's a long ways off," he said. "Best to forget about it now, figure to take care of it when it gets here."

She smiled up at him, then frowned. "But you're tired as I am . . . I know that."

"Sort of used to it . . . anyway, I aim to do some sleeping myself. Don't figure we'll have any trouble till daylight, but if something does start stirring, I'll wake you. The big thing is not to worry."

Roxie gave him another worn smile and, reaching out her arms, caught him around the neck. Drawing him down, she kissed him.

"I won't . . . Good night."

" 'Night," Lockett replied huskily, and, rising, moved to the front of the barricade.

XVII

Draping the blankets over the side of the barricade, Lockett continued on to where the horses were standing, heads slung low, in the knee-high weeds and grass that fringed a small pond. Of his own volition the chestnut had joined the two Raker mounts and seen to his own watering and grazing. Loosening the gear on all and using halter ropes, he led the animals to a fairly large cottonwood tree at the upper end of the stock pond and picketed them securely. It was not likely they would stray since both grass and water were available, but with the promise of gunfire in the offing they could become frightened and bolt and they would be facing enough problems without finding themselves afoot should it become necessary to leave fast.

Pulling his rifle from the saddle boot, he returned to the barricade and settled down near the center of the forward wall. He had made that particular side more substantial than the others as Cushman and his killers could be expected to come in from that direction. They could fool him, of course, hit from the remaining sides as well, all of which he'd built up to fair strength. But the primary attack he felt certain would come from the front.

Hanging the blankets around his shoulders to stay the increasing chill of the night, Dade checked his pistol, and then the Henry rifle. Three weapons, including the one taken off Abe—and forty-three cartridges according to the count he'd made earlier. He smiled ruefully as he leaned the long gun against the low wall. Not much of an arsenal with which to make a stand against a gang of killers of the sort Cushman would bring— but with a little luck they just might make it. If not, well, a man couldn't expect to live forever. He had to die sometime, somewhere, and one way was as good as another so long as he was on the move and not flat on his back in a bed just rotting away. Funny thing about it was, however, he'd be getting himself plowed under for the kids of the man he'd set out to kill. That was a big laugh when you stopped to think about it. After all that time he'd spent in the pen piling up hate and making plans to track Raker to the ends of the earth if necessary, and take his vengeance, he now wound up sitting alone in the half dark, waiting to swap lead with a bunch of hired gunslingers for Raker's own son and daughter and the two-bit ranch the lousy sharp had bought with their money.

Dade shook his head in wonderment. How had he managed to jockey himself into such a bind? There'd been moments in the past when he'd gotten himself into tights, but they had been of his own making. Lockett shifted his attention to Clint. He was not resting well, stirring restlessly and muttering in a low voice. The boy needed a doctor, that was sure, and unless they could somehow get him to one the next day, it would likely be too late.

His eyes moved on to the girl. She lay curled on her side, her smooth, almost angelic face turned toward him. The soft, lustrous moonlight on her skin gave it a creamy glow, accented her dark brows and lashes, caused her hair to look almost black. She had changed in the short time he had known her, Dade realized. That first day she had seemed a young woman completely out of her accustomed element and over her depth in trouble. Her natural place in life could only have been in some civilized city where lawn parties and masquerade balls and fine homes were the usual. She had fooled him some. The veneer of polite society had been thin, had likely begun to wear from that very first day when Charley Raker had brought her and Clint West from Indiana to join him on his ranch. It was probable that matters had gone fairly well at first with only an occasional hint to her of the harsh and raw realities that went hand-in-hand with living on the frontier. Trouble piled upon trouble, anxiety, fear, and the ever-present threat of hooded night riders had combined to alter her make-up and stiffen her resolve to fight for what was rightfully hers and her brother's. And then when this last attack had come, leaving the ranch in blackened timbers and gray ashes, with Renzo Clark dead and Clint but little better off, the last transformation had taken place. She was now fully acquainted with the facts of life, aware that she was in a land where a man—and in her case, a woman—was compelled to stand and fight and be willing to die for what was right. A time ago Roxie Raker likely would not have considered such a brutal course, but that was in the distant past, and, come morning, he could expect to have her at his side at the barricade exchanging bullets with Cushman and his gunmen. The Roxanne of now bore small inner resemblance to that one of yesteryear.

Clint Raker awoke with a start. He raised his aching head slightly, focused his haze-filled eyes upon the blanket-wrapped figure hunched on a box a few paces away. Lockett, he realized—on guard, watching and waiting for Ed Cushman and his men. He stirred angrily, brushed at his eyes and tried to ignore the giddiness that gripped him. He should be the one out there, not this grim-faced stranger who had ridden into their lives so unexpectedly and taken a hand in their troubles. Although Roxie was a bit older than he, it was he who had always been the head of the family and assumed the responsibilities that ordinarily a father would shoulder. But their father had rarely been home and he knew him mostly from letters containing money sent from some odd-sounding town far away in the West, or an occasional hurried visit while he was in the city on business. His mother never quite gave up on the hope of their settling down as a complete family some-day, somewhere, but it never came to pass as she died one winter of lung fever. After that he and Roxie had gone to live with an aunt but that, too, was an uncertainty as the aunt had problems of her own to contend with. It had been a relief and a sort of rebirth actually when their father sent word and the necessary funds to bring them out to join him on the ranch he'd bought.

Clint stirred, rubbed nervously at his face. It was

moist with sweat, clammy as was his entire body. The pain was only a dull ache now and the hot gnawing in his leg was of small consequence, but he couldn't shake off the weakness that followed those moments when he would alternately burn with fever and then tremble with chills. He was saying nothing about it to Roxie or Dade Lockett. They had enough to worry about as it was. He'd simply fight it out and by morning force himself to take a hand in repelling the attack Lockett expected. He wasn't too sure in his own mind that Cushman would launch such an attack; why should he? The ranch was lost, only burned wood and ashes remained of it. The livestock had been slaughtered and likely what was left of their herd had been stolen or perhaps also killed. But he was in no position to buck this stolid, hard-jawed man who had been so intent, at first, on fulfilling some quest of his own, and then suddenly and with no reason had changed his mind and decided to stay on and help them.

Clint's thoughts wandered as he felt a spasm of chill sweep through his body. Clenching his fists, holding his arms rigidly to his sides, he sought to control the trembling, failed, and rode it out. Then, weak and gasping, odd words spilling from his lips, he lay motionlessly until once again his senses were back to normal.

Lockett—just why had he changed his plans? There had been a few moments before the decision had been made when he thought he'd recognized pure hate in the man's deep-set eyes. It was as if it involved him and Roxie, but that was foolish thinking; he'd never seen or heard of Dade Lockett until he'd ridden into the yard that morning a few days ago and driven off Cushman's riders. Was it Roxie who had brought about the change? Had he fallen in love with her, now wanted her for himself? A wry smile pulled down the corner of Clint's mouth. The thought—the very idea that his sister could ever marry a man like Lockett—a girl well brought up by a gentle mother in genteel surroundings was utterly ridiculous. Why, he was no more than a cold-blooded killer devoid of all human feeling and accustomed to getting what he wanted by whatever means necessary. There was no other explanation for his actions. Certainly no man, especially not an utter stranger, ever walked in willingly and offered to lay down his life for two persons he didn't know. It would be up to him to stop Lockett, not permit him to ruin Roxie's future—if there was to be one for any of them.

He'd best get some rest now, at least try to. When morning came, he'd take steps to get Roxie out of there. It would be easy if Cushman didn't show up with the idea of making an attack; he'd simply force Roxie to take what they could of their belongings, and with the money they'd received from the sale of the cattle to Pogue head out for

Mule Springs and there catch a stagecoach for Indiana. If the rancher did ride in with his killers ready to complete the job of wiping them out once and for all, he'd call for a truce and stop everything before it got started. After he explained to Cushman that they were moving on, leaving it all to him, they would be able to depart in peace—and Dade Lockett, thus shut out, would continue on his way to fulfill whatever purpose it was that had brought him here in the first place. Mean-while, he'd get some sleep—if possible. He'd need all his strength.

Roxie opened her eyes slowly. It was still half dark, that dull gray hour before sunrise and cold was biting deeply into her body. Drawing the blankets tighter about her, she peered through the gloom at Dade. He was a hunched shape perched atop one of the boxes he'd dragged up to the front of the barricade. She wondered if he was asleep. Likely he was only partly so, probably being one of those who possessed the faculty for resting and dozing without ever completely losing conscious-ness. There was a vast difference in men, she had discovered, particularly between those she had known back home in Indiana, and the ones she'd met after coming to the ranch. Where had he come from, and where was he going—and why? That puzzled her along with the reason for his abrupt decision to forsake his own purpose and stand by her and Clint in their struggle against Ed Cushman.

Lockett had given her his reasons, to be sure, but they were a bit beyond her understanding.

Learning much of Dade Lockett, his past and future, was not an easy task. He kept such things to himself, and the deep reserve, almost a hurt in his eyes, prevented one from prying. It didn't matter anyway who or what he was; he was heaven-sent and had it not been for him appearing when he did matters would have been far different at that moment than they were. Whether it would have been better or worse for them was difficult to tell. That her own life would have been scarred and unalterably changed after being forced to be the bush mate of half a dozen of Cushman's men was unquestionable. She would have survived, she supposed; she had heard of other women being raped and later picking up the threads of their lives and going on. It seemed you didn't give up.

Renzo Clark, that old and trusted friend of her father's and subsequently of Clint and her, and who had been of such help, would still be alive. Clint would be suffering with no more than a simple leg wound instead of being half out of his mind from the clubbing he'd taken. Maybe it would have been better if Dade Lockett hadn't shown up—but there was no point in thinking about it now. What had happened was done with and there was no turning back; all they could do was meet what came next and hope for the best. She held little fear. That emotion had long since been driven from her being and she looked ahead to things in a philosophical, come-what-may sort of determination. She would have the answers, meet the emergencies—with Dade Lockett's help—and somehow come out the winner. She was certain that was how it would end; in fact, she was determined that it should.

Her glance drifted to her brother. Poor Clint! He had hated the life their father had imposed upon them, preferring the city where he could work at some regular job, wear clean, stylish clothes, and be a part of what some foolishly called the social whirl. She had been a part of it once, too, but now, looking back, it all seemed so shallow, so useless, and she wondered if it had ever really appealed to her. It had been important to her mother and it had been drummed into her daily that a girl must participate in such activities, that she must be seen often in all the right places with the right beaux as her escorts. What a contrast between the boys she had been associated with there, and who so often professed their undying love for her, and Dade Lockett. She smiled, thinking of the start it would give the people back home if they could see him, talk with him, and know how she felt about him.

Roxie sobered at that thought. How did she feel about Dade Lockett? Was she in love with him—a man she'd met only a few, short days ago, one she knew nothing about other than that he was willing to die for her. Did that mean he was in love with her—or was it another example of that peculiar gallantry she'd learned that most Western men accorded women, placing them on a pedestal and risking all to see that no harm came to them? Whatever Lockett's motivation, it was something that would be determined later. As for her own feelings toward him, that would have to wait; the only matter for consideration and of importance now was the showdown with Ed Cushman, turning him back, killing him if necessary to maintain possession of what was rightfully hers.

Roxie stirred. How easily and naturally the resolution to kill the rancher had slipped into her mind! It had been as simple as drawing a breath —and why shouldn't it be? The right to protect what was God-given and law-sanctioned in this still raw land where . . . —she brought her thoughts to a halt. Lockett had straightened, moved forward off the box, letting the blankets slide from his shoulders. He was gazing off toward the treesto the east. "Well, reckon the ball's about to commence," she heard him drawl softly.

XVIII

There appeared to be at least a dozen men in the party. Lockett, squatting behind the barrier, studied the distant, indefinite figures stoically. They had appeared suddenly at the edge of the trees a long two hundred yards away. In the weak light he could make out few details other than that they were not masked, were sitting their saddles quietly as if awaiting orders from Ed Cushman. Dade heard a sound, glanced to his left. It was Roxie. She was up and had crowded in beside him. Wordlessly he reached for the rifle, handed it to her, and drew his pistol.

"So many," she murmured, gripping the Henry's barrel with both hands.

"Sure never figured on him bringing an army," Dade said. "A half dozen maybe. Looks like he's got twice that many."

"Not wearing hoods, either. Guess that means he doesn't plan on leaving any witnesses."

Lockett nodded. "That'll be the way of it. Now's the time to change your thinking if you're of a mind to do it. Expect we could make it to the horses were we to move right fast. Doubt if there's any use trying to talk to Cushman, once he starts."

"I'm finished with talking . . . begging," Roxie said in a cold voice. "And I won't run."

"Reckon it's too late anyway."

The riders were in motion, pushing forward like a line of cavalry with the pale orange flare of sunrise a brightening fan behind them. Near center and slightly to the rear of the forage formation was Cushman. It was no longer difficult to distinguish the rancher from his men.

"Like as not they'll split into three bunches,"

Dade said. "Part of them'll come at us from the sides, the rest from the front."

"I'll be ready," Roxie said, levering the rifle half open to be certain there was a cartridge in the chamber. The gun was fully loaded, and snapping it shut with a decisive click, she glanced toward her brother. "Clint . . . you awake?"

Raker drew himself to a sitting position. "I'm awake."

"You feeling all right?"

"I'm fine. Don't worry about me, I'll do my part."

Lockett breathed a bit deeper. Clint sounded better, even stronger. Maybe he'd be able to hold up his end after all. "Keep your eyes peeled for the ones that'll come in on us from your side," he said. "Roxie'll be watching her side. I'll take care of the front."

"Heard you say something about trying to talk to Cushman," Clint said, bracing an arm against one of the trunks and pulling himself partly upright. "I think we should do it. I'm willing to try."

Dade, eyes on the slowly advancing riders, said—"Probably too late."—and he looked at Roxie.

The girl shrugged. "Do what you like, Clint," she said. "I won't knuckle under to him . . . and I won't agree to anything but his getting off our land and leaving us alone."

"That's what I want, too!" Clint said, his voice

rising. "You leave it to me . . . I'll get it for us! You hear, Lockett? Want you to stay out of it. I'll do the talking."

"Suit yourself," Dade replied. "Best you be a mite careful, however. That bunch'll be plenty trigger-happy. Expect you ought to have yourself a white flag of some kind."

"I know what I'm doing," Raker declared, resting on the trunk.

The raiders were drawing nearer, walking their horses at a slow, measured pace. As the light strengthened, distinction became even more complete. Each man had drawn his pistol, was holding it with the barrel pointed upward in the fashion of cavalry preparing to charge. Evidently Cushman had once had some connection with the military.

"Dade . . . !"

At Roxie's quiet call he glanced at the girl. She nodded at Clint. Lockett shifted his attention to the younger man. He was leaning forward across the domed trunk, face shining with sweat, eyes unusually bright in the sunlight.

"Best you keep low," Dade warned.

"I know what I'm doing," Clint said again. "I'm going to stop all this before it goes any farther. And when it's settled, I'm taking you away from here . . . away from him! I'm not letting him drag you down . . ."

"Clint!"

Raker's voice broke off at Roxie's withering tone. He swung his feverish features to her, shook his head, turned back to face the approaching riders, now moving into range. Lockett nodded to the girl, raised his pistol. She smiled grimly, leveled the rifle.

"I'll take care of things . . . everything," Clint muttered.

Abruptly he lunged forward and, steadying himself with one hand on the barricade, pointed the weapon he was holding in the other at the sky.

"I want to talk!" he shouted, triggering the pistol in an effort to halt Cushman, gain his attention.

"No!" Lockett yelled, and threw himself at the man in an effort to drag him down and out of harm's way.

He was a fraction too late. A half a dozen shots crackled through the early light, picking up the echoes that rolled out across the flat. Clint jolted as bullets drove into him, knocked him back against the old trunk. Dade caught at Raker's sagging body, pulled it down below the level of the barrier. Clint had died instantly, every bullet fired having found its mark. Snatching up the pistol Raker had dropped, he pivoted, still on his knees, and moved back to Roxie. She was watching him intently.

"Is he . . . ?"

"Dead," Lockett replied flatly, and began to fire

his weapon at the raiders, now opening up in earnest.

Roxie, silent, bent forward, rested the rifle's barrel on the top of the barricade, added her efforts to his. Cushman's men were coming at a trot now, their line still unbroken. Taking his cue from Roxie, Dade steadied his pistol on the edge of the barrier, centered his sights on the rider straight ahead, and pressed off a shot. His mouth tightened with satisfaction as he saw the man flinch, sag in his saddle.

A yell went up then from the raiders—probably from Cushman. At once the riders broke into a fast gallop, firing their weapons steadily as they came. Bullets began to bang into the corrugated metal laid across the front of the barricade, some ricocheting shrilly off into space, others thudding into nearby timbers, sending up showers of black dust and splinters. Firing carefully, conscious of their lack of ammunition, Lockett sought to make every shot count. He caught another rider near the end of the line, toppled him from his horse. A third pulled off, clutching at his leg. Dade glanced at Roxie. She was levering the old Henry steadily, seemingly unaware of the rifle's kick-back against her shoulder.

Abruptly the raiders wheeled, hammered their way back across the open ground to the trees. Dade reloaded quickly, and then crawled to where Clint lay. Taking the man by the shoulders, he dragged him onto the pallet, covered him with a blanket. Roxie, also taking advantage of the lull to feed cartridges into the Henry's magazine, completed the chore, then moved to his side.

"I should've watched him closer," he said, looking around at her. "Just never figured on him shooting that pistol."

Dry-eyed, expressionless, Roxie shook her head. "Don't blame yourself. He wasn't in his right mind."

"Reckon not," Dade said, picking up the cartridge belt still lying on the ground beside the pallet and hanging it over a shoulder. "But I ought've figured . . ."

Shots rang out again, cutting into Lockett's words. The forage line had formed again, was making a second charge. They would split this time, come at them from three sides, Dade thought—and that could be the end of it. He looked at the girl, again kneeling behind the barricade, rifle ready.

"Reckon hell's a-coming," he said. There was no time to waste on gentler words. "Like for you to know that what Clint was talking about's true . . . only I sure wasn't aiming to drag you down none."

The hard lines that had so recently become a part of Roxie's expression softened slightly. "I know that."

"Had more in mind building up this place if we could get the chance. If not, then maybe moving on, finding us another valley somewhere and starting a home . . . that is, if that's how you'd want it."

"It is, Dade . . . and I was hoping it would be here, too . . . Is this good bye?"

"Sort of stacking up that way, but I reckon we can give them a fight to the finish."

At once he began to fire, now using both pistols. Roxie also opened up with the rifle. The line of riders slowed at the sudden, concentrated outpouring of lead. A horse went down. Two more of the raiders buckled, swung off to the side, both from bullets triggered by the girl. She had finally gotten the hang of the Henry's sights. The charge broke. Cushman's men wheeled, again retreated for the trees. Strangely they had not split into separate groups as Lockett had expected. Either they had been turned back before they had the opportunity, or else the rancher was not as adept a cavalryman as he'd thought. But it was an opening that offered salvation, and Dade seized it instantly.

"Let's be getting out of here while we got the chance," he said. "Be no stopping them next time."

Roxie faced him. "I'm not ready to quit . . . not now, not ever," she said coolly.

"Not much sense staying. Doing that'll be playing his game. Smarter to back off, then go after him again on your terms. Just about out of bullets, anyway."

The girl frowned, stared off toward the trees. The raiders were gathered in a circle, apparently listening to instructions from Ed Cushman.

"What can we do?" she asked hesitantly.

"Make a run for the horses. We keep low they won't spot us. Once we get in the saddle we can line out for the hills, find a place to hide."

Roxie, lips set tightly, looked down at Clint, allowed her gaze to slide over the boxes and trunks and piles of family belongings. "I would as soon die right here fighting for what's mine," she said slowly, "but maybe your idea of leaving and getting even with Cushman later is a better one. What about Clint?"

"Can't do him any good. We can come back later and bury him if they don't."

She nodded, turned toward the rear of the barricade, began to gather up items from a box containing food. Dade reached for her arm, pulled her away.

"No time for that," he said, glancing toward the trees. "Grab your rifle, and let's go."

"But we'll need provisions."

"Have to make do with what I've got in my saddlebags," Lockett said, and urged her toward the rear of the barrier. "Keep down low," he said as they started for the coulée. "They'll be on our trail soon enough."

XIX

They reached the horses without arousing a cry from Cushman and his men. Lockett made swift appraisal of the two Raker mounts, chose the husky bay that looked to be the stronger. Stepping hurriedly in close to the animal, he began to tighten the gear.

"Bridle him," he said over a shoulder to Roxie.

She was staring back at the ruin of the ranch house when he spoke, as if taking a last look at what had once been home for her. The knuckles of her hands showed white as she gripped the rifle and there was a set grimness to her face. She turned at once at his words, and, sliding the Henry into the empty boot of the saddle, began to work the bit and headstall into place. Dade, moving fast, completed the job on the bay, wheeled to his own mount. It took only moments to ready the chestnut, and, freeing the remaining Raker horse so that he might wander, he glanced toward the trees.

"They're coming," he said tensely, and stepped into the saddle.

Roxie was already on the bay. She followed his gaze, the coldness of her features increasing. Her hand dropped to the butt of the rifle.

"Cushman . . . ," she murmured. "I could wait . . ."

"There'll come another day," Lockett cut in, wheeling up beside her. "Right now we're getting out of here."

He did not wait for her reply but grabbed the bay's reins close to the bit, brought him around. Roxie forgot the rifle, took up the leathers.

"Where . . . ?"

"Head out for those buttes," Dade answered, pointing to an area of broken, gray-faced hills a mile or so to the west. "We make it to there without them seeing us, we'll be in good shape."

But it was a false wish. They were scarcely started when a yell sounded back in the clearing. Lockett swore, threw a glance in that direction. The raiders were sweeping across the hardpan of the yard, stringing out in pursuit.

"Run for it!" he shouted to the girl, and raked the chestnut hard with his spurs.

Roxie bent lower over her horse, and side-by-side she and Lockett raced across the flat that separated them from the bluffs. Gunshots began to break out when they neared the area. Roxie turned, looked back. Dade shook his head at her.

"Too far . . . they're just wasting lead!"

The girl crouched again over the bay's out-stretched neck. Shortly they swung into a broad arroyo that fronted the row of formations. Immediately the horses began to slow, laboring in the loose sand. Dade scanned the bluffs anxiously. Cushman and his men could quickly narrow the distance between them, bringing them within bullet range if they were compelled to follow the wash for any length of time.

The first of the ragged-faced buttes was just ahead, the beginning of the row of almost identical steep-fronted hills. Lockett studied them closely, searching for a break in the frowning façades, a wash, an intersecting gully, anything that would permit them to pull up out of the sand and disappear, if only briefly. He located such an opening just as the raiders turned into the far end of the arroyo—a fairly narrow but not too steep cleavage between adjacent hills.

"Through there!" he yelled to Roxie, and pointed at the escape route.

She veered the bay toward the gash. Guns were now hammering relentlessly at the head of the arroyo, filling the early morning with rebounding echoes. Here and there spurts of sand indicated that those men using rifles were now within range. Dade wheeled in behind the girl, guiding the bay into the wash. The footing was not too stable and immediately the chunky little bay began to scramble in the loose shale and the sand blown in by the winds. But he managed to keep from going down and within moments was topping out onto the flat above. Lockett, only a length behind on the chestnut, was quickly at Roxie's side.

"Can't stop," he said in a tight voice. "They've seen where we turned off and will be following."

She nodded her understanding, glanced around. "Where can we go?"

Lockett, after a hurried survey of the country, pointed toward the lower end of the buttes. "Somewhere down there. Ought to be a place we can hole up. You go on . . . I'll meet you by those trees. Got some slowing down to do."

She looked at him, puzzled. "Slowing down?"

Dade grinned, drew his pistol and nodded at the wash up which they had just come. "First man in there gets a surprise. Now, move on . . . and stay back from the rim so's nobody'll see you from below."

Roxie rode on at once, and Dade, cutting the gelding about, walked the horse quietly to the wash. He could hear Cushman and the others urging their mounts through the loose sand.

"Keep at it! Keep at it!"

The rancher's voice was an impatient, strident sound on the warming air.

"We lose them, by God, you'll spend the day . . . night, too . . . tracking them down!"

"We'll get them, Mister Cushman!" someone shouted reassuringly.

"See that you do . . . and don't be forgetting there's a little extra cash for the man that does!"

Lockett waited in silence, listening to the thudding of hoofs, the creaking and popping of leather as the riders drew nearer. The rancher was determined to leave no one alive who was in any way connected with the Raker family; he wanted no witnesses, as Roxie had observed. Apparently he did not fear the men who rode for him; likely he had something on all those he employed for such lawless purpose and in that way maintained control over them.

"Went up through here!" a man shouted from the arroyo. "Little wash. Got a kind of a trail."

"Well, god dammit, follow them! If they climbed it, we sure as hell can, too."

Dade rode nearer to the edge of the gash. Leveling his pistol, he waited until he heard the noisy entering of the first rider, and then moments later a wild thrashing about as the horse struggled for solid footing. Leaning forward, Lockett aimed his weapon at a flat rock far down in the gully and pressed off a shot.

A yell went up from below, the sharpness of it slicing through the echo of the gun's blast. It was succeeded by a frantic crashing as the rider apparently fought to control his mount. More shouts, interspersed with curses and protests, lifted, accompanied by a dry crackling of brush and the steady rattle of displaced rocks and gravel spilling into the arroyo. There was a solid thump. The rider and his horse had evidently fallen, and judging from the fresh burst of oaths, had slid downward, piling into those who had followed him into the wash and swept them back into the arroyo.

Lockett swung off at once and put the gelding to a fast gallop. He could see Roxie in the distance, her bay loping easily along over the grassy mesa. As he surged in beside her, she turned a questioning look to him.

"Worked fine," he said. "A right smart of a mix-up going on at the bottom of that draw when I left."

Roxie smiled faintly, sobered. "Will they give up now, do you think?"

"Not Cushman. I don't figure him for the giving-up kind. Plain can't afford to, not after doing what he's done."

"Then we'll have to stop somewhere . . . fight him again?" There was no fear or resignation in her voice; instead, there was a note of eagerness, almost one of hope.

"You can bet on it," Lockett said, gazing off in the distance. "Those hills over to the right . . . you ever been there?"

Roxie shook her head. "I've never done any riding in this part of the valley . . . it was always closer to home."

Lockett nodded, continued to scrutinize the sprawling, low formations as the horses pressed on. Then: "Expect they're what we're looking for. Country looks rough and there's plenty of brush and trees."

"I remember someone saying there were old silver mines over here somewhere," Roxie said.

146

"That'd be fine. Can't think of anything I'd rather see than a mine shaft. But I reckon we don't have a choice other than heading that way and taking our chances. One thing sure, we've got to get off this flat. If Cushman can't get up through that wash, he's bound to send his men around the ends."

At once Lockett began to veer their course toward the ragged hills in the near distance. They should be able to find a cave, or a deep cañon—or possibly an abandoned mine shaft—that would enable them to elude Cushman. The buttes would have provided the same sanctuary had they been able to reach them before the rancher spotted them.

The wooded formation drew nearer. Lockett began to relax somewhat. The hills were higher and more extensive than they had appeared at first glance. They should have no problem locating a good hide-out, and there lie low until things cooled off a bit.

"There's two of them . . ."

At Roxie's quiet words Dade glanced around quickly. Two riders were coming up onto the mesa from the south. Cushman had done exactly as he'd expected—only sooner; he had sent men to circle the buttes in order to gain the mesa above. There would be others showing up at the opposite end. He swung his attention to the north, swore. Three riders were coming into view at that point. Lockett settled his attention on the slopes ahead. They had a long lead on the rancher and his party, and while their whereabouts would now be no secret, they still had a good chance of losing their pursuers.

He nodded to Roxie, grinned. "Just keep riding."

XX

They reached the foot of the hills and ducked at once into a brush-filled wash. Dade, riding in front of Roxie, rode straight on until a second cleft, cutting in at right angles, drew his notice. Immediately he wheeled the chestnut into it, and with the girl following closely urged the horse up the steep grade.

Far back on the mesa men were yelling back and forth, and shortly a gunshot sounded—indication to all of Cushman's party that their quarry had again been sighted. They would immediately answer the summons, racing to regroup at the base of the mountain and from there press the search. With the chestnut heaving mightily, Lockett gained a narrow ledge on the face of the slope, halted, waited until Roxie and the bay had moved in behind him. Lifting a hand for silence, he listened. At once the rapid tattoo of horses pounding across the mesa from the south reached them. It was the two riders they had seen earlier.

"Watched where we turned in," he said. "More'n likely they'll be trying now to head us off."

Roxie laid her hand on the butt of the rifle slung from her saddle. "I've got bullets enough to take care of them," she said in an emotionless voice.

Lockett studied the girl thoughtfully. She had spoken as if using a gun on a man meant nothing, that killing was the answer to any problem, and readily acceptable. But he reckoned she had a right to be feeling that way; it was only a state of mind, a groove of bitterness into which she had been plunged by the loss of her brother and their ranch holdings. It would pass, he was certain; Roxie was a fine, well brought-up girl with a good education. She would shake off the urgent need for vengeance that possessed her along with the idea that a bullet was the way to set all things right, and become her own self again—he was certain of it. Or was he? Such beliefs had been his, he realized; he had started out to exact revenge from the man who had wronged him and would have done so had not someone beaten him to it. How, then, could he be so sure that Roxie would not have those same instincts, that she would forget her need to kill Ed Cushman? Was it simply because she was a woman?

He shook his head, finding no answers to his own thoughts, and returned to the moment. "Can't do it that way. One shot from that rifle and we'd draw them all."

"Then what can we do?" she asked in a quick voice. "I don't intend to let them get close enough . . ."

"We won't," Lockett broke in, a bit startled by the harshness of her tone. "Just keep following me, quiet as you can. And forget about using that gun."

Roxie only shrugged, kicked her heels into the bay's flanks, and started him forward in the wake of the big chestnut. The shelf led them across the slope for a time and then began to sink lower, make its way into a fairly wide arroyo that slashed down from the peaks and ridges far to their right and above them. Dade gave the higher regions consideration. If they could make it up to the area, which appeared extremely wild and broken as well as being thickly covered over with oak brush, mountain mahogany, and other tough growth, they would have their problem solved. But doing so without exposing themselves as they crossed the periodic breaks of open ground would be the drawback; at such times they would offer easy targets for the guns of Cushman's riders.

"They're coming."

Lockett heard the click of a horse's hoof against a rock at the same moment Roxie did. It would be the pair that had come up from the south end of the mesa; none of the others could have had time to move in so close. Dade looked around hurriedly. The trail across the slope they had followed turned sharply downward a few yards farther on, branching off at a fork, previously unseen, that struck for higher levels. Apparently the two raiders were climbing the lower trail with the thought in mind of continuing on up the mountain.

"They're not sure where we went," he said in a low voice, and put the gelding into motion on a course straight ahead.

Roxie moved in behind him and they walked their mounts hurriedly but quietly as possible, taking the turn to the right when they reached it that would eventually end at the towering peaks far above.

"They'll see us," the girl began uncertainly.

Lockett did not slow but pointed to a dense stand of cedars this side of a broad meadow through which the trail made its way. "Not if we're in there."

They pressed on, gained the cover with the thud of the raiders' climbing horses a solid sound behind them. Motioning for Roxie to remain quiet in the saddle, Dade took up a position on the opposite side of the path.

"They'll be tracking us," he whispered. "When they come by, I'll take care of them both. You keep back."

Roxie said nothing, only moved the bay deeper into the brush that crowded the shoulders of the trail. Lockett, pistol in hand, listened intently. Far down the hillside he could hear Cushman and the others talking, but at such a distance the words were unintelligible. They were climbing the slope, he knew he could be certain of that. Leaning forward, Dade rested one hand on the chestnut's neck, seeking to keep the horse quiet. The two men had reached the fork in the path, had halted to examine the tracks left by the bay and the gelding.

"Headed up," one said. "Trying to reach them high rocks."

"I can see that. Going to be hell chasing them out of there, was they to make it."

The other rider swore. "Hell, they can't be that far ahead of us! Come on, let's keep moving."

There were a few moments' hesitation on the part of his companion, then: "Reckon we ought to wait for the boss and the boys?"

"Not me! You can if you want. I'm aiming to collect me that extra reward Cushman was talking about."

At once the other said: "Dang nigh forgot! Goes for me, too."

The thump of hoofs resumed along with the faint clatter of sliding gravel, the quiet swish of disturbed branches whipping back into place. Lockett glanced at the girl. She was hunched over her saddle, had drawn the Henry from its boot, and was holding it ready in both hands. He pulled the extra pistol he now carried from its place under his waistband, held both up for her to see, and shook his head warningly, signifying that he was well equipped to do the chore of halting the men and disarming them.

The sound of the approaching horses became loud. Tense, Dade raised one of the weapons butt first, prepared to use it as a club. The other he held in usual fashion, barrel pointed straight ahead. He would knock the first rider senseless with the one, still be in position to hold his partner at bay with the second.

Abruptly the riders were in view—two lean-faced individuals with eyes intent on the trail up which they were moving. The man in the lead was as he'd hoped he'd be—no more than an arm's reach away. The other, however, was keeping to the opposite shoulder of the path. Lockett swore silently. Such complicated matters called for a change of plan; he'd have to knock out the man behind first. Poised, he let the pair draw abreast, pass. As the rear horse moved by, Lockett suddenly jammed spurs into the chestnut, sent him lunging forward. Both men hauled up in surprise, whirled to face him. Dade lashed out with the pistol in his right hand, caught the outlaw nearest on the side of the head. The man groaned, pitched sideways off the saddle. Instantly Lockett spun to meet the second rider. In that same fleeting moment he saw Roxie swing the Henry rifle by its barrel. It arced through the air. The stock of the weapon struck the man at the base of his skull and the crack of bone was like the snap of a dry twig. He rocked forward as his startled horse shied away, and then as his arms dropped limply, he fell to the ground.

Lockett was off the chestnut immediately. The rider he had knocked from the saddle was on his hands and knees beside the trail. Blood was dripping from a gash laid open along the side of his head by Dade's pistol. Stepping up beside him, Dade plucked the man's pistol from its holster, tossed it off into the brush. He turned then to the one felled by Roxie. She, too, had dismounted and, holding the broken stocked Henry in her hands, was looking down at the man, her features utterly devoid of expression. Lockett squatted, examined the limp figure briefly, and drew himself erect.

"Dead. Was quite a wallop you gave him."

Roxie passed the rifle to him. "I've ruined your gun," she said.

He stared at her wonderingly for a breath of time, and then glanced at the rifle. "No matter. It was getting old," he said, and tossed it aside. Moving forward a few paces, he looked off down the slope. "Best we keep going. Won't take Cushman long to catch up, find these two."

Roxie nodded, turned to the horse the dead man had been riding, and crossed to where the animal, reins tangled in the brush, was waiting. Jerking the rifle from its boot, she took the belt of cartridges hanging from the saddle horn, and returned to Lockett. "These the bullets for this gun?" she asked, holding them close for his inspection.

Dade checked them, nodded, and watched her sling them over a shoulder as she dropped back to the bay. Sliding the Winchester into the scabbard once filled by the Henry, she swung onto her horse. "Which way?" she asked in a cool, business-like way.

Lockett glanced again down the slope. There was still no sign of Cushman or any more of his men, only the faint, muted sounds of their progress as they worked their way uptrail carefully. He switched his attention to the rider he'd knocked cold. The man no longer was on hands and knees, but now lay sprawled full length at the edge of the brush.

"Reckon that depends on what we're aiming to do," Dade said, facing the girl. "We could go higher, find a place to hole up till dark, then get out of the country."

Roxie met his eyes squarely. The hardness of her had grown more intense and there was a coldness that reminded him of a hired killer he'd once known. "I'm not leaving the country," she said quietly. "Not until I've killed Ed Cushman."

XXI

Dade Lockett considered the girl in silence. The change from the Roxanne he had first met that evening in the yard of the Raker Ranch and the remote, cool Roxie who now looked down at him from her saddle on the bay was as vast as the distance separating the towering Rockies and the equally cloud-piercing Sierra Nevadas. That she was capable of carrying out her declaration he had no doubt; the manner in which she had handled Cushman's rider, knocking him from his horse, killing him, and then calmly brushing aside the fact, was proof of that. But it was all wrong; it was not woman's work.

"I can't let you do something like that," he said. "Ain't right."

"Right," Roxie echoed. "Why isn't it? What's the difference if I avenge a wrong done me and my family, or if it was my brother doing it?"

"Ain't sure but there is . . . him being a man and . . ."

"Poppycock. He's gone . . . dead, killed by the man who murdered my father. I'm the only one left so it's up to me."

"No, squaring up's not the thing for you to be trying to do. Not right."

"Are you trying to say that revenge isn't right?"

"Well, maybe I . . ."

"You know that's not it, Dade. You were on your way to square up with somebody, as you call it, when you stopped to help Clint and me. I know that now, just from the way you acted and talked because I've been seeing the same thing in myself ever since Clint was shot down and I found out for sure about my father. Now, isn't that the truth?"

Lockett, caught between a rock and a wall of granite, unable to express himself or explain his beliefs, turned on a heel and moved to where the chestnut stood.

"Well, isn't it?"

Dade settled himself on his saddle. If he answered her question, told her about her father and what had lain between them and that he had planned to kill him for his wrongdoing, would it help any? Would it make her understand? He decided it would not. "Reckon it was something like that," he murmured.

"That proves it then," Roxie shot back, a triumphant note in her voice. "It was someone who had harmed you, just as Cushman has me . . . maybe even killed a person who was very dear to you. Isn't that how it was?"

Lockett shrugged. "It was just a jasper I once knew. Left me dying on the ground when he could've helped."

"So, since you're a man, it was all right for you to seek vengeance, but because I'm a woman, even though I've got greater cause than you, I've no right to feel the same way?"

Dade pivoted the gelding about, headed uptrail. He was weary of bandying words, and if they didn't get moving, they'd find Cushman right at their heels. There was no arguing with Roxie, he could see that—and no time to do so if there was. Later, once they were safely beyond the rancher's reach, he might be able to talk a little sense into her. It was loco, plumb loony for her to think she could go gunning for Cushman.

They climbed steadily, pointing for a dark bank of cliffs well to the west. Once there they not only would have a wide, sweeping view of the slopes below and all that stirred upon them but there should be many natural fortifications they could select as a hide-out. He could not blame the girl for her desire to even up with Ed Cushman. It was a natural feeling and one he well understood. Only it was not for a woman, particularly one like her to have such desires. Women simply didn't involve themselves in killings—he wished he could make her see that. Oh, sure, there were those who carried Derringers about in their reticules or the pocket of a lace dress and avenged themselves for various reasons on some dandy, but they were the fancy women—not fine, genteel girls like Roxie. Why couldn't he make her understand that?

Time wore on as the line of cliffs grew taller, darker. There were no sounds of pursuit although he was sure the rancher and his men had come upon the two who had been in advance of them by that hour. Either Cushman was not certain of the direction that he and Roxie had taken or was reluctant, being caught below on the slope and therefore at a disadvantage, to press any farther. He hoped that was it, that Cushman, satisfied he had nullified the Raker claim to the land he wanted by killing off all but one member of the family—a mere girl—had turned back and was letting it drop. It would solve a lot of his worries, Dade thought, if that were true. He could forget about the rancher and his raiders, keep Roxie on the move and get her clear out of the country, and by then she would have maybe come to her senses and given up the idea of killing Cushman.

"I don't think they're following," he heard her say in a worn voice. "Can't we stop and rest for a while?"

Lockett glanced at her. She was slumped in the saddle, wearied to the verge of collapse. He pointed to the cliffs. "I was wanting to make it to there. They'll never find us once we get that far. Take maybe another hour. Figure you can hold out that long?"

Roxie nodded listlessly and they moved on. The horses, too, were beginning to show the effects of the grueling climb, and Dade, picking the route as carefully as the lay of the land would permit, chose the gentlest course. Within the promised length of time they reached the base of the lengthy stretch of palisades that reared high above the country below, and cutting due north Dade led the way toward what appeared to be a large cañon. The bright green splash of cottonwood trees indicated the presence of a spring or mountain stream. It proved to be the latter, breaking out of the dark, rich earth, crossing a small meadow lush with thick grass, and then disappearing again into a welter of sun-scoured boulders.

They halted at the edge of the water, dismounted. Lockett led the horses a distance below, and allowed them a brief drink. As he turned to picket them, he saw that Roxie had settled herself on a nearby log, was brushing ineffectually at her hair with her hands. The rifle she had appropriated from the slain rider lay across her knees, ready for instant use. He sighed heavily, seeing in that an index to the new Roxie; never again would she allow herself to be caught helpless and unprepared.

"This is a beautiful place," she said. "A house back there on that little rise, the rest of the sheds and things near the trees . . . Living here would be wonderful." Her voice faltered, and she added: "If they'd only let us."

Dade, busy at stripping the gear from the horses, paused. "If you're thinking of Cushman . . . not everybody's like him. Far as the land goes, it's probably open to homesteading."

"I know, but it would be a hopeless thing, same as my father's place. As soon as it was fixed up and doing well, somebody would start wanting it, and sooner or later they'd drive us off."

"There'd always be somebody who'd try. Out here you have to fight to get what you want, then fight to keep it . . . and it's not always some other man you're up against. Can be a drought or a blizzard, the wind . . ."

"Those things you can fight," Roxie said quietly. "It's men like Cushman, big and strong with plenty of money to hire night riders . . . killers that ordinary folks like us can't beat."

Lockett only shrugged. Straddling the saddles over the fallen pine, he pulled at the strings anchoring his saddlebags, and freed them. It was growing late, and hours back he had become convinced that Cushman and his party had given up the chase—at least until the next day. A small fire, some hot coffee, and the few bites of food that he still had on hand—and they would both feel better. Perhaps, after a little rest they could saddle up and move on.

"Dade . . . I'm going back."

He slowed his stride, turned wearily to her. "Back to what's left of your ranch . . . that what you mean?"

She nodded. "I can't let Cushman drive me off. My father worked hard to build up that place, actually died for it . . . all so that I would someday

161

have something good and worthwhile. I'd be letting him down . . . betraying him, if I didn't fight to keep it."

"We been all through this," Lockett said. "I was hoping you'd come to your senses. You can't fight Cushman. You saw that this morning. What makes you think it'll be any different next time?"

"One thing," Roxie replied, hands dropping to the rifle. "Cushman won't be there. I plan to kill him first."

XXII

Lockett moved on to a small cleared space in the grass, squatted. Setting the saddlebags aside, he began to assemble small stones into a circle for a fire pit.

"I had hoped you'd forgot that, too," he said in a low voice. "It's the smart thing for you to do . . . forget it. Take it for a licking and move on. We can go somewhere else, start over."

"No, I can't do that."

The rocks arranged to suit, Lockett dug into the saddlebags, obtained the sack of crushed coffee beans and the tin he used to boil water in. Filling the blackened container with water, he struck a match to the dry limbs he had placed within the rock circle, and then propped the tin over the flames. "Maybe it's something you'll have to do.

You or anybody else shoots a big man like Ed Cushman, the law'll step in."

"Let it. Right is on my side."

He faced her, shook his head slowly. "Haven't you learned yet that being in the right doesn't always count," he demanded in a frustrated voice. "There's plenty of times when somebody being in the wrong turns out to be stronger than somebody in the right."

"But the law . . ."

Dade pushed his hat to one side, gently touched the area under the bandage where the rustler's bullet had left its wound. The place was healing, he supposed, but it was becoming increasingly tender. "Law's just a man . . . sometimes a good one, sometimes a bad one, and most of the time they're beholden for their job. They can't always be blamed if they look out for themselves."

"You're only saying what I've come to realize . . . that you have to look out for yourself . . . protect what's yours."

Lockett fed more wood into the fire. Somewhere up on the slope behind them a dove was calling into the hush. "Might be all right if you were bucking just somebody that didn't amount to much . . . but Cushman, he's somebody big. Hate to say it, but it makes a difference. Have you stopped to think what'll happen if you do get in close to where you can put a bullet into him? That won't be easy but if you make it, every lawman in the country'll be on your trail . . . along with all the bounty hunters and drifters, looking to pick up a few dollars' reward."

"If you'd found the man you set out to kill, wouldn't it be the same for you?"

The water in the tin was beginning to simmer. Opening the sack of coffee, Dade poured a quantity into the container, and nudging it to a back corner of the rocks, he placed the battered spider he carried over the center of the flames. Taking a chunk of slightly rancid bacon from its oily wrapping, he cut it into slices and dropped them into the pan. To these he added several hard biscuits crushed between his palms, a lone potato discovered in the bottom of the saddlebag, and a piece of onion. Over it all he poured water.

"Be ready pretty soon," he said, more to himself than the girl.

"Wouldn't it?"

She hadn't forgotten the question, as he'd hoped. "No, it'd be different. The man I was looking for was a nothing . . . a nobody. The law wouldn't care about him."

"But if he'd been Cushman . . . ?"

"If it was somebody big like him, then I'd get moving, and stay moving. Only thing I could do."

"And I can't . . ."

"No, by God, you can't!" Lockett snapped, suddenly finding himself on solid ground. "Places I'd go to keep out of the way you couldn't go.

Things I'd do to bury myself from scalp hunters and the lawmen, you'd not be able to swallow. You'd be like a duck sitting in a rain barrel, and mighty damned fast they'd have you dead or up before some hanging judge friend of Cushman's. You'd be lucky if you got off with no more'n spending the rest of your life in the pen."

Roxie sat silent for a time, then: "At least I'd have made Cushman pay."

"Nothing's worth being cooped up behind the walls of a pen," Dade said. "I know, and before I'd let them put me there again, I'd take on the whole United States Army."

She considered that thoughtfully, eyes on Lockett as he began to stir the stew with his skinning knife.

"It doesn't matter . . . none of that," Roxie said finally. "I have to do it . . . and I can. It will be simple to hide out near his ranch, put a bullet in him when he passes by. You won't need to go, Dade. It's best I do it alone."

Lockett set the spider off the flames, procured a tin plate, a wooden spoon from the saddlebags. Dividing the contents of the frying pan into the plate, he passed it to her. "I figure you're making a mistake," he said, "but I'll be siding you . . . there and from here on out. About time you got to remembering that . . ." He stiffened suddenly, drew himself upright. The clacking insects down the trail had abruptly ceased their racket. A moment later a horseshoe chinked dully against a stone. Lockett set the frying pan back on the fire, spun to Roxie.

"Over there . . . quick," he snapped, pointing to the nearby trees.

She rose at once, hurried to the small grove with its undergrowth of brush, filling with shadows now as the day waned. Lockett waited. It could be a false alarm—not Cushman or any of his men but some pilgrim cutting through the mountains. But he was taking no chances.

"You . . . there by the fire . . . get your hands up!"

At the harsh command Dade raised his arms. He hadn't been wrong; it was the rancher. Taut, he watched Cushman, accompanied by two other men, move into the open and advance slowly. All had drawn their weapons and were leveling them at him.

A dozen paces away they halted. The rancher looked around, eyes narrowing. "Where's that woman?"

"Gone," Lockett said. "You got here too late to finish up your murdering."

The husky man to the rancher's left took a half step forward. "She's the one who'll be facing a murder charge. Brother of hers, too, only we took care of him this morning."

Lockett centered his attention on Cushman. "What kind of a deal's that? Ain't true and you damned well know it."

"They shot two of my men. Got witnesses to prove it."

"That's a lie, Cushman. The only murdering that's been done was by you and your outfit."

The squat rider shook his head. "That's only talk . . . and the charge includes you, too, whoever you are. Seen you there this morning. Where's the girl hiding?"

"Said she was gone," Dade repeated.

Cushman swore angrily, triggered the weapon in his hand. The bullet plowed into the ground at Lockett's feet, sprayed dirt over his boots.

"You trying to make me believe that . . . and me standing here looking at two horses? Where is she? Speak up, or by God, I'll put the next slug in your belly!"

The third man in the party holstered his pistol, turned to the rancher. "Reckon I know how to make him talk. Just let me work him over a mite."

"Not worth the trouble, Tip . . . he's good as dead anyway," the rancher said. "It's a cinch she ain't gone. Like as not she's hiding over there in them trees. You and Tillman take a look . . . I'll finish off this bastard," he added, and raised his weapon.

"I'm here, Mister Cushman," Roxie said from the edge of the grove.

The rifle in her hands blasted as she spoke. The rancher clawed at his chest, rocked back. Tip reached for his pistol. Lockett drew, fired, spun the rider half around with a bullet. He heard the Winchester bark spitefully again as he turned, saw the man called Tillman stagger, fall heavily across a clump of sage. Motion caught at the corner of his eye and he swiveled his attention to Tip. The rider was plunging off into the brush. Dade whipped up his gun once more but it was too late. Tip had disappeared into the brush.

As the rolling echoes faded slowly, Lockett stared at the lifeless figure of Tillman sprawled face up, empty eyes fixed on the sky. A coldness swept over him. He glanced to Roxie, now moving in beside him, her gaze on Cushman.

"Is he dead?" she asked tonelessly.

Dade nodded. "Both of them. Other one's hit but he got away."

A shudder passed through her as she looked down at Tillman. "I didn't want to shoot him but he started to . . ."

"Don't think about it," Lockett cut in roughly, and wheeled about.

There was no time to waste. He had misjudged the rancher, assumed he'd called off the hunt. Instead, he'd kept at it, and that meant the remainder of his party was somewhere on the mountain. Not only would they have heard the gunshots, but Tip would summon them and they would soon be closing in.

"We've got to get away from here," he said,

grasping the girl by the arm. "Give me a hand saddling up."

Roxie frowned. "Why? We can go back to the ranch now. Cushman's dead."

Lockett pointed to Tillman. "Forget doing that. Take a good look at him. The badge you see there inside his pocket says he's a lawman . . . a deputy sheriff."

The girl's lips tightened into a thin line. "A . . . a lawman?"

"The star didn't show until he went down," Lockett said, taking up the saddles and crossing to the horses. "Must've been a friend of Cushman's. Probably came along to make things look good . . . or it could be he did figure to haul us in to stand trial on that trumped-up murder charge."

"But Cushman was about to shoot you."

Dade said: "Yeah, did for a fact, but it won't make any difference. He's a lawman and he's dead."

The bay was ready. Lockett began to work on the chestnut. Roxie was gathering the cooking equipment, hurriedly stowing the items into the leather pouches.

"What's that mean?" she asked.

"It means we ain't got a prayer in this part of the country, and a mighty small one everywhere else. Kill a lawman and you're dead . . . that's an old saying and the badge-toters work plenty hard at keeping folks believing it."

"Then where can we go?"

"We'll light out for Mexico. If we're lucky, we'll make it," he said, helping her onto the bay. "If not . . . well, it's been nice knowing you."

He pivoted to the chestnut, vaulted onto the saddle. For a few moments he was silent, listening for sounds on the slope that would tell of other men drawing near. He could hear nothing. That was the way it would be from that time on, he realized; they must forever be on guard, fearful of what lay beyond the bend in every trail they followed, of every corner they turned. Their lives would depend on it. Coming about, he faced Roxie. She was erect on the bay, features calm, at peace. She had not returned the Winchester to the boot, instead was resting it across her lap. Lockett ducked his head at the weapon, smiled grimly.

"That's your best friend now. Just keep remembering it's the difference between living and dying when you're a wanted killer . . . like us."

"I won't forget," she murmured, and, swinging in beside him, rode out of the clearing.

But hope, too, is a many-splendorous thing, and minutes later, when they reached the crest of the first rise, Roxie paused, looked off toward the north where the ranch lay.

"Maybe someday we can come back," she said wistfully. "After all, the land will still be there."

"Maybe we can," Lockett agreed as they rode on.

Wanted: Dead or Alive

I

With the furious storm raging about him, Ben Jordan halted. He was high in the towering Mogollon Mountains of New Mexico Territory, struggling to follow a trail that cut a precarious course along a rocky ridge. He probed the wet half darkness with anxious eyes. Although it was only midafternoon, it seemed night was almost upon him. He was soaked to the skin, despite his slicker, and chilled to the bone from the snow-tinged rain. Water cascaded from him and the weary buckskin he rode in a hundred small rivulets. The trail had become a sea of flowing mud, the entire mountainside a sheet of glistening water. Arroyos were running full, and had become wild, turbulent rivers of boiling, brown slush that swept everything before them. Lightning flashed vividly, now and then striking one of the towering pines that studded the slope, creating an eerie glow and setting up a hissing and crackling that blended with the continual grumble of thunder.

Jordan had no idea of how far he was from a settlement, or even if there was one in the area. It had been hours since he had noted a miner's cabin or squatter's shack. But the trail he followed appeared to be a main course; it would lead eventually to somewhere. At this point, however, it made little difference; he wanted only to get in out of the hammering rain to dry and warm himself. It was days since he had ridden out of Mexico and the comfort of the hot Sonora sun. Now, wet and cold, he was having vague regrets, wishing that he had not accepted Tom Ashburn's offer and that he had not given up the ranch in the Barranca Negra, since that morning when Mexican bandits swooped down, attacked, and killed his father and stepmother.

Perhaps he should have stayed put on the ranch deep in the black-walled gorge; maybe he should have toughed it out, continued the never ending war with the renegades that had begun the day his father, Dave Jordan, and he, then only a small boy, had settled in there. Matters had improved somewhat a few years later when the elder Jordan had met and married a Mexican woman; the *gringo patrón* and his son had become more acceptable to the natives at that point. But in the end it mattered little. The bandits' bullets recognized no distinction, and the letter from Dave Jordan's old friend, Tom Ashburn, arriving two months later was most opportune. It offered him the job as foreman on his vast Lazy A spread in northeastern New Mexico. Ben had lost no time accepting. He gave away what was left of the ranch in the Barranca Negra, packed what few possessions he owned in his saddlebags, and rode out.

In his heart he knew it was the right thing to do. Although he had come to love the country he grew up in, there was nothing there for him; the ranch was a poor, starve-out affair at best. Ben Jordan knew that, admitted it, but change always comes hard to any man. Sitting there, high on the storm-swept mountain, wet and cold, he told himself again that he had made the right decision and he would abide despite the bitter welcome being extended him by the elements. He stared ahead. He could see no sign of shelter through the whipping gusts. All that was visible were the swaying, tortured pines shifting under the storm's impact, the wetly shining rocks, the deeply grooved trail that was now an onrushing stream. Lightning glared beyond the ridge to his left, and was followed instantly by a clap of thunder. The buckskin trembled beneath him. At once the rain seemed to increase and somewhere behind him came a new roaring as an arroyo, filled to capacity, broke free of its bounds and began to pour down the slope in a new channel.

Jordan urged his pony on. The footing was slippery, dangerous, and the horse moved reluctantly. If there was no hope of reaching a settlement, then he must soon find shelter of some sort for the buckskin and himself. They were both about finished. A low butte facing away from the slanting rain would afford some protection. He was avoiding the thick stands of trees, prime targets, it would seem, for the jagged streaks of lightning.

A hundred yards farther along Jordan again pulled to a halt and dismounted. It was too much for the buckskin to carry a rider and maintain his footing in the swirling mud and water. Walking out ahead of the worn horse, Jordan pressed on, able to follow the trail now only because of the lack of brush and rock in its course.

A half hour later Jordan saw ahead a lower crest, actually the summit of a saddle looping between two peaks. There the trail dropped off the high ridge along which he was traveling, and appeared through the murk to angle off the rim and slice diagonally across a broad swale and enter the forest. He did not like the idea of going into the trees but the hollow itself was low and considerably sheltered from the full force of the howling storm.

Hopeful of finding at last the protection he sought, he pushed on, keeping well back from the edge of the ridge which here dropped off steeply into the dark depths of a cañon. Although the footing was uncertain, the ground was fairly level, and he moved on, leading the buckskin at a good pace. And then suddenly the world was nothing more than a vacuum of blinding, blue light filled with tremendous sound. He felt the buckskin wrench the reins from his hand, heard him neigh in terror. Jordan was aware of a powerful force striking him, slamming him flat into the swirling water and mud.

Half blinded, he struggled to his feet. A peculiar prickling sensation filled his body and he was slightly stunned. He looked about. Lightning had struck a tree no more than fifty feet away, and had split it down the center, smoking and sizzling in the pouring rain. There was no sign of the buckskin. Jordan wheeled, hurried to the rim of the cañon. He waited for the next spread of light. It came at once. He saw the luckless horse far below, wedged between two massive boulders. There was no doubt that the fall, when he had shied and gone over the edge, had killed him instantly.

Ben Jordan stood quietly on the brink of the chasm for several minutes while a sense of loss possessed him. The buckskin had been a good horse, a faithful companion. But there was nothing he could do for him now. And he was now afoot, with all his gear lost, with no hope of replacement until he reached civilization.

He moved on, following the trail across the long swale, still heading for the trees lying on its far side. The rain continued its onslaught, freighted with frequent and vivid flashes of lightning and rolling, crackling thunder. When he reached the lowest point of the hollow, a twenty-foot-wide arroyo blocked his route.

He hesitated momentarily, then ventured into

the knee-deep torrent cautiously. The current was strong, tugged at him relentlessly. Legs spread to steady himself, he made his way slowly. He reached the center, braced himself for the final effort—and then, suddenly, he was going over.

Something moving beneath the surface of the boiling water, a small log perhaps, or a bush ripped free of its moorings, had caught at his feet and tripped him. The force of the arroyo spun him about and thrust him backward. He fought to remain upright, failed, and went down into the churning, roily water. Choking, gasping, he managed to roll over, striving frantically to get his feet under him again as he bobbed erratically in the rushing current.

He touched ground, and steadied himself. Bucking the arroyo's force, he managed to pull himself upright again, and stagger his way to the edge of the wash. He dragged himself out of the surging flood, and halted, sucking deeply for breath. His clothing was plastered to him, and seemed to weigh a hundred pounds and his feet were awash inside his boots. He sat down, emptied them, and noticed at that instant that he had lost his gun.

He rose, turned up the slope, dismissing the loss with no further thought; recovering the weapon would have been impossible. Worn to exhaustion, he trudged on. He must stop now. He was physically incapable of going any farther. A bush, a low tree, a ledge of rock, anything would serve as shelter.

A sudden flare of light shattered the darkness, and illuminated the entire slope. Hope surged through him. In the brief break he thought he had seen the outlines of a cabin. He waited for the next flash, eyes straining into the gloom. A jagged finger ripped the murk once more. A long sigh escaped his lips. It was a cabin—shelter at last! Even if uninhabited it would provide protection from the storm, a place to rest, to remove and dry his clothing. and wait out the storm. He struggled up the grade, slipping, falling, hurrying desperately to reach the structure. As he drew nearer, he saw that it was a crude, log affair, that it appeared to be in fair condition. Beyond it a short distance stood a second building, a shed of some sort. His spirits lifted higher. Someone likely was there, possibly a miner. There would be food, a fire, dry clothing.

He stumbled up the last of the incline, reached the level upon which the cabin had been built. He lurched toward the doorway, now seeing faint light seeping through a shuttered window. His hand grasped the wooden latch, and lifted it. The door opened, and he half fell as he entered. His head came up swiftly and his pulse quickened as he stared into the muzzle of a pistol.

II

"Don't . . . move . . ."

The command came from a man hunched in an opposite corner. The words were halting, labored.

Jordan froze. A lantern placed near the crouched figure spread a small circle of light before him. Ben looked sharply at the man. His brush jacket had been thrown back. The entire right side of his chest was soaked by blood. There was another wound in his leg. The pistol in his hand wavered uncertainly.

Ben closed the door with his heel, started to rise. "Here, better let me . . ."

The hunched shape stiffened. "Don't try . . . ," he began, and lapsed into silence. After a moment he motioned with his weapon. "Get in the light. Got to see if . . ."

Jordan advanced slowly, stopped within the lantern's yellow glow. "You're in a bad way," he said. "Let me help."

The man stared at Ben with hot, glittering eyes. He was a thin-faced, dark individual. "You're . . . you're not one of them," he said finally, and let his arm fall as though the pistol's weight was more than he could manage. "Who are you?"

"Name's Jordan. Up from Mexico," Ben said,

dropping to his knees beside the man. "What happened to you?"

There was a long minute as though the man were having difficulty concentrating. Then: "Outlaws. Jumped me late yesterday afternoon. Gave them the slip but caught a couple of bullets . . . Thought . . . thought you were one of them."

Jordan examined the man's breast. It was a bad wound, one that left nothing to be done. Death could be only a matter of hours.

"Not me," Ben said, pulling the jacket into place. "Got trapped in the storm. Lost my horse over a cliff when lightning hit close by. I was looking for shelter when I saw your cabin."

"Don't belong to me," the wounded man said. "Like you . . . come across it after I got hit . . . and was looking for a place to hole up. Name's Woodward . . . Walt Woodward."

Jordan reached for the man's hand, shook it gently. He glanced about the cabin. It was bare, and apparently had not been lived in for some time. Several insistent leaks drip-dropped from the ceiling and the glass in a window high on the rear wall had been broken out.

"Little heat would feel good," Ben said, his eyes pausing on the fireplace and a scatter of split wood and pine knots near it. "I'll get a fire going, then we'll see what we can do about those wounds of yours."

Woodward smiled weakly. "Be a waste of time,"

he said. "Been around, seen how these things go."

Jordan was busy at his chore. "We'll give it a try, anyway. Never can tell."

But he knew there was little point to it. Not even the expert attention of a physician could help Walt Woodward now. Not only had he lost far too much blood, but the bullet in his chest had damaged his lung.

When the fire was going well, Jordan turned, began to prowl the cabin. He located a gunny sack, stuffed it into the gaping window, closed out the driving rain. The storm still raged, slamming against the cabin in fitful gusts and blasts.

The flames in the fireplace mounted, filled the room with warmth and light. Jordan kneeled beside Woodward again. The man was propped in the corner, his back resting against a pair of saddlebags. Ben pointed to them.

"Any grub in there? Coffee?"

Woodward shook his head. "No. No food. Could sure use a drink of water. You got any?"

Jordan said: "No. Lost everything when my horse bolted. But I can fix you up."

He found a tin can left by some previous tenant. Holding it beneath one of the steady drips, he rinsed out the dust, then allowed it to fill. He handed it to Woodward.

"May taste a bit rusty . . ."

Woodward seized the can, drank greedily. When he had finished, he set the container on the floor beside him. He studied Jordan with bright, feverish eyes.

"From Mexico, eh? You a 'breed? Don't look like a Mexican."

Ben, faintly angered, said: "No, I'm neither, not that it makes any difference. Just happens I grew up down there."

"Headed for where?"

"Northeastern part of the territory. Going to work for Tom Ashburn, the Lazy A Ranch."

Except for the suffering Woodward, it was pleasant in the cabin, out of the shrieking storm. The room had warmed, and was now filled with the soft glow of the fire. Ben took up the can, and filled it again with water, and then set it near the flames to heat.

"Let's get some hot water. I'll see what I can do for . . ."

"Forget it," Woodward said. "Just not in the cards for me."

Jordan stared into the dancing flames. "You mentioned outlaws . . . what happened? They try to hold you up?"

Woodward shifted his position slowly, painfully. "Fire feels good," he murmured. Then: "Yeah, four of them, four men. Tried to rob me. Made a run for it. Got away except . . . except maybe I didn't really get away after all."

Jordan was silent, wondering why outlaws would attempt to halt Woodward unless the man were carrying something of value. He did not appear to be a man of wealth. And if there were other reasons . . .

"You're . . . you're wondering why," the wounded man said, reading Jordan's thoughts. Lightning crashed somewhere back up the slope, briefly filling the room with a lurid white light. Woodward waited until the roll of thunder died. "I'll tell you why, Jordan. Money . . . cash money. Quite a lot of it. That's what they wanted."

Ben glanced up in surprise. "Why tell me? Aren't you afraid I'll . . . ?"

"Afraid you'll take it from me, that what you're trying to say? Maybe, but I don't think so. You're not the kind to rob a dying man of all he's got . . . not when he has a wife at home waiting for him to show up."

Woodward paused, out of breath. He managed a half smile. "The truth, Jordan . . . I was on my way home . . . carrying the money I got from selling a ranch of mine . . . down Arizona way . . . every cent I have in the world . . . it's here in these saddlebags. Twenty . . . twenty thousand dollars."

"Twenty thousand dollars," Ben echoed softly.

"Figure you're a man I can trust," Woodward said, his voice sinking lower. "I want my wife to have that money. She needs it. Something to keep her the rest of her life. No country for a woman alone . . . broke. There's a thousand in it for you if . . . if you'll see to it . . ."

Jordan frowned. "I don't want any of it."

Woodward forced a smile. "Knew you'd say that. Reason I'm asking you. As a favor, Jordan . . . to a dying man. Will you see she gets it?"

Ben stared into the flames. "I don't know," he said slowly. "Not sure I can, or want to. I've got a job waiting for me. I ought to be there now. And I've lost my horse."

"Won't be out of your way none. And I give you my horse. He's in the shack behind the cabin. Maybe not in too good a shape . . . but he'll take you where you're going."

Jordan considered. "Where is your wife?"

"Town by the name of Langford . . . about a day's ride on the other side of the Lazy A outfit."

"You know Ashburn?"

"No. Heard of the Lazy A, that's all."

Woodward paused, coughed deeply and softly. Ben dipped a finger into the can of water. It was just beginning to warm.

"There'll be no problem," Woodward continued. "Just ride in. Ask somebody . . . anybody where Ollie . . . Olivia . . . Woodward lives. They'll show you. Give her the saddlebags and . . . that's it. I want you to keep a thousand for your trouble."

Jordan said: "No, but the horse will be a favor."

"He's yours . . . along with the gear . . . good saddle . . . rifle . . . pistol, too. I see yours is missing."

"Lost it fording an arroyo."

185

Woodward nodded, waited. "You giving me your promise?"

Ben said: "My word on it."

Walt Woodward sank back gratefully. He wiped at his lips with the back of his hand. "One bit of luck . . . ," he murmured, "having an honest man show up here. Could've been somebody who would've taken the money and rode on. I'm obliged to you, Jordan."

"Forget it," Ben said. "I appreciate the horse and gear. Losing mine was a blow."

"I'd like to say one more thing . . . about the money. Don't trust anybody. Hand it over to my wife . . . nobody else. I want your promise on that, too . . ."

"You've got it."

Woodward sighed heavily. His fingers tugged at the edge of his sheepskin brush jacket. "Might as well have this, too. Won't do me any good . . . where I'm going. And you'll need it. Gets cold in these hills . . . at night."

Jordan said—"Thanks, again."—and let it drop.

Woodward pulled himself around, seeking more comfort. "I want to warn you about those outlaws. Four men . . . got on my trail outside Tucson. Never shook them until yesterday."

"How'd they find out you were carrying all that cash?"

"Who knows? Must have got tipped off by somebody . . . but it's what they're after . . . no other reason. Recognized them. A man named Bart Crawford's the leader. Big fellow . . . riding a black horse . . . and Cleve Aaron. He's one of them. He's on a bay. Arlie Davis is forking a bay, only it's a small horse . . . like an Indian pony. Fourth man will be on a gray. They call him Gates."

"Sound like you know them pretty well."

"Ought to . . . I've been up against them before. Real hardcases, every one of them. When you pull out of here, keep your eyes peeled. They'll still be looking for me."

"I'll watch," Jordan said.

The water in the can had begun to simmer. Picking up a small stick, Ben pushed it away from the fire. He glanced at Woodward. "Is there any extra shirt or something in your saddlebags? I need to make a bandage."

Woodward said: "Never mind, Jordan. I'm feeling all right. Doctoring won't do me any good now . . . could use another drink." Ben started to empty the can. The wounded man said: "Leave it . . . being warm, maybe . . . it'll melt some of the ice . . . in my belly."

Jordan picked up the container. It was cool enough to hold. He passed it to Woodward who wrapped his hands about it.

"Feels good," he murmured. After a moment he began to sip the tepid water. "Little whiskey in this . . . sure would . . . help."

Ben tossed the remainder of the wood on the fire. He was dry now, and beginning to grow drowsy. He yawned, stretched out full length before the flames. He glanced at Woodward. "Sure there's nothing I can do for you?"

"Nothing," Woodward replied. "Reckon I'd . . . better let you get . . . some sleep." He reached out his hand. "Want to say it . . . again, Jordan. Obliged to you."

Ben took the man's fingers into his own. They were cold despite the warm can he had been holding. "It's all right. And don't worry. I'll see that your wife gets the money."

"A . . . great relief," Woodward said, sighing. "Good night . . . Jordan."

III

Ben awoke cold and stiff. He lay quietly for a minute listening. The rain had finally stopped. It was still dark but he guessed the hour must be somewhere near dawn. The fire had gone out and a damp chill again possessed his body. He thought then of Walt Woodward and sat up quickly.

Woodward was hunched in his corner. He had pulled the saddlebags from behind his back, had them laid out across his legs along with the sheepskin jacket. The man's face was a sallow mask, his eyes deep, shadowy pockets.

Jordan rolled to his feet swiftly, and crossed to where Woodward sat. He reached out, shook the man's shoulder gently. Woodward aroused. His hand dropped to the pistol lying on the floor at his side. Then he relaxed.

"Jordan . . . ," he muttered. "Jordan . . . thought for . . . a second it . . ." The words trailed off.

Ben crouched nearer to the man. "Woodward! Woodward! Listen to me. The storm's quit. We can get out of here. Is there a settlement around close? I'll try to get you to . . ."

"Don't bother . . ." The man's voice was no more than a low croaking sound. "Don't bother. Just get . . . the . . . money . . . to my . . . wife . . . you promised . . . me . . ."

Woodward's head sagged forward abruptly and he started to topple. Ben caught him, laid him back. He felt for a pulse, and found none. Walt Woodward was dead.

Jordan got to his feet. He stood for a time looking down at the man's tormented face, and then turned away. The cabin was cold. A fire would feel good but there was no wood left, and outside any wood would be soaked. He stared into the gray ashes of the fireplace, considering his next move. It would be senseless to take Woodward's body on to Langford and his widow. With only one horse it would be a long, drawn-out, near impossible task. And there was no point. Better to bury the man here and move on, and fulfill his promise to deliver the money to Olivia Woodward.

He wheeled to the door and went outside. The sky had cleared and the first rays of the sun were beginning to spray upward from the eastern horizon in flaring fingers of color. The air was cold and damp and water lay about in low places wherever he looked. But it would not long remain, he knew. Once the sun began to climb and send forth its sucking heat, the moisture would disappear.

He walked to the rear cabin and entered. Woodward's horse, a handsome sorrel gelding with white forelegs greeted him with an anxious whicker. Ben comforted the animal, then led him into the open, and picketed him on a small patch of grass a few yards up the slope. The sorrel was a fine-looking horse, much better than the buckskin.

Leaving the gelding to graze, Jordan hunted around until he found a broken spade and with that dug a shallow grave. He buried Woodward, covered the mound with rocks to keep away the wolves and coyotes. Then, wearing the dead man's jacket, and with the bulging saddlebags heavy with gold coins and packets of currency, he mounted the sorrel and rode down the mountain.

The trail was again visible, the rainwater having drained away, and he had no difficulty in following it except when he would come upon a gash cut at right angles to its course where an arroyo, surging downward from the high peaks, had slashed a channel. He had no idea how far it was to the next settlement but, as before, he figured the trail would eventually bring him out at some point. He was not particularly disturbed about it since a northerly course would take him in the right direction and lead him finally to the Lazy A Ranch of Tom Ashburn.

Food was the pressing problem; he had not eaten since the previous morning and hunger was now a gnawing pain within him. Around noon he saw a long-eared jack rabbit. Using Walt Woodward's rifle, he killed it. He halted then, and roasted the animal over a low fire. The meat was tough and stringy, almost tasteless for lack of salt, but satisfied his stomach, and he rode on an hour later feeling better.

As the miles passed, he appreciated more and more the qualities of the sorrel, and as well the country surrounding him. Everywhere the land was green and beautiful, much different from the dry wastes of the Barranca Negra. He wondered if the country where Tom Ashburn had his ranch was like this, and found himself hoping it would be. It should be no chore raising fine cattle in a land so lush. Grass covered the ground in a deep, green blanket anywhere a man looked. Water was plentiful. It was strange that he saw no ranches, no farms, then remembered that the area was devoted mainly to mining. Men searching for gold or silver had no time for anything else.

He pressed on, the sorrel seemingly tireless. They topped out one succeeding rise after another and the realization gradually came to Ben Jordan that he would be forced to spend the night in the open again. But that was no problem. Being under a roof with Walt Woodward was the first time he had not slept on the trail in over a week. He glanced at the sky, thankful that no rain-heavy clouds hovered about. It would be cold, but not wet.

Again he had to think of food. He began to watch the brush and scrubby growth that fringed the deep forest, alert for another rabbit, preferably a cottontail or a young jack this time. Venison would taste good but he rebelled at the thought of wasting a whole deer for only one or two meals.

He killed another rabbit a short time later, a young jack, and halted there to skin and cook it. He would get the meal out of the way, he decided, and at the same time allow the gelding to rest. Then he would ride on until full darkness over-took him before he bedded down for the night.

He had just finished eating, and was stamping out the embers of his fire when he chanced to look back over his trail, rising and falling as it climbed in and out of the long swales and topped out the ridges lying in between. At first, he saw nothing, only the deep, rich green of the land, and then suddenly riders came into his vision. Interest stirred through him and was followed quickly by alarm. They were at a considerable distance but were moving toward him at steady pace, coming along the exact path he had taken. Of course they could be simply fellow pilgrims, headed in the same general direction, but Walt Woodward's money was making him suspicious, jumpy. And then, as they moved out into the last of the bright sunlight and he had a good look at them, he knew his fears were warranted. There were four men in the party.

IV

Ben Jordan swung to the saddle quickly and wheeled into the deep shadows off trail. He could not be certain they had seen him yet, but that they were following him, tracking him by the hoof prints left by the sorrel in the soft ground, there was no doubt. He studied the men, striving to identify them and thus rule out all possibility of error. He waited until they crossed the next shallow valley, climbed the grade, and were again outlined on the horizon. A big man on a black horse—that would be Crawford. Two on dark brown animals; a fourth on a gray. He was not wrong. They were the outlaws.

He moved off at once, putting the gelding to a

lope. He had a good lead on the four men, and darkness was not far off. If he could reach rocky ground, a place where the sorrel would leave no prints, there was a good chance of losing Crawford and his bunch. But as the miles wore on that hope dwindled. The heavy rainfall had soaked the country generally, and there was no hard ground within reach.

He began to curve then toward the higher hills, aiming for the ridges and peaks. It would be rougher going with plenty of granite ledges and benches that would not mark his passage. He rode on, pushing the gelding, now beginning to labor as he moved upgrade. Daylight was disappearing slowly. Jordan, grim, looked ahead. Another mile, perhaps two, and he would be at the foot of the mountain. And by then it should be night.

He reached the first upthrust of solid rock, and halted. Slipping from the saddle of the heaving sorrel, he dropped back a dozen yards to a huge boulder that stood out away from the edge of the trees. He climbed to the top and there, after his own rapid breathing had calmed, listened in the darkness.

Somewhere, far to the south, a pair of coyotes were setting up a wild chorus. An owl hooted into the blackness and a rain frog chirped his warning of more storms to come. There was nothing else. If Crawford and the others had swung off the trail as he had done, it seemed logical to expect some sign, some noise that would indicate their approach. He could hear nothing. He remained perched on the rock for another quarter hour while the light of a pale moon rising above the low hills to the east grew stronger, and then gave up. He dropped to the ground and made his way back to the sorrel.

He mounted at once. He would take no chances, not with his life and Walt Woodward's $20,000, although all indications were that he had thrown the outlaws off his trail. He would continue on for another hour at least, and make camp. Thus he would put a safe distance between himself and Crawford.

He found a good camping place a few miles, and a long hour, farther along. It was a shallow cave, hollowed by wind and rain from the face of a high butte. A cautious man, even when he felt reasonably certain he was in the clear, he built no fire and left the sorrel saddled and ready to ride. He gave his precautions no thought, simply doing these things from instinct, and perhaps from a smattering of habit, for in the Barranca Negra a man learned to hold himself in readiness for an emergency at all times, or else he was not destined for a long life. Ben Jordan hoped to enjoy the same thing in this new land across which he was riding. He intended to live, to take on the fine job his father's old friend, Tom Ashburn, had offered him, and no outside influence in the guise of four hardcase outlaws was going to prevent him doing so. He had been sucked into something he would have gladly avoided, if there had been a choice, but since there was not, he would now see it through to the finish, and stay alive.

Using Woodward's blanket roll, he made himself as comfortable as possible in the cave. The night was cold, the ground hard, and his hunger was still far from satisfied, but he took it in stride. All things came to an end, eventually, he had learned, and tomorrow he would likely reach a settlement where he could stuff himself with a good meal, rest on a soft bed, and perhaps . . . Ben Jordan came suddenly alert. An unusual noise had prodded his senses to wakefulness, setting small flags of danger waving in his mind.

He lay still for a long minute, his ears tuned to the darkness, hand gripping the butt of his revolver. It could have been a prowling animal, possibly the sorrel. He heard it again—the sharp, metallic click of iron against rock. It was the sound of an approaching horse. Crawford? Jordan sat up instantly. It was black as jet inside the cave, only a little better beyond in the feeble moonlight. Clouds had begun to pile up and were scudding swiftly across the sky, gathering for more rain.

Picking up the saddlebags and blanket, Ben moved into the open. He took each step with extreme care as he worked his way toward the sorrel picketed fifty feet or so to the left. Almost there, he raised himself to full height and glanced toward the stand of oak brush, seeking to pinpoint the horse's exact position. He saw the silhouette of the gelding, and at the same instant heard a man's hushed voice speak.

"There's his horse. It's him, sure enough. I'd know that sorrel anywhere."

There was a brief silence and a second voice said: "Where you reckon he is?"

"Hunkered up against that cliff, I expect. Bart and Cleve are movin' in from that side. Smart thing for us to do is set tight. He'll make a run for the horse."

"Just what I was figurin'."

Ben remained crouched behind a clump of brush, listening, waiting, trying to think of a plan, a means for escape. Crawford and the one called Cleve Aaron were sneaking up to the cave, according to what he had just heard. That placed them behind him now. Gates and Arlie Davis would be the two hiding in the darkness ahead, blocking his course to the gelding. He could not drop back—and he could not go on.

"Gates?"

"Yeah?"

"Just can't figure it out. Known damn' well I plugged that jasper. Hit him square . . . but here he is, ridin' just like nothin' had happened."

"Maybe you just thought you got him."

"You seen the blood, same as me."

"Sure, but it could have been a flesh wound, somethin' that didn't do much damage."

"Don't make sense. I seen him grab at his chest, dang' near fall offen his horse . . ."

"Then who the hell we been follerin', his ghost?" Gates demanded impatiently. "We seen him ridin', and we know he's around here somewhere. Ain't that proof enough you didn't wing him?"

"But I know I . . ."

"Forget it, and keep your trap shut for a bit. We don't want him findin' out we're hidin' here."

The fact that he was riding Woodward's sorrel was not the only reason they were mistaking him for the man, Ben thought with a tight smile. He was wearing the sheepskin jacket that had been Woodward's, also. Recognizing it wiped all doubts from their minds. His thoughts came to an abrupt halt. A sound back in the direction of the cave brought him sharply to the moment. Crawford and Aaron would break out into the open soon. They would discover the cave was empty, and press on toward the sorrel. He must move, and move fast or else become trapped in a deadly game of hide-and-seek.

He raised himself again, swept the surrounding brush with a probing glance. Gates and Arlie Davis were somewhere to his left, on a direct line between him and the gelding, judging from their voices. If he could circle wide, come in to the sorrel from the far side—it was worth a try. He moved off at once, keeping low and taking time to create no sound. Every few yards he paused, listened, and now and then he would search out the silhouette of the big horse to be certain he was not going too far.

Inch by inch, it seemed to Ben Jordan, he made the circle. He had heard no more sounds back at the cave and Gates and Davis were remaining stone silent. He crept on, always fearful the saddlebags would scrape against the brush and betray him, or that he would put his weight upon a dry branch, and create a loud popping noise that would be heard by all four of the outlaws. But finally he completed the arc. He was in front of the sorrel now, and could approach the horse head on. He hunched forward, and rested himself on his elbows, breathing hard. It had been a tiring effort, but he had been lucky. He had not aroused Gates and Arlie Davis. He turned his head toward the cave, disturbed because there had been no sounds from Crawford and Aaron. Were they still there, or had they closed in? Were they also standing watch over the sorrel?

He resumed the tedious crawl, reaching a point where he dared advance no farther. His sudden appearance was certain to startle the horse, and cause him to shy and draw the attention of the outlaws. He considered that, but could find no answer to it. He had to gain the gelding's side, and jerk the short tether rope free and get on the saddle.

His hand touched a rock, one the size of his fist. He picked it up, a thought racing into his mind. If he could turn the outlaws' attention to another direction for only a few moments . . . ? He drew himself to a crouch, made ready to race to the sorrel. He cocked his arm, threw the rock toward the cave.

The instant it struck, setting up a loud, dry clatter, Jordan surged toward the gelding. The horse saw him and jerked back. Ben seized the tail of the tie rope with his left hand and pulled, gathering the reins with his right, all in one motion. He vaulted onto the shying sorrel's back, and fought to bring the frightened animal under control.

"Hey . . . here! He's over here!"

It was Gates's surprised voice. Jordan ignored the nearness of it, and sawed at the bit to bring the gelding about to head him off and away from the outlaws.

"Over here! Over here!" Gates yelled again.

Jordan got the sorrel pointed right, sent him plunging recklessly down the slope, praying he would not stumble and fall, would not run straight into a cañon or a dead end.

A gun blasted through the darkness. Another. Someone was yelling—Crawford probably— shouting for the others to keep shooting, for someone to bring the horses, to watch the sorrel, not lose him.

A fresh volley of gunshots smashed through the night, and set up a chain of rolling echoes. Jordan bent low over the saddle, urging the gelding on. The big horse responded with a burst of speed, then suddenly began to slow. The dark formation of a bluff loomed directly ahead, blocking his path. Desperately Jordan cut to his right. A stand of scrub oak barred the sorrel's path; he cleared it in a long jump. Guns blazed through the darkness immediately. Jordan realized the outlaws had spotted him, and were now rushing down slope, trying to head him off. He hammered at the sorrel's flanks for more speed. The big gelding seemed to sink lower as he lengthened his stride. And then Ben Jordan felt the sudden, solid jolt of a bullet driving into his left arm, just below the shoulder. He sagged forward in the saddle, shocked by the impact. He grabbed for the horn and hung on.

V

The sorrel plunged heedlessly through the rock and brush for a good half mile, finally broke out onto wide, grass-covered flats. By some miracle he had not fallen although there had been three or four times when the big red horse had stumbled, but always he had recovered and raced on. Near the center point of the plain they intersected a road. It was little more than paralleling trails in the pale moonlight, but Jordan swung the gelding onto it, and they rushed on through the night, the horse running free and easy over the smooth, spongy ground. Ben threw a glance over his shoulder.

The outlaws were in pursuit. Two followed the route he had taken, the other pair were higher on the slope, keeping pace with him. But he had a good quarter mile lead and the sorrel showed no indication of slowing. Jordan settled down to a race. His arm was beginning to pain him now that the anesthesia of shock was wearing off. He examined the wound as best he could. The outlet had struck just below the bone, had passed entirely through the fleshy part of his arm. It had bled considerably and Jordan further stanched the steady oozing by cramming his handkerchief inside his sleeve and forcing it about the openings in a makeshift pressure bandage. It would serve until he could get the outlaws off his heels but he knew he must have proper medical attention soon.

He looked ahead. The road appeared to run on indefinitely, faint, twin lines of gray in the deep color of the grass that stretched northward through the half light. But the valley through which he fled seemed to be narrowing, crowding in closer to create a sort of pass. There was no possibility of Crawford and his men overtaking and blocking his flight—thanks to the sorrel—but the darkly shadowed hillsides did offer a solution to a problem that would eventually present itself. He must rid himself of the outlaws soon, for with daylight, the men would bring their rifles into use and his lead was not sufficient to put him beyond a long gun's reach. If they failed to hit him, they would get the gelding.

He began to drift the sorrel off the road gradually angling toward the darker shadows to the right. It would be slower going over the rougher ground but the sacrifice of speed would be well worthwhile, if his plan worked. The break in the horse's stride immediately sent shooting pains stabbing through Jordan's injured arm, but he clenched his teeth and rode on; if luck were still with him it would soon be over.

When he was well off the road, he pressed the sorrel to a faster pace, hoping his disappearance from the open had worked its desired effect. He looked back. He could not see the two men who had been behind him on the flats because of the long shadows, but the pair high up on the slope were now swinging down, hurrying to rejoin their companions.

Jordan grinned tightly. So far it was going as he had expected. He wanted Crawford and the others to believe he had cut off and was seeking a hiding place somewhere on the hillside. While they were thus diverted, searching about for him, unsure whether he had actually turned off or not, he would continue on through the pass. If he could make his way through, relying on darkness to cover his movements, he would gain precious time.

He reached the foot of the slope that led upward to the narrow gash between the two hills. Here the good fortune he had hoped for was evident; the shoulders of the road were brushy, shot with deep shadows. Keeping within the wild growth, he gained the crest and halted. He looked back. There was no sign of the outlaws. They had taken the bait and were now somewhere in the trees on the rock-strewn hillside miles below, hunting for him.

Jordan sighed in weary relief and walked the tired sorrel through the opening, thankful he had not actually sought to escape back in the valley for one man, posted in the pass, could have effectively blocked his way with no difficulty when he did attempt to ride through. The gelding fell into an easy lope down the grade, again staying to the smooth surface of the road. Now and then Jordan twisted about on his saddle for a look at the slice in the summit of the ridge, but when, an hour later he saw no indication of Crawford and his men, he concluded that he had finally shaken them, and he worried no more about the matter.

Near dawn he broke out of the rolling foothills onto another wide flat. On the far side he saw smoke trailings winding into the morning sky and recognized the low, blurred outlines of a settlement. Somewhat faint from the loss of blood and lack of food, and groggy for sleep, he struck out across the alkali-streaked plain.

When he reached the outskirts of the town, a cluster of two dozen or so buildings strung out on either side of a single street, he halted and glanced over his shoulder, the old inborn caution still very much alert with him. No riders were in sight. Crawford and his friends were yet beyond the pass, he guessed. But eventually they would realize he had tricked them, and would resume the chase. They would reach the town, make their inquiries, and likely make a house-to-house search. Accordingly he must move with care. It would be smart to by-pass the settlement entirely, but this he could not do; his arm needed attention, and he must have food.

Jordan circled to the rear of the first structure. A man, chopping wood, glanced up at his approach, eying him with frank curiosity.

Ben halted the sorrel. "There a doctor around here?"

The man studied him. "You hurt?"

Jordan, keeping his blood-stained shoulder turned from the man, said: "Friend of mine got himself shot up pretty bad. Ought to take the doc to him."

The man nodded. "Sure. Doc's place is right on

down the street. Third house from the end, on this side."

"Obliged," Jordan murmured, and moved on.

He located the physician's residence, still keeping to the rear of the buildings, and rode into the yard. A small barn stood at the back of the lot, and, not hesitating, he guided the sorrel into it, halted him in one of the empty stalls. Two other horses were under the roof and a buggy was parked near the doorway. He threw an armload of hay into the manger, and bucketed out a quantity of grain for the gelding, and then headed for the house with Woodward's saddlebags slung across his good shoulder. He felt oddly light-headed and he was unsteady on his feet, but he managed to reach the door.

At his knock a thin, elderly man wearing dark trousers, vest, a striped shirt with no collar attached, peered at him through steel-rimmed spectacles.

"Yes? I'm Doctor Hensley. What's the trouble?"

"My arm," Jordan replied. "Needs some fixing up."

Hensley continued to stare. "I'd guess you could stand something to eat, too. And a little sleep." He stepped back, holding the door open. "Come on in."

Jordan followed the physician through the quiet house to his office quarters fronting the street. Hensley pointed to an iron and worn leather examining table.

"Sit there. And peel off that jacket and shirt," he said, and left the room.

Ben stripped to the waist, doing it slowly, painfully. By the time he was ready, the doctor was back, bringing a water tumbler half filled with whiskey.

"Drink this," he ordered, handing the glass to Ben, and began to examine the wound. "Nice. Clean. You're lucky, mister. Didn't even nick the bone."

Jordan nodded, downed the liquor. It struck him like a small thunderbolt, but he began to feel better almost at once as tension faded from his long body and relaxation set in.

"Lay back," Dr. Hensley said, taking the empty glass. "Take me a few minutes to dress this, then I'll stir you up a cup of coffee." He paused, smiled down at Ben. "When did you say you'd eaten last?"

"Didn't mention it," Jordan answered, "but it's been a couple of days since I had a full meal."

"See what I can do about that, too," the doctor said, turning to a cabinet filled with bottles of medicine.

Stretched out on the table and lulled by the whiskey, Jordan felt drowsiness creeping over him. He struggled against it for a few minutes, and finally gave in.

Ben awoke with Dr. Hensley shaking him insistently. He was still on the table, but the medicine man was finished with his arm. He moved it experimentally. There was only slight pain and a bit of stiffness.

Hensley said: "How does it feel?"

"Fine," Jordan replied. He turned his head toward the chair where his shirt and jacket had been hung. Woodward's saddlebags were there. He shifted his eyes then to the window. The sun was still bright and a pall of dust hung in the street. "How long have I been asleep?"

"Couple of hours. Dead to the world. How about some coffee?"

"Could sure use it," Ben said, sitting up. The abrupt motion set his senses to spinning. He hung there, face tipped down, the strong, pungent smell of medicine in his nostrils, allowed the giddiness to pass. When it was gone, he grinned wryly at the doctor. "Guess I moved a little too quick."

"You'll be all right in a few minutes. You need something in your belly, more than anything. There's a restaurant down the street." The physician paused, studied Ben thoughtfully. "Any reason why you can't use it?"

Jordan said: "No, reckon not. But until then I'll sure appreciate some coffee."

Hensley wheeled, disappeared into the interior of the house. He returned in a few moments, carrying a thick mug of black coffee and a plate of sweet rolls. "This ought to hold you until you can get to that restaurant," he said. He placed the food on a table near the window and stood back as Jordan settled on a chair and began to eat. The whiskey was still having its way with him, but the steaming coffee and rolls would quickly dull its effects.

When he had finished the first cup and was sipping at the second, Hensley said: "Would have let you sleep longer but saw some men ride into town. They've been parading around like they were looking for somebody. They friends of yours?"

Jordan sat his cup on the table quietly, felt the tautness begin to build within him once again. It could be Crawford and his men. If they had not spent too much time searching for him before they realized they had been tricked, they could have arrived. Or it could be someone else—riders who happened to be strangers to the doctor.

After a moment Ben said: "I doubt it. How many in the party?"

Hensley said: "Four."

Ben stiffened as granite-hard tension closed in about him completely. Four men, that tallied. Still it could be coincidence. "They stop here?"

Hensley turned, replaced two or three bottles in the cabinet. He shook his head. "No. Like I said, they've just been riding up and down the street. Appear to be hunting for somebody." He glanced out the window. "Fact is, here they come again."

Jordan swung about, threw his gaze into the dusty pall suspended between the buildings. It was Bart Crawford and his three hard-faced companions.

VI

Crawford, a dark, grim man with a square-cornered jaw, rode center and slightly in front of the others. To his left was Aaron, hat pushed to the back of his head revealing a shock of brick-red hair. The one on the gray horse was Gates, a sallow-faced man who looked as though he would be more at home at a faro table than on a saddle. At the near end of the line, and apparently the youngest of the crowd, was Arlie Davis. He was easing himself by leaning forward in the stirrups while his eyes, like the rest, probed along the street in a ceaseless quest.

"They looking for you?" Hensley asked quietly.

Jordan waited, watched until the outlaws had passed the house and were moving slowly on toward the end of the street. He said then: "Reckon so but they're not friends."

"They the reason for that bullet hole in your arm?"

Ben nodded. He was considering the advisability of taking the physician into his confidence, or perhaps going to the town marshal and asking his protection. Immediately he knew it would be a bad move, and far too risky. The local lawman could prove to be of little help, unable to stand up against such men as Bart Crawford and the

210

others. And he was reluctant to involve the physician or anyone else in his trouble. Besides, he had made his promise to Walt Woodward that he would personally see to the delivery of the money. To bring in others would only serve to complicate the problem. Jordan rose, pulled on his shirt and brush jacket. He looped the saddlebags over his shoulder. There was the faint clink of coins as the pouches slapped against his body. Hensley's expression did not alter.

"How much do I owe you, Doc?"

The physician shrugged. "Couple of dollars will do it. Sure you can ride?"

Jordan said—"I'm sure."—and handed over the specified amount. "I put my horse in your barn and fed him when I first rode in. I owe you for that, too."

"Forget it," Hensley said. "Lots of people around here pay me off with hay and grain. Always have plenty." He glanced toward the street. "Here they come again. Which way are you headed?"

Jordan studied the medical man thoughtfully as if considering the wisdom of a reply. Finally he said: "North, or I guess you'd say northeast."

Hensley said: "Give them five minutes and they'll be at the other end of town. Then pull out and they won't spot you."

"Obliged to you," Ben said, and started for the door. He paused. "Anybody asks, I'd appreciate your saying you haven't seen me."

The medical man shook his head. "If it's the marshal, I'll have to tell him the truth. Matter of principle. Anybody else wants to know, it's none of their damned business."

"Good enough," Jordan said, and moved on.

He crossed to the barn, backed the gelding out of his stall, and mounted. Pulling up to the door, he halted. After several moments he rode from the yard, again keeping close to the buildings until he reached the end of the line, and there angled off toward the north. He veered to the right, putting himself from view of anyone on the street. If Crawford and his men made another return sweep and glanced on ahead, they would undoubtedly see him, at least they would see a horseman riding toward the north. If he could put enough distance between himself and the settlement, there would be a question in their minds as to whether he was the man they sought, or was just another rider crossing the flats. He could only hope that he would be far enough away to create that question when the moment came.

But luck was not with him this time. Shortly after noon, as he was nearing the far side of the flats, he saw the outlaws on the road behind him. They had just emerged from the settlement, appearing only as small, dark shapes in the distance. Yet there was no doubt as to their identity. Either they had discovered he had been in the town and ridden on, or else they were simply assuming that would be the fact since it was the only course left open to him. Most likely, however, some citizen had noted his passage and, when asked, volunteered the information. That they would have learned nothing from Doc Hensley Ben was dead certain.

He began to look ahead, hoping for some means once more to throw them off his trail. It was yet hours until darkness, and night promised little salvation anyway. It had not turned the outlaws aside before. There was little reason to expect it would now.

At the end of the plain a finger of trees extending down from the hills formed a dark, green barrier and Ben hurried the sorrel to gain this shelter as quickly as possible. Once inside he would be lost to view insofar as Crawford was concerned, and if he so desired he could then alter his directions and thereby confuse the outlaws.

A vast cloud of dust rising above the hills to his left drew Jordan's attention a quarter hour later and set him to thinking. From all indications it was a cattle drive. It was late in the summer for it, but a man didn't always follow the pattern, and likely there was some particular reason for it. Regardless, it presented a possibility; why not join the herd, perhaps take on a job of riding—long enough to sidetrack Crawford and his men?

He swung off the road at once, slanted toward the yellowish pall. Two hours later he caught up with the drive, one of fair size moving slowly toward the east. He sought out the trail boss, a man named Slaughter; he was told by a dust-plastered cowhand. Slaughter was a huge man. He rode heavily in the saddle. His face was sweaty and also well caked with dust although he was in front of the cattle when Jordan finally found him. He favored Ben with a hard, irritable glance.

"Now, what in the hell's on your mind?" he demanded.

Jordan grinned. A contrary herd had a way of getting under a man's hide. "Looking for a job. How you fixed for trail hands?"

Slaughter swore. "What I got ain't worth the powder it'd take to blow them off a bunk! Lump the whole bunch together and a man wouldn't have one good cowpuncher. That's how I'm fixed! You handle cows before?"

"Longhorns. Since I was big enough to climb onto a saddle."

"You're hired," Slaughter said bluntly. "Fall back to swing, on the north side. Tuck's having trouble. Can't seem to keep the critters caught up with the rest. See if you can straighten it out."

Jordan nodded and wheeled away, inwardly satisfied. This should throw Crawford off his heels. The outlaws would never think to swing wide of the road and check a trail herd; they would believe him still ahead of them some-where in the darkness. He would help Slaughter for a day and then ride on. He should have no more trouble now.

He found Tuck, a squat, moon-faced young rider at the edge of the herd. Two more cowhands were moving about and all were having their problems with the steers that were continually bolting from the sea of heaving bodies and making a run for the brushy slopes of the hills a short distance away.

"You a new hand?" Tuck asked, mopping at his ruddy features.

Jordan said: "Yeah. Slaughter sent me over to give you some help."

"Need it," the cowpuncher said. "Orneriest bunch of bones and hide I ever seen!"

"Think I see what's causing it," Ben said, his eyes on an old blue-nosed gray longhorn that seemed bent on shaping up a herd all his own. "Bear down on 'em, push 'em hard," he said, and spurred the gelding toward the old mossy horn.

He wheeled in close to the gray, and began to haze him from the herd. The activity aroused the pain in his injured arm but he gave it no attention, concentrating on driving the big steer away from the herd and off toward the hills. The remainder of the cattle swept on. Tuck wheeled back to Jordan's side.

"What's the deal?" he asked, watching the gray amble off into the brush.

"He's the one holding you back," Ben said.

"We get rid of him, we'll have no more trouble."

Tuck frowned, scratched at his neck. "Slaughter ain't goin' to like losin' even one lousy steer."

"He won't lose him," Jordan said. "Watch."

Just within the fringe of brush, the longhorn halted, wheeled about. Head swung low, he stared at the passing herd, unhindered now by his presence. He shook himself, bellowed his summons, but the cattle moved on unheeding. The old gray watched for several minutes, occasionally bawling his displeasure, and then finally he gave it up and began to follow.

Tuck grinned at Jordan. "You some kin to these danged tick farms?"

"About as close as I can be without being one of them," Ben replied. "He'll catch up when we haul in for the night. If he tries the same stunt tomorrow, we'll run him off again."

The cowpuncher spat dust. "Might be better to put a bullet in his head and tell Slaughter the coyotes got him." He reached for his canteen, unscrewed the cap, and offered it to Jordan. "You signin' on for the whole drive?"

Ben took a swallow of water. "No, heading on north. Going to work for Ashburn on the Lazy A."

"Too bad," Tuck said. "We can use a man with your kind of savvy."

It was full dark when they bedded the herd for the night. They were still west of the road Jordan had been following and his guess was that the outlaws had long since passed that point and were miles beyond. It would be smart to stick with Slaughter and his trail herd for another full day, Ben decided. By then Crawford and his bunch would be well out of the way.

Slaughter rode by to pass the word that half the crew was to stay on watch while the remainder went in for the evening meal at the camp. Jordan waved Tuck toward the chuck wagon electing to be one of those who waited, and it was near 9:00 p.m. when the round-faced rider returned to relieve him.

He swung off through the night toward the blazing campfire where the cook had set up his kitchen. He hoped he would be one of those chosen to take the late turn at night hawking as he was beginning to feel the need of rest and sleep. If he could have only four or five hours on a bedroll, he would be good as new again. He had made up his mind to ask Slaughter for just such an arrangement, but as he drew near the camp his eyes caught sight of riders halted at the edge of the broad circle of light thrown by the leaping flames. He swung in behind the chuck wagon quickly, his face going taut, his muscles beginning to tighten as a wild suspicion ripped through him. When he was a few yards from the canvas-topped vehicle, he stopped the sorrel, and dismounted. At a crouch, he eased in silently, careful not to stumble and not to draw the attention of any of the men in the camp. He reached the wagon, kneeled down, and glanced through the spokes of a wheel. A wave of exasperation, almost desperation, moved through him. The riders, still on their horses, were only too familiar—Crawford and his three followers.

VII

The outlaws faced Slaughter. The big trail boss stood with his legs spread, his back to Jordan. Several of his riders had gathered about him in careless but watchful silence.

"What's got you thinking he came here?" Slaughter demanded, blunt and impatient.

"Not sure he did," Crawford replied. "Just had a hunch he might. Man on the run tries all kinds of fancy tricks."

He had not fooled the outlaws for a solitary moment, Ben realized. Crawford, personally acquainted with the problems of a man on the dodge, had recognized the possibilities a trail herd presented and deemed it wise not to ignore but to investigate. "A tall man, wearin' a sheepskin jacket. Rides a sorrel with white forelegs."

Slaughter was still for several moments. "What do you want him for?"

"Bank robbery," Crawford said. "Been chasin'

him clear across Arizona and half of New Mexico. About had him two or three times, but he's mighty slippery. Got away from us."

Jordan listened in amazement to the bald effrontery of Bart Crawford. The outlaws were passing themselves off as lawmen! They were making it appear that he—or, in reality, Walt Woodward—was the criminal! A surge of anger rocked Ben Jordan. He started to rise, to rush out into the open and confront Crawford and his gang, denounce them as liars before Slaughter and the others. And then he realized that would be a foolish gesture. He could prove nothing. He was a stranger to the trail boss and his riders, and it would be his word against that of Bart Crawford, backed by Aaron, Davis, and the narrow-faced Gates. Slaughter would have little choice but to believe Crawford. And he did have $20,000 in his saddlebags, something that would bolster Crawford's accusations despite any explanation he would make. Fuming, feeling utterly helpless to protect himself, Ben Jordan listened to the conversation between the two men.

"Figure he's shot up some," Crawford said. "One of my boys here thinks he winged him a couple of days ago."

"The man I hired didn't look like anything was bothering him," Slaughter stated flatly. "Fact is, he . . ."

"There was a place on his sleeve," a cowpuncher, sprawled out on his bedroll and propped on one elbow, volunteered. Ben recognized him as the first man he had encountered when he reached the herd.

"What kind of a place?"

"Sort of ragged like. Maybe a bullet hole. And somebody's washed it up, like they'd cleaned off blood."

Crawford glanced at Cleve Aaron, then at Gates and Davis. "Could've been him," he drawled. "What kind of a horse was he ridin'?"

There was no immediate answer. The cowpuncher sank back onto his blankets. Slaughter drew a sack of tobacco and a folder of papers from a pocket, and began to roll himself a smoke.

"I'm askin' what kind of a horse?" Crawford snarled. "Speak up! You want me to charge the whole bunch of you with interferin' with the law?"

The trail boss shrugged. "Do what you damn' well please, friend. Threatening won't get you nowhere. I don't figure the man I hired is the one you're looking for."

"What kind of a horse?" Crawford pressed in a cold voice.

"He was riding a sorrel," the man on the blanket said. "Had white stockings."

Gates and the other two outlaws drew themselves upright in their saddles, looking expectantly at Crawford.

"Where is he?" the renegade leader asked.

Slaughter waved his hand toward the swale where the herd was bedded. "Out doing his trick at night hawking. He'll be coming in for supper pretty quick."

Arlie Davis, breaking the silence he and the others had maintained throughout the conversation, said: "Reckon, we'd better get over there. Could be he'll pull out again."

Crawford thought for a moment, shook his head. "Nope, don't figure he'll do that. He thinks he's safe here. And trying to find him in the dark could tip him off. Best we wait." He brought his attention back to the men around the fire, touched each with his hard glance. "Nobody leaves, understand? Anybody tries to warn him . . ."

"Won't be anybody doing that," Slaughter said, "because we don't figure he's your man. Jacobs there's got his ropes all crossed up about the 'puncher he saw." The trail boss paused, confronted with extending a standard courtesy he cared little to observe in this instance. "Reckon you might as well step down. Coffee and grub over there at the chuck wagon."

Slaughter turned away. Crawford's voice, sharp and suspicious, split the hush. "Where you think you're goin'?"

The cattleman did not halt, simply glanced over his shoulder. "I'm taking a turn around the herd, then I'm crawling into my blankets."

Crawford spurred his black across the camp and pulled up short in front of the trail boss. "What I said goes for you, too, mister!"

Slaughter, a man with his temper always lying close to the surface, reached up impulsively. He grasped the front of Crawford's coat, dragged him from the saddle. He swung the outlaw half around, shoved him, and sent him sprawling into the dust. "Don't be telling me what I can't do!" he raged. "This happens to be my camp, and you, lawman or not, sure ain't running things here!"

Davis and Cleve Aaron had moved quickly, and were now at opposite ends of the circle thrown by the firelight. Gates was motionless. Each now held a cocked pistol. In the tight silence Bart Crawford pulled himself to his feet, his eyes on Slaughter's huge shape. He hung there, half crouched, poised as though ready to spring. And then he relaxed suddenly. He picked up his hat, dusted himself. "I'll overlook that, mister," he said in a low voice. "This time anyway. But you're not ridin' out. You or nobody else . . . not until Woodward shows up. After that you can do as you damn' please."

A man on the opposite side of the fire cleared his throat nervously. "Cattle's a mite jumpy, Mister Slaughter," he said. "Some sort of a ruckus would sure start them a-running."

The big trail boss glanced at the threatening figures of Gates, Arlie Davis, and Aaron. He shrugged angrily. "All right, all right. Have it your way."

Jordan watched Slaughter wheel and cross the camp to where a lantern hung from a mesquite bush. There the trail boss squatted down, drew a tally book from his pocket, and began to flip through the pages.

Crawford studied the man in glowering silence for several moments, and then turned to the rest of his party. He motioned and they drew together again and dismounted.

Ben Jordan withdrew into the shadows as the four outlaws started across the camp for the chuck wagon behind which he was crouching. The cook, hunched by the fire, sucked at his blackened pipe and made no effort to rise and accommodate the guests; common courtesy required Slaughter to invite the strangers to climb down and eat, but it did not necessarily include being waited on.

Jordan reached the sorrel, and stood for a time with his eyes on the camp. The tough, brassy ways of Bart Crawford had infuriated him. He would like nothing better than to call the outlaw's bluff, and expose him and his three men for what they were. He could imagine Slaughter's irate reaction. But it wasn't practical, or even possible. He had nothing with which to back his contention. He could do nothing but let the matter drop —and move on.

He took up the gelding's reins and led the horse

away from the camp a good distance before he swung into the saddle. He could take no chances on Crawford, or anyone else, hearing the sound of the sorrel's hoof beats. He glanced at the stars in the black canopy of sky overhead, squared his directions, and struck off once again into the northeast. Tom Ashburn's Lazy A spread could not be far now.

VIII

Two days later Ben Jordan found himself near his destination. He had seen the landscape change gradually from high, rugged mountains with towering peaks and deep cañons, to endless, rolling plateaus, rich with grass and gentle to look upon. Far to the east a new range of hills had appeared, seemingly more massive than those through which he had traveled, and so distant they were only a bluish smudge on the horizon. But the Lazy A would be found in a wide valley, he had been told when he chanced upon an itinerant peddler of housewares, and the mountains to the east were another world. Tom Ashburn's ranch was a fine place, with good buildings, plenty of shade provided by giant cottonwoods, and all the clear, cold water it could ever use. In fact, the Lazy A was the finest spread in the territory, as Tom Ashburn was also the finest of men.

The peddler had been right, at least so far, Ben thought as he topped out a low rise near the middle of the afternoon and started down a slope that led to the ranch. The house was a long, well-kept structure, neatly painted and trimmed and further beautified by a wealth of vines and flowers. Huge, spreading trees, vivid gold now in the crisp fall air, overshadowed it all.

Several corrals and a small garden plot lay to the rear of the main building, while other structures, the bunkhouse, wagon shed, barns, and the like stood off to one side. A small pond a short distance beyond those mirrored the sun and, looking more closely, Jordan could see several canals cutting away from its circular shape to form other convenient water holes. Water, that was the answer, Ben thought, remembering the scarcity of it in the Barranca Negra. If a man had plenty of water, he could grow anything. How many times had he heard his father make that statement? And how many times had he personally realized its truth? It was the key to success, to life itself in the vast frontier West, and a man rose or fell according to the supply available to him. But it was a problem that would never plague Tom Ashburn. In one glance Ben saw the glitter of a half a dozen springs surging up among the cottonwoods, all independent of the distant pond.

As he rode below the rim, Jordan cast a final look over his shoulder at his back trail, a gesture that had become habit with him since his first encounter with Bart Crawford and his men. The endless flats were empty and the comforting thought settled in his mind that at last he had shaken the outlaws, that, with a modicum of luck, he never again would see them. And the time was near when he could deliver Walt Woodward's money to his widow and discharge that obligation. The saddlebags with their store of currency and gold coins had become a wearisome burden since he had accepted them and he would be thankful to rid himself of the responsibility.

He circled Ashburn's house, came in to it from the front. Two men and two women stood on the gallery that crossed its width. They glanced up as he swung in and slanted toward the hitch rack. The older of the men stepped off the porch immediately, a quick smile cracking his weathered face. He extended a heavily veined hand.

"Ben Jordan, sure as a mule's got long ears!" he shouted. "Ain't seen you in ten, twelve year, but I'd know you anywhere. You're the spitting image of your pa!"

Ben dropped from the sorrel and enclosed the old rancher's fingers in his own. He did not remember Ashburn too well, for he only faintly recalled the man's visit long ago to the Barranca Negra. But he said: "Good to see you again, Mister Ashburn."

"Mister Ashburn," the rancher echoed. "I'm

Tom to you, boy." He stepped back, a lean, bent man with faded eyes and seamy face. His hair and drooping mustache were snow white. "Come on and meet the rest of the family."

Ben hung Woodward's saddlebags across his shoulder and followed the rancher to the porch. Ashburn seized him by the arm.

"Folks, this here's Dave Jordan's boy, Ben. He's who I've been waiting for. My wife Ellie," he added, nodding to the older woman who smiled gravely and shook Jordan's hand. "My daughter Sally."

Ben's glance had been drawn to the girl from the start. She was young, well built, and had light brown hair and blue eyes that had a bright, dancing quality to them. She took his hand in a firm grasp.

"I'm pleased to know you, Ben Jordan."

Ben swallowed, bobbed his head, suddenly conscious of his appearance, of his awkwardness in her presence. But he managed a grin, saying: "My pleasure . . ."

"Feller there is Oran Bishop," Ashburn went on, turning to the young cowpuncher waiting quietly off to one side. "He's been sort of filling in for you, until you got here."

Bishop was a man with about the same number of years behind him as Ben, twenty-four. He was a husky, six-foot blond, handsome in a rugged sort of way. He was fairly well dressed. He took Jordan's hand and said—"Howdy."—in a cool voice that carried no promise of friendship.

"Reckon you've been quite a spell in the saddle," Ashburn said when the introductions were over. "Long ride up from Mexico. Have any trouble finding the place?"

Ben said: "None. Met a wagon peddler who put me on the right road."

"Good. Didn't figure you'd have any problems. I've been around here so long now 'most everybody knows where the Lazy A is." He wheeled to Bishop. "Oran, expect you'd better go move your duds and gear out of the foreman's cabin. Ben'll be wanting to settle in." He came back to Jordan. "You got a wife, maybe some family that'll be coming along later?"

Ben shook his head. "No, I'm all there is to it." He glanced at Bishop. "No need for you to move out. We can share the quarters."

Bishop said: "No thanks. I'll get back in the bunkhouse with the rest of the hands."

There was a trace of bitterness in the man's voice and Ben realized resentment lay strongly in his mind. Likely he had expected to step in and fill the job of ramrod for the Lazy A when the opportunity arose. That he would exhibit little cordiality to an outsider was to be expected. Jordan gave that a moment's consideration and shrugged it off. He regretted Bishop's attitude but he could not allow it to matter. Had Tom Ashburn felt the man capable he would have selected him for the foreman's job and not sent all the way to the Barranca Negra for a stranger.

Ashburn said: "I'll show you around the place. You can meet the rest of the crew tonight." In his quick way, he wheeled to Bishop. "Oran, you take Ben's horse and turn him over to the wrangler. Put his stuff in the cabin. Forgot to ask," he added, turning back to Ben. "You eat yet, boy?"

Jordan said: "I'll do until supper."

"Good. Now, figure to eat your meals with us here in the main house. Like to have my foreman around where I can yammer at him."

Ben slid a glance at Bishop. That such an arrangement did not set well with him was apparent. Probably he had been enjoying that privilege to this moment, but now he was being relegated to the general dining quarters where he would take his meals with the remainder of the hands. Again Ben Jordan shook off the problem. It was something he could not worry about. Tom Ashburn was calling the shots.

Bishop reached forward. "The saddlebags," he said irritably. "Pass them over if you want me to put them in your cabin."

Jordan stepped away. "Never mind. I'll just take them along."

Bishop frowned. His eyes narrowed slightly at the rebuff. "There something special about them?"

"Just a habit I've got." Ben grinned, and moved off across the hardpan with Ashburn.

IX

That evening, when the crew had gathered for their meal, Tom Ashburn conducted Ben to the long, narrow dining hall that extended off the kitchen. All of the men would be there, except three or four staying with the herd, the rancher explained. Those he could meet later. As they walked into the room and halted at the head of the table, all conversation ceased.

"Want you to meet your new foreman," Ashburn said. "Name's Ben Jordan." The rancher made the rounds then, introducing each man individually. When he had completed the chore, he said: "Reckon you've been wondering why I sent all the way to Mexico for a ramrod. One reason was . . . I figure a man who can raise cattle, look after a farm, and still keep his skin whole while doing it in that Barranca Negra country, sure wouldn't have no trouble doing a good job up here. That, and the fact that his daddy was the best damn' cowman I ever knew."

One of the crew, a slim Mexican named Cruz Rodriguez, looked up with interest. He smiled. "The Barranca Negra, *señor*? It's a place I know well. How are the *banditos* these days?"

"They grow worse," Jordan said with a smile. "And there are more of them each year."

Rodriguez shrugged. "In Mexico if you would fill your belly regular, you must be either a *soldado* or a *bandito*. Nothing else pays well."

Jordan laughed along with the crew. There was a great deal of truth in what the Mexican had said. "We'll have to get together and talk about it, *amigo*," he said. "I grew up ducking bullets from both sides."

He moved around the table then, shaking hands with each man, all of whom were cordial enough except Oran Bishop and another young cow-puncher named Ross Colby who evidently was a close friend of Bishop's. Both maintained a cool, aloof attitude.

When that was finished, he returned with Ashburn to the family quarters and spent another two hours listening to the rancher talk first of the old days in Missouri before Dave Jordan migrated to Mexico, and then about ranching in general. Ben had seen nothing of Sally, or Mrs. Ashburn since supper, and when at last he arose, tired and in need of sleep, they still were not there. Tom Ashburn had apparently ruled them out of the evening's confab, decreeing that it was to be strictly man talk.

"We'll do some riding tomorrow," the rancher said, watching Ben retrieve his saddlebags from behind a chair. "Want you to get a good idea what the place is like. You can take over the next day."

Ben nodded. "Certainly the finest ranch I've ever seen."

"Thanks," Ashburn said, suddenly sober. "Took a lot of blood and sweat, but it was worth it. Problem now is to keep it fine. That's the way it goes, it seems. A man puts in half his life building something good, then spends the rest trying to hang on to it."

"You've been having trouble?" Jordan asked, halting in the doorway.

"Not much. A little rustling going on now and then. Got a few nesters. I figure you won't have a problem taking care of both. Anyway, we'll jaw about it in the morning. Good night, son."

"Good night," Ben said, and moved out into the cool darkness.

He made his way to the small house assigned to him, a squat, compact building that stood halfway between Ashburn's main structure and the crew's bunkhouse. Apparently the previous foreman of the Lazy A had been a married man for there was kitchen equipment available as well as the usual living facilities. After entering, Ben closed the door and dropped the latch into place. He struck a match to one of the lamps, and then drew the shades. He began then to search out a suitable hiding place for Woodward's money. He could not continue to walk around with the leather pouches slung over his shoulder; already they had been cause for suspicion in Oran

Bishop's mind—possibly also in Ashburn's. And the sooner he fulfilled his promise to Walt Woodward, the better for all concerned. Having the money was a worry and he would not rest easily until he had turned it over to Olivia Woodward. He could not afford to let it affect his position at the Lazy A. Tomorrow he would ask directions to the town of Langford, get Ashburn's permission to make the trip, and have done with it.

He prowled about the two rooms of the cabin, decided finally to place the leather pouches under a board in the floor that he managed to loosen. He completed the concealment by changing the furniture around somewhat, ending up with a small rug and a chair placed over the cache. He had no personal belongings to place in the closet and in the drawers of the scarred dresser. What little he had owned had been lost when the buckskin had gone over the cliff high in the Mogollon Mountains. When he made his visit to Langford, he would buy the items he needed—a razor, shaving and washing soap, and some extra clothing. Meanwhile he would make do as best he could.

He had just sat down on the bed and was beginning to undress for the night when he heard a knock. He arose, lifted the bar, and faced Ross Colby.

"There's a man outside who'd like to see you," the young cowpuncher said.

Jordan's first thoughts were that Bart Crawford had again caught up with him. He looked out into the dark yard. "Only one?"

"That's right, only one."

Ben pushed past Colby and stepped into the shadowy area that lay between his quarters and the bunkhouse. He heard the dry crunch of gravel, wheeled. He had a quick glimpse of Oran Bishop's set, angry features, and then a rock hard fist smashed into his jaw and sent him reeling to the ground. He struck on his left shoulder, sending a wave of pain through his body as his weight crushed down upon his wounded arm. He lay quietly for several moments, aware of Bishop's taut shape standing over him. Two or three men were now coming from the bunkhouse and Ben could hear Ross Colby laughing. Anger began to build within Jordan. Ignoring the throbbing pain, he sat up.

Beyond Bishop, watching and waiting in silence, were the Mexican, Rodriguez, an old cowpuncher, Amos Wall, and a third man he had not met. Colby still was near the doorway of the cabin from which a shaft of yellow lamplight laid an oblong onto the yard.

"Get up," Bishop snarled. "You're going to have to whip me, mister, to get my job!"

The blond cowpuncher's fury was so intense his voice trembled. Ben pulled himself to his feet. "Your job?"

"Would've been, if you hadn't come along," Bishop said. "I was all set . . ."

"That's a dang' fool thing to say, Oran," Amos Wall broke in. "If Tom'd wanted you, he'd 'a' picked you instead of sending clear to Mexico for Jordan."

"Keep out of this, old man," Bishop said without turning. "We're deciding right here who'll ramrod this outfit. And when it's done with, I'm loading him on his horse and sending him back to Mexico."

"You're a damned fool and there's no reason for this," Jordan said then, his anger leveling off to a brittle hardness. "So's you'll have it straight, I never asked for this job. Had no idea Ashburn even was looking for a man until I got a letter from him."

"So you say."

"It's the truth, but it's neither here nor there now. I like what I've seen of this place and I figure to stay. If you think you can change my mind for me, you're welcome to try."

Bishop rushed in suddenly. He swung a quick left, missed as Jordan ducked away, tried to recover with a right. Ben blocked the blow with his left arm, gritted his teeth as fresh pain rocketed through him from his wounded shoulder, and drove his own right fist into Bishop's ear. The cowpuncher staggered, went to one knee, caught himself. He swore vividly, pulled himself upright.

"Another thing. Something else. You keep your eyes off Sally."

He lunged again. Jordan, favoring his left arm, spun away, chopped a right to Oran's neck as he closed. Bishop howled and wheeled off.

From the half darkness Cruz Rodriguez's soft, accented voice said: "I think you pick the wrong *hombre* this time, Oran."

Ross Colby no longer laughed. He slouched against the wall of Jordan's quarters, watching with a stilled face.

"Damn you!" Bishop growled, anger now a wild surging torrent claiming him mentally and physically. "I'm not letting you get away with this, not with anything! Don't know what it is but you're hiding something . . . trying to fool Tom."

"I'm not trying to fool him, or anybody else," Jordan said, circling warily. "I'm here to work. Nothing else."

"You're a liar!" Bishop shouted, and once more moved in.

Ben fell back a step, was aware that his foot came up against something. He almost went down. From the tail of his eye he saw Rodriguez cross swiftly and take up a position next to Ross Colby. He realized that Colby, endeavoring to help Bishop, had tried to trip him. But there was no chance to do anything about that; besides, Rodriguez had apparently noticed it and was assuming the chore of keeping Colby out of the fight. He ducked beneath Bishop's swinging arms, crowded in tight, and hammered a half a dozen rapid-fire blows into the blond cowpuncher's belly. Bishop struck out blindly, desperately. Jordan took a sharp blow to the head, another across the mouth that started a warm flow of blood from his lips. Fury broke loose within him then, and, ignoring the pain in his arm, conscious of a stickiness along his side, he ripped a second flurry of fists into Bishop.

Oran began to gasp, started to fold forward. Ben straightened him up with a stinging blow to the chin. Bishop sought to turn away, his breathing coming now in loud, rasping grunts, his mouth gaping open. Jordan spun him back around with a smash to the side of his head. Showing no mercy, paying no heed to the pain that screamed within him or the wetness that told him his wound had reopened, Ben Jordan punished Bishop without let-up. The cowpuncher was weaving on his feet, helpless. He rocked back and forth, staggered forward, was driven back to his heels, only to be caught up again. Finally his knees began to buckle. He started to sink slowly, wilting as though his legs were made of smoke.

Ben felt hands close about his shoulders, drawing him off. Amos Wall's voice said: "That'll do it, boy. Reckon he's had more'n enough."

Sucking for breath, his body quivering from the stress, Jordan allowed himself to be pulled away.

Oran Bishop lay sprawled on his back, mouth open, chest heaving. Ross Colby came forward, kneeled beside him. He stared into the cowpuncher's face. "Get some water somebody," he said.

One of the crew brought the bucket from the bunkhouse, dashed a quantity of its contents against Bishop's head. Oran groaned, thrashed about briefly, and opened his eyes. He lay still for several moments, and then finally struggled to a sitting position. He looked around, dazed.

"What . . . how . . . ?" he stammered.

"You just got hell knocked out of you," Wall said laconically. "And by a man with only one good arm."

Jordan pulled away from the old cowpuncher, dismay flooding through him. He had hoped to keep his wound a secret, thereby avoiding any speculation on the part of the crew, or by Tom Ashburn. But there was no hiding it now. The left sleeve of his shirt was soaked with blood.

Bishop got to his feet, stared. "I told you," he said, glancing at the small circle of men. "He's hiding something. He's been shot."

"Doesn't concern you, or the job," Jordan snapped. "It's a personal matter."

"Personal . . . with the law, maybe?"

"The law had nothing to do with it."

"Reckon it ain't none of our business, anyway," Amos Wall broke in. "And if you're looking for advice, Oran, I'd say you'd be smart to forget it."

Bishop was silent for a few moments, then bent and picked up his hat. Pulling it on, he faced Jordan. "Reckon this means I'm fired."

Ben shook his head. "You can quit if you're of the notion, but I won't fire you."

Bishop stared, surprised and at a loss for words.

"Just one thing," Jordan continued, "if you stay, you do your job and keep out of my way. I'll take no more of your lip or your foolishness. Or yours," he added, swinging his glance to Ross Colby.

Colby murmured, looked down. Beside him, Ben saw Cruz Rodriguez beaming at him through the poor light, his broad teeth gleaming whitely.

"What's it to be?" he demanded, coming back to Bishop.

The blond cowpuncher shrugged. "I'll stay," he said, his tone low and surly.

"Then get that chip off your shoulder and figure on doing a job, or else you are finished. You're one man I figure on watching close."

Bishop wheeled, started for the bunkhouse. Wall stepped up to Jordan. "Come on, boy, let's see what we can do about that arm of yours. It's bleeding right good."

Ben moved across the yard toward Rodriguez who stood holding open the door to his quarters. Halfway he paused, turned. "One thing more," he said, "there'll be nothing said about this. Not to the rest of the crew . . . or to Tom Ashburn. That clear?"

The men nodded. Colby said—"It's clear."—but Oran Bishop gave no indication that he had heard, and simply walked away, morose and sullen in his defeat.

X

They prepared to ride out shortly after breakfast that next morning, Tom Ashburn, Jordan, and Sally. Ben was surprised and secretly pleased the girl was coming with them. He was finding himself more and more interested in her and had been hoping for a chance to talk to her. There had been little opportunity during the two meals they had shared. He watched her stuff a lunch into saddlebags and swing lightly onto her pony. She rode astride, and used one of the heavy stock saddles, just as did any of the Lazy A ranch hands. She was wearing a corduroy skirt split up the center, a white shirt with a bright yellow scarf gathered about her neck. Soft, high-heeled boots and a broad-brimmed, flat-crowned hat completed her attire. As she settled herself on her pinto, Ben felt a tightness fill his throat; she made a picture he knew would never fade from his mind.

Ashburn came from the house grumbling at the

stiffness of his joints, and mounted up. He cocked his head at Ben. "Getting old sure as hell. There was a time when I enjoyed crawling out early and piling onto a horse. Now it's a right smart chore."

Jordan grinned his understanding and the three of them wheeled out of the yard, the rancher and his daughter waving to Ellie Ashburn as they passed the kitchen door. They rode abreast and in silence, the men flanking the girl until they were out of the hollow in which the ranch buildings lay and had gained the plateau above it.

"Told the boys to drift the lower herd on west," Ashburn said as they broke out onto the flats. "Lots of new grass over there. Been no grazing on it since spring."

"How many head you running?" Ben asked, his eyes drifting lazily over the vast expanse of gray-green ground cover. It was like a monstrous field with only a few trees scattered here and there to break the horizon.

"Pretty close to four thousand."

Jordan whistled softly. Sally turned and gave him her smile.

Ashburn said: "Most I've ever had. Been holding back on selling. Market's climbing. I figure next year will be the time to turn 'em loose."

"What's the price now?"

"Fifteen, sixteen dollars, thereabouts. Ought to go to eighteen, maybe twenty by spring."

Ben considered that for a time. On his and his

father's place they had never owned as many as four hundred head of stock, much less four thousand, and the highest price he could recall having received for a steer was $9. "Big difference in ranching up here," he said. "How much of a herd do you figure to sell off?"

"Only the three- and four-year-old stuff. They'll be prime, and just right for the market."

"Wonderful country," Ben murmured. "Should be no problem raising cattle up here."

"You like what you see?" Sally asked.

His eyes settled on her. "Everything," he said, a faint smile tugging at his lips. "Everything."

Sally blushed slightly and turned away.

Ashburn said: "Swing north. Expect we ought to have a look at the line shacks up there. Recollect somebody saying there was some fixing up needed before winter sets in."

"It gets pretty bad around here?" Ben wondered.

Ashburn nodded. "One of the drawbacks. Big snows. And plenty of wind. Have to watch the herds mighty close. Seen them drift thirty, forty miles, if we don't keep on them. Sure makes it mean when we round up."

"How much acreage have you got, anyway?" Ben asked, surprised by what Ashburn had said.

"I own a hundred sections. Got another fifty thousand acres of free range I'm using."

"Nobody on it?"

"Not now. Been two or three families try it."

"You have to move them off?"

"Didn't need to. Land itself took care of them. This is good cow country, and nothing else. Too much heat in the summer, too much bad weather in the winter. And it's a long way to water when the rain don't come. I tried to tell them they can't make a go of farming out here, but nobody ever listens. Got to find out for themselves. Worst thing is they break the ground, try to seed it. All they raise is a crop of dust, and that's bad for everybody. But I won't fight 'em. I figure every man's got a right to a piece of this country, same as I had. Only thing, if they'd listen to some of us that's been around for a spell, we could spare them a lot of sweat and heartbreak."

Ben nodded. "My pa always said the only kind of advice a man will listen to is the kind he wants to hear."

"Sure the gospel truth," Tom Ashburn agreed.

At noon they ate lunch in a small grove of trees where a spring trickled from a ledge of rock in a clear, cold stream. They had bacon and sliced beef sandwiches, prepared for them earlier by the cook, and topped them off with slices of layer cake made by Sally. Ashburn brewed the coffee himself, maintaining no woman alive could boil up a cup strong enough to suit him.

Three hours later they caught up with the herd that was being moved to the western side of the range and paused there to have a few words with the riders who were handling the chore. It was Ben's first close look at Lazy A cattle and he could not help mentally comparing these fat, sleek animals to the lean, rangy brutes he had labored so hard to raise in the wilds of Mexico.

"Boys sure have took to you," Tom Ashburn observed, when they were again moving on. He gave a sly look. "It have anything to do with that swelling on your lip and that bruise on your jaw?"

"Just a bit of a misunderstanding," Jordan said, skirting the subject.

"A misunderstanding with Oran Bishop is at the bottom of it, I'll bet!" Ashburn snorted. "Well, he's going to be one of your problems, you can bank on it. A good boy but he just ain't ever growed up."

"We'll get along," Ben said. "You have a winter range?"

The rancher shrugged. "Not much difference in the land. Usually let cold weather catch the stock wherever it happens to be. You got some kind of a scheme?"

"I was wondering why it wouldn't be smart to put everything as far north as we can. Then when the snow hit, they'd just naturally drift south. Grass there would be in good shape then, and it might cut down on a lot of work when spring roundup comes."

Ashburn wheeled to Sally. "See what I was talking about? Man's either a natural cowman, or he ain't." He swung back to Ben. "That's smart thinking. You start doing it . . . moving all the stock north . . . soon as you're ready."

"Maybe a little late now to do any good this year."

"No, don't figure it is. Snow won't hit until late November, maybe even December. You can expect a couple months yet of good weather."

"Then we'll get at it tomorrow. The sooner we move that beef off the lower range, the faster the grass will come back."

Ashburn murmured in satisfaction. Ben was aware of Sally's glance on him, of the smile on her lips, and the pleasure in her eyes. She seemed as proud of his suggestion as her father had been—a suggestion that appeared no more than common sense to him. And the north range, as far as they rode into it, was in excellent condition; indeed, it seemed hardly to have been worked. Ben doubted if there had been a steer on it for months.

"Settles it for sure," Ashburn said. "It happens when a man don't look after things himself. Crew gets lazy. Want to stay close to the bunkhouse so's they can ride in every night at dark. You change all that, Ben. Keep 'em living in the line shacks, if you've a mind to. I'll back you all the way." The rancher paused, swept the land with a fond, remembering gaze. "Place has been good to me," he said. "And I've been worrying some about its going to hell. Reckon I can forget that now and start sleeping easy." He shifted on his saddle, turned to Jordan and the girl. His face was calm, settled, reflecting the ease he felt. "I'll be leaving you here. Had enough of this blasted horse for one day. Sally, you take Ben on over to the brakes. I want him to see the bad part as well as the good. So long."

Ashburn rode off abruptly, hunched forward on his horse, a man turned weary by the years.

Sally and Ben continued on, making a wide circuit of the land, traveling along the edge of the wild, brushy area Ashburn had mentioned. Cattle were never permitted to graze in that section, Sally told him. Too many were lost in the brakes and it was always a temptation to rustlers. When he had taken his look, they swung back to the south for the ranch. The afternoon sun was warm and they rode slowly, easily. After a time the girl spoke.

"You've seen it all, or most of it," she said. "Do you still think it's so fine?"

"The best," he answered. "A man can be proud of a spread like this."

"It can also be a prison," Sally said quietly. "It has held my father here for thirty years. And I guess it will keep him until he dies."

"Not much reason to leave it," Jordan said. A rider silhouetting the horizon claimed his attention momentarily. "Or do you think there is?" he finished.

The girl shrugged, her face turned from him as she looked toward the smoky hills far to the east. "Sometimes I think so. Sometimes I wish I could go away, leave and never see this ranch again. I guess if I had been born a son instead of a daughter, it would be different." She hesitated, added: "Do you plan ever to return to Mexico?"

The rider had disappeared. Ben was silent for several moments. "Maybe. I don't know. My parents are buried there and the land, for what it is worth, is still mine. The way I feel now I want no more part of the Barranca Negra."

"I've never seen my father like this before," Sally said quietly. "I think he's found the son he's always wanted at last. He'll want you to stay here."

Jordan glanced at her. "And you?"

She moved her slim shoulders. Her face, profiled to him, was delicately molded, soft-looking. "I would like it, too," she replied in complete honesty.

"I was told last night to keep my eyes off you."

"That Oran Bishop!" she cried angrily. "That sounds like him. He has no right . . ."

"I don't intend to pay any attention to him," Ben said, and checked his words suddenly. The lone horseman had appeared again. He was still too distant to recognize but there was no doubt now in Ben Jordan's mind that he was deliberately maintaining his position and pace to coincide with theirs. It was as though he were keeping a close watch over them. It could mean nothing, or it could mean a great deal. Jordan decided there was no point in taking any chances.

"I think we'd better be getting back to the ranch," he said, touching his horse with spurs.

Sally looked at him in surprise. "Why?"

He grinned at her. "Be suppertime," he said as they broke into a gallop.

It was full dark when they reached the lip of the swale and started down the long, gentle slope to the ranch. Lamplight glowed in the windows of the houses, warm and friendly. There had been no more sign of the mysterious, distant rider and the thought of that had faded from his mind. Ben was thinking of how fine a line a man could make on a spread such as the Lazy A—with a wife like Sally—and wondered if he dared hope. It was possible, he decided, but before he could do anything, he still had his promise to Woodward to fulfill. That could easily be discharged now.

"How far is it to Langford?" he asked.

She glanced at him curiously. "Langford? About a day's ride northeast. Why?"

"Some business there I've got to attend to."

"That's fine!" Sally exclaimed, pleased. "I've been meaning to make the trip myself. There are some things I need to buy. We can go together. When?"

"Soon as I can get the crew to working at what I want done."

"Let's make it this week," she said as they rode into the yard. "I would have gone today, but changed my mind."

Jordan reached out, caught the pinto's bridle, and halted him. Sally looked at him questioningly.

"Thanks for that," Ben said.

She smiled at him. "I enjoyed it, too," she said, and dropped from her saddle. She started across the yard but paused. "Come on up to the house when you're ready. I'll have Mattie set out supper for you."

"Sure thing," Jordan replied, and turned the horses over to the hostler.

He swung toward his cabin, whistling softly under his breath. As he rounded the feed barn, he pulled up sharply. A dark figure emerged from the rear window of his quarters, leaped to the ground, and raced for the deeper shadows alongside.

"You!" Ben shouted, breaking into a run. "Stop . . . or I'll shoot!"

But when he reached the corner of the structure, the intruder had disappeared into the night. Jordan's face hardened. He had been right. The rider he had seen in the hills had not been there by accident but for a reason. Someone had wanted close tabs kept on him—someone who was interested in something inside the cabin. Sudden fear lifted within Ben Jordan as realization came to him. He spun, ran swiftly to the door.

XI

Even in the darkness Jordan could see the place was a shambles. Drawers had been pulled open, the bed stripped, furniture overturned; every conceivable nook that might conceal anything had been investigated. Ben glanced at the small rug he had pulled across the loose floor board. It appeared undisturbed. Closing the door, and still in the dark, he dropped to his knees. Brushing the carpet aside, he lifted the plank. Relief flowed through him as his groping fingers felt the worn, smooth surface of leather, sought and touched the packets of currency, and toyed with the gold coins. If it had been the money the intruder was looking for, he had failed to find it.

Jordan gave that consideration. It had to be the money, or, at least, the saddlebags, for he had brought nothing else with him when he rode into Ashburn's. And who would be so interested in what he was carrying in the leather pouches? He replaced the floor board carefully and pulled the carpet and chair back into place. The saddlebags were the only thing anyone could be after; it was hardly possible that any of Ashburn's hired hands knew he was in possession of a small fortune. That added up to one answer. The trespasser was searching for something he did not know the exact nature of—an article he felt would have bearing on Jordan's presence. That brought Ben's thoughts to a dead stop on Oran Bishop. He had been the only man to take note of the saddlebags, to remark on the jealous care that Jordan accorded them. It would be Bishop then, possibly curious as to what made the pouches so valuable, and hopeful they would contain something with which he could discredit Ben in the eyes of Tom Ashburn. The rider in the hills, watching to be certain Jordan did not return unexpectedly early, could have been Oran's friend, Ross Colby. It was all an outside guess—but it made sense.

Suddenly angered, Ben left his cabin and walked the short distance to the bunkhouse. He pushed open the door and entered. Several of the cow-punchers had already crawled into their bunks. Cruz Rodriguez and three others sat at a table playing poker for matches. They glanced up as Jordan halted before them. The Mexican smiled, sobered quickly when he saw Ben's face.

"¿Qué pasa, amigo?"

"Who just came in here . . . during the last five minutes?" The riders looked at each other. Rodriguez said: "Nobody. Who do you look for?"

Jordan shook his head. "Not sure." He moved deeper into the room, made a slow tour of the bunks. Bishop and Colby were among those absent. That would mean they were part of the crew night hawking the cattle. He halted near

251

the door. "Any of you seen Oran, or Ross Colby since you rode in?"

"They come to the herd at dark," Rodriguez said. "We leave to eat. They stay. I have not seen them since."

That had little meaning. The two men could have slipped away unnoticed. One of the cow-punchers started to rise.

"You want them, Mister Jordan? Be right pleased to go get them for you."

Ben said: "No, let it go. I'll see them in the morning. Good night."

He left the bunkhouse but halted when he reached the yard. All was quiet and for a time he stood there, his shoulders squared against the night sky while he lost himself in thought. One thing came through to him, quick and clear: he must get Walt Woodward's money off his hands. It was dangerous to have it around any longer.

He wheeled, headed for the main house where a lamp still burned in the kitchen. He would tell Ashburn he needed to make a trip into Langford that next morning. He would get it done at once. But Tom Ashburn had already gone to bed, as had Sally. Jordan ate his meal of cold, sliced beef, warmed-over biscuits, and coffee in solitude, deciding he would talk to the rancher first thing that following morning. And it was probably best that he not take Sally with him. He was only assuming the intruder who had searched his quarters had been Oran Bishop. There could be another, someone who had learned he had the money, somebody besides Bart Crawford and his outlaw friends who were out to get the $20,000 he had sworn to deliver to Olivia Woodward. There could be danger.

He finished his supper and walked back into the yard. Far from sleep, he strolled on to the barn, looked in briefly at the sorrel contentedly crunching his ration of grain in one of the stalls, and then, keeping to the shadows, circled the yard to its opposite side where he could stand in the brushy windbreak planted years ago by Ashburn. There, unseen, he could watch his cabin. The intruder might pay a return visit, Ben reasoned, if he thought no one was around.

The night was cool and quiet. Off to the east a coyote barked and fell silent. An owl swished across the yard on motionless wings, and then came to a halt somewhere beyond the cook's vegetable garden. Inside the bunkhouse someone laughed and Cruz Rodriguez said something in quick Spanish. The light in the kitchen winked out as Mattie, the cook, wound up her chores and went off to bed.

A faint breeze began to stir, drifting in from the west, fresh with the scent of grass and juniper, almost sharp with a breath of winter. Jordan glanced to the sky, a vast, black arch studded with low hanging, glittering stars. A cold sky, he thought, and snow could not be too far off. It would come sooner than Tom Ashburn had predicted. He must get the crew busy and prepare for the days when the weather would turn bad and neither man nor beast would find it possible to move about.

Tomorrow. He would start the crew gathering the herds that next morning, get them moving north to fresh grass. His thoughts halted. He would not be there. He must make the trip into Langford and rid himself of the responsibility that lay so heavily on his shoulders. It would take two days, even more if he had trouble locating Olivia Woodward. He could arrive there and find her out of town, or possibly moved away. Yet if he were to fulfill his new obligations to Tom Ashburn, he could not afford to waste even one day.

He stepped from the windbreak of tamarisk, and crossed to the bunkhouse. The card game had broken up and now Cruz Rodriguez squatted on his heels, back pressed against the wall of the building as he smoked a final cigarette. He looked up and grinned, as Jordan approached.

"You find sleep comes hard, *señor*," he said, stating it as a fact rather than a question. "Perhaps it is because the Barranca Negra teaches a man always to keep one eye open for death."

"Down there, if a man is not careful, it comes too soon," Jordan agreed.

"But there are other things that trouble you, no?"

Ben nodded. "Got to make a trip to Langford. I'll be gone a couple of days, maybe more. I want all the stock moved onto the north range. I'd like to have the crew get at it in the morning. I want you to pass the word along."

Rodriguez stared at the glowing tip of his cigarette. He placed it between his lips, inhaled, and then exhaled a cloud of smoke. "Up here, *amigo*," he said quietly, "one such as I . . . a Mexican . . . does not give an order."

Ben stirred impatiently. "It's my order, not yours. I'm only asking you to repeat it since I won't be here myself."

Rodriguez flipped the cigarette into the yard. "It shall be as you wish. I will repeat the order."

"If anybody balks, tell them they'll answer to me when I get back. The main thing is I want the stock grazing up there before bad weather hits so the rest of the range gets a chance to shape up for winter."

Rodriguez said: "I understand, *señor*. This journey you must take to Langford . . . it is important?"

"Has to be done," Jordan replied. "No way out of it."

"The *patrón* . . . Ashburn, he knows of this?"

"I figure on telling him in the morning."

The Mexican was silent for a long time. Then: "And you will return, *amigo*? He is a fine man and he thinks much of you. I would not like to see him sad."

"I'll be back, Cruz. Depend on it."

"It is enough," Rodriguez said, thrusting out his hand. "*Adiós. Buena suerte.*"

"*Adiós*, and thanks," Ben said, enclosing the man's fingers in his own. He turned then, walked to his quarters.

Not bothering to remove his clothing, Jordan stretched out on the bed, his pistol placed nearby for instant use should the intruder return again. Sleep came quickly to him now that the decision to deliver Woodward's money had been made.

He awoke at the first gray streaks of dawn. Washing himself from the bowl and pitcher on the dresser, he made himself ready to travel. That done, he paused in the center of the room to formulate a plan. He would first have his breakfast and tell Tom Ashburn of his need to go to Langford. Then he would return to his quarters, take the saddlebags from their place of concealment, get the sorrel, and leave. It could be done with a minimum of wasted motion and time—unless he had trouble with Sally. But there was a possibility she would not be there for the early meal. She had been tired; she could sleep late.

He stepped to the door, pulled it open—and came to a quick stop. Four riders were pulling into the hitch rack in front of Ashburn's house, four grim, dusty men. He knew them all—Crawford, Aaron, Gates, and Arlie Davis.

XII

Ben Jordan withdrew into the room quickly and closed the door. The outlaws again. He had thought they were off his trail, and that he had lost them for good. How could they have tracked him to Ashburn's? In those tight, frustrating moments, he searched his mind for an answer. Tuck—one of Slaughter's men. They had been talking. He had mentioned that he was headed north to take a job on the Lazy A. Crawford must have questioned all of the trail herd crew. Jordan swore angrily. This changed everything. Of course, he could talk to Tom Ashburn, and call upon him for help. And the Lazy A hands would likely stand by him in a showdown. But as it had been with Slaughter, Jordan was reluctant to involve others in his own trouble; a man skinned his own cats and looked for no one else to give him a hand.

He wheeled to the cache where he had hidden the money. There was only one thing he could do now—leave, get off the Lazy A before the outlaws saw him. Throwing the saddlebags over his shoulder, he let himself out the rear window, hurried across the open ground to the barn. The hostler was nowhere in sight and Ben threw his gear onto the sorrel in quick, practiced motions. Mounting, he rode through the wide doorway, dropped back behind the bulky structure, and circled the ranch, keeping the tamarisk windbreak between the buildings and him. When he reached the end of the dense, feathery growth, he halted. The ranch, clearly visible, lay below him. Crawford who had come off the black, stood now, one foot on the porch of Ashburn's house while he talked to the rancher. Near the door Ben could see both Sally and her mother. Three of the hired hands, one of them Oran Bishop, were coming around the side from the dining hall, apparently curious as to the purpose of the four strangers. They would not be long discovering that he had fled, Ben realized, and immediately pulled off below the crest of the rise, and struck northward at a good lope. It would be wise to put as much distance as possible between him and the Lazy A within the next half hour.

He pressed the gelding hard for the first ten miles, and then, topping out a high ridge, he looked back. There were no riders in sight. A sigh of relief slipped from his lips. If luck were with him, there would be doubt as to where he was; they might think he was somewhere on the range with the herd, since no one had seen his departure. If it worked that way, the outlaws would lose several hours—ample time for him to reach the town of Langford and rid himself of the money.

He saw the settlement, three dozen or so graying shacks and buildings, huddled in the center of a brushy swale, shortly after noon. The gelding had made surprisingly good time, eating up the miles with his tireless, long legs and easy stride. Pleased that the journey had been much shorter than he had anticipated, Jordan rode on the crest of the hill where he had paused, and then started down the final two-mile stretch of lane that led into the town. If all went well, he should be able to turn back for Ashburn's place before dark, that very day.

He reached the bottom of the slope, the halfway point, passed one or two run-down shacks, once homes of squatters but now deserted, and loped on. He would go first to the general store; store-keepers always knew where everyone lived and could tell him where to locate Olivia Woodward. Unexpectedly the sorrel checked his run and slid to a halt. The big red horse reared, startled by the sudden appearance of three riders who burst from the depths of the dense brush that lined the road.

Ben Jordan's hand dropped instinctively to the pistol at his hip, and fell slowly away as he looked into the muzzles of the guns held by the trio. One, a husky, dark man, with a somewhat better appearance than the others, pushed out ahead.

"Forget you've got that hogleg," he said, moving in close. He studied Jordan for several moments. Then: "Where'd you get that horse?"

Anger whipped through Ben, not only at being accosted in so high-handed a manner, but at his own carelessness. Just as the end of his problem was in sight, he had allowed himself to get tripped up. "Not that it's any of your business," he snapped, "he was given to me."

"I'm making it my business," the dark-faced man said. He reached into his pocket, produced a star. "Name's Sharpe. Deputy town marshal." He waved his hand at the pair behind him. "Frick and Rosen. They're working with me. We've been on the look out for that sorrel. What's your name, mister?"

Jordan breathed easier. "Ben Jordan . . . and I can explain about the horse. It belonged to a man named Woodward, Walt Woodward."

"I know him," Sharpe said.

"He got shot up. I found him dying in a shack, back in the hills. I'd lost my horse so he gave me his."

"Why?" Sharpe's tone was cool, suspicious.

"I just told you . . . and I agreed to do him a favor."

"Favor?" Sharpe repeated, his voice lifting. Frick and Rosen moved up beside him, rifles still cocked and leveled at Jordan's breast.

"Something personal," Ben said.

The lawman studied Jordan in suspicious silence. Finally he said: "Maybe you could have killed him, stolen the sorrel."

"No," Ben rapped impatiently, realizing in that same moment that he had no proof of any sort, except the $20,000. "It was just the way I've said it."

Sharpe rode forward, lifted Jordan's gun from its holster, thrust it into his own belt. He leaned to the side, elbow on the horn of his saddle. "This favor you're talking about, what was it?"

Jordan hesitated, and then shrugged. Telling the whole story would likely be the only way he could prove his innocence. A man, killing another for his horse, would not be delivering a small fortune in cash to the widow. And he was talking to the law; there could be no danger.

"He asked me to carry some money to his wife . . . widow. He'd just sold out a ranch, he said. Made me promise to see she got the cash."

"Twenty thousand dollars?" Sharpe said.

Ben stared. "How'd you know that?"

Sharpe shook his head. "The Woodwards are friends of mine. Personal friends. I knew about the deal from the start." He paused, cast a sideward glance at Frick and Rosen. "We've been worrying about Walt. The money in those saddlebags?"

Jordan nodded. "I'd be obliged if you'd take me to Missus Woodward. I want to get it off my hands."

"No use you having to bother about it any longer," the lawman said. "I'll see she gets it."

"I appreciate that, too, but I'll have to do it personally. I gave my word to Woodward."

"We'll do it my way," Sharpe said quietly and

261

firmly. He motioned to Frick. "Tubo, get the saddlebags."

"Now, hold up a minute!" Ben said. "I don't see where it makes any difference to you . . ."

"You walk easy, mister!" the lawman cut in sharply. "I'm still not sure I swallow that yarn you handed us about finding Woodward dying, and him giving you his horse."

"Then what the hell am I doing here, bringing his widow all that money?" Jordan shouted, furious. "If I had killed Woodward and stolen his horse, I'd be going the other way fast as I could!"

"A point in your favor," Sharpe said calmly. "I'll tell it to the marshal. Get the saddlebags, Tubo."

Jordan sat motionless, helpless, as Frick pulled the pouches free and handed them to Sharpe. The deputy unbuckled one side, checked the money. He nodded as if satisfied. "All here, far as I can tell," he said. He turned to Rosen. "Barney, take Jordan here in and lock him up until we get things cleared around. I want to talk to Missus Woodward about it, see what she thinks."

Jordan sighed in disgust. "You're wasting a lot of time, time I sure don't have to spare, Deputy. I can't afford to lay around in jail for two or three days. I've got a job to get back to."

Sharpe considered that for several moments. Then: "Reckon you're right. I won't keep you waiting any longer than I just have to. And you give me your word you'll hang around until I straighten this out and I won't lock you up. Just you check in at the hotel. Guess the word of a man honest enough to ride clear across the territory with another man's money ought to be reliable."

"Sure ought," Barney Rosen agreed.

"Won't take no longer'n tomorrow morning. Main thing is for me to explain it all to Bardett . . . he's the marshal. And I've got to see what Missus Woodward wants to do about that horse."

"Her husband gave him to me."

"I know that. You told us. But you'll need a bill of sale. Woodward was pretty well known around here and people will be recognizing that sorrel of his. You'd better have some papers proving he's yours, or you're liable to get strung up for horse stealing."

Ben shifted on the saddle. No matter what his personal thoughts were, it seemed he had no choice but to do as the deputy directed. "All right," he said. "I'll be at the hotel. But hurry things along. I want to be on my way home by tomorrow morning."

"We'll sure move fast as we can," Sharpe said. "Hotel's down at the end of the street. I'll go first off and see Missus Woodward." He reached down, plucked Jordan's gun from his belt, and returned it. "Might as well have this back," he said, and started to move off. He drew up suddenly. "One thing more, don't think you ought to mention anything about this money to anybody. Risky business having twenty thousand dollars just laying around. Sure wouldn't want anything to happen to it before the widow Woodward could get it stashed away in the bank."

Jordan said: "All right, Deputy. Whatever you say." And he rode on toward a scattering of buildings.

XIII

Jordan entertained no thoughts of registering in Langford's hotel. He would allow the deputy until nightfall to satisfy himself that all was honest and aboveboard and then, whether Sharpe liked it or not, he was returning to the Lazy A. If there were matters still to be cleared up, the lawman could come to him at Ashburn's. He felt he had fulfilled his promise to Walt Woodward —at least he had done so to all practical purposes—and that ended it. He angled the sorrel into a hitch rack in front of a café, the only one in the settlement, it appeared, and dismounted. He had eaten no breakfast and now hunger was making itself known. The café was far from clean but he settled down at the counter and ordered himself a meal.

It was good to have the responsibility of Woodward's money off his hands, and with it the knowledge that Bart Crawford and his men would not again be dogging his trail. Yet there was something about the whole affair that left him vaguely dissatisfied and disturbed. He was not feeling the tremendous relief that he had imagined would be his, once the chore was finished; instead, there was a gnawing discontent, a sense of having left a job partly undone. But there had been no other way. Sharpe was a lawman, a deputy marshal according to what he had said, as well as the badge he carried, and he had claimed to be a close friend of the Woodwards. The fact he knew the exact amount of money in the saddlebags further verified that statement. Still, he wished now he had insisted more forcefully on delivering the money himself to Olivia Woodward. Sharpe and his two helpers could have accompanied him, if there were doubts in their minds as to his intentions. Ben stirred restlessly; that was the way he should have handled it.

His food came and he dallied and toyed with it for a full half hour, taking no pleasure from it. When he had enough, he arose, paid his check, and returned to the street. On the opposite side, a few doors down, he saw the marshal's office and jail. Leading the sorrel, he crossed over. The lawman's headquarters were empty, the single cell vacant. Ben turned, walked back into the open. A man, standing in front of a saloon a short distance farther on, looked at him inquiringly.

"You hunting for Marshal Bardett?"

Jordan said: "Yes. Any idea where I can find him?"

"Nope. Sure don't. But I reckon he's around somewheres. Might be he's out in the country."

The dissatisfaction within Ben Jordan continued to grow. "What's his deputy's name?"

"Ain't got no regular man. Once in a while appoints himself a special deputy when they's something that's got to be done like moving pris'ners.

"Know one called Sharpe?

The man thought for a moment, shrugged. "Don't recollect the name, but could be. Like I said he hires on somebody now and then. What's the trouble? You needing help?"

Jordan gave him no reply. After a time he said: "How about Missus Olivia Woodward . . . know where she lives?"

"Ollie? Sure." The man grinned broadly. "Down to the end of the street, turn left. Green house setting off to itself."

"Thanks," Ben said, and swung onto the sorrel.

Jordan found the Woodward home with no difficulty. He tied the gelding to a fence post, made his way along a path to the door, and knocked. There was no immediate answer and after a time he repeated the summons.

The panel opened. A heavy-eyed woman, her face smeared with cosmetics she had not troubled to remove the previous night, straw-colored hair falling in disarray about her shoulders, and clad in a faded robe that she clutched at the neck, stared out at him. Once she had possessed beauty but it was gone now, replaced by that brassy hardness common to saloon women. "What do you want?" she demanded harshly.

"Are you Missus Woodward . . . Olivia Woodward?"

"That's me," she said. "Who are you?"

"I knew your husband," Ben said. "Name is Jordan."

He watched Olivia Woodward's haggard face for some reaction. If the deputy had been there, had delivered the money to her, she would recognize his name as that of the man who had brought it. Her features remained stolid. "Come on in," she said, retreating into the shaded, over-furnished room. "Where is Walt?"

Jordan, pushed by his own fears, entered. "Have there been three men here to see you . . . one of them Sharpe, the deputy marshal?"

Olivia Woodward's eyes narrowed slightly. "Sharpe, the deputy?" she repeated as though startled. "No. Why would he be coming here?"

"You know him?"

"Yes, I know him."

Jordan took a deep breath. "He's bringing you the money your husband sent you. Twenty thousand dollars." Ben paused. "I've got bad news, Missus Woodward. Walt's dead."

The woman stared. "Dead? You sure?"

"I was with him when it happened. Outlaws shot him. I buried him myself. Before he died, he made me promise to deliver the money he got from the sale of your ranch to you. Twenty thousand dollars, he said it was."

"You say Al Sharpe has it now?"

Jordan nodded. "They . . . Sharpe and a couple of men he called Frick and Rosen . . . stopped me at the edge of town. Thought I'd stolen your husband's horse. When I explained what I was doing, Sharpe took over the money, said he was a personal friend of yours, and he'd take it to you. Told me I'd have to wait around until he cleared up things. He a friend of the family?"

"Yes, for a long time."

"Said he'd bring the money straight to you. I've been dodging outlaws all the way across the territory to keep my promise to your husband. Wish now I hadn't turned it over to Sharpe."

Olivia Woodward smiled. "It will be all right," she said. "I'll get it. Al must have gotten side-tracked on the way. When did you say you gave it to him?"

"About an hour ago."

She rose, moved to the door, and opened it for him. "I want to thank you for all the trouble you went through, Mister Jordan. And don't worry about your promise to Walt. You've kept it."

"I wish I could make myself feel that way,"

Ben replied, moving into the open. "But if you're satisfied, I guess I should be. What about the horse?"

"Horse?"

"The sorrel. Walt gave him to me, but I've got no papers to prove he's mine. The deputy said I had better get a bill of sale from you."

"Of course, and I want you to have him. Tell you what, the least I can do for you in return, is cook you a good supper before you leave. You get your bill of sale made up and be back here about dark. I'll sign it, then we'll eat."

"Sounds fine, but you don't need to go to all that trouble . . ."

"No trouble. You do what I say. Risking your life to bring that money . . . a good supper will be little enough pay."

Jordan walked on into the yard. "See you at dark, then," he said, smiling, and continued on to where the sorrel waited.

It was all finished now. He could stop stewing about it. Olivia Woodward, while seemingly not particularly saddened by her husband's death, had exhibited no alarm when she had learned that Deputy Sharpe was in possession of her money and had failed so far to deliver it. But she was right, of course; he could have been delayed for some cause. And he guessed he was pressing things too hard. It had actually been little more than an hour since Sharpe had relieved him of the saddlebags. He was pleased that the sorrel was to become his legally. Now he need fear no subsequent problems in that matter. He would go to a livery stable, obtain a blank bill of sale, and fill in a description of the horse. With Olivia Woodward's signature properly affixed, the transfer would be above question.

He mounted, turned back up the lane, heading for Langford's one street. He had three or four hours to kill before dark and the hour at which he was to return to Olivia Woodward's. The smart thing would be to go somewhere, get a little sleep, if he intended to spend the night riding back to the Lazy A. The livery stable where he planned to get a bill of sale—he could crawl into the loft and take a short nap in the hay.

He reached the corner, halted, his eyes searching for such an establishment. He stiffened suddenly. Five men, riding abreast, turned into the far end of the street and came slowly, purposefully onward. Crawford and his friends again—and with them was Oran Bishop.

XIV

A smile cracked Ben Jordan's lips as he watched the grim-faced outlaws approach. The laugh was on them now. The money was safe where they could not touch it. They were too late. And then

Jordan frowned. What was Bishop doing with them? There was no denying the ill-feeling that existed between him and the cowpuncher, but he did not think Oran so bitter that he would seek to gratify it by siding in with outlaws such as Bart Crawford. Drawing back until the corner of the building where he had halted shielded him from the men's view, he watched as the riders moved along the street and came to a stop in its center. Several persons emerged from the doorways of the weathered stores and stared at them curiously. There appeared to be a discussion between the five, something that had to do with the marshal, for all glanced now and then toward the lawman's office.

Jordan contemplated riding out into the open, moving up to them and having his moment of victory, but the presence of Oran Bishop among the group held him back. He could find no logical reason for the blond cowpuncher's being with them unless—Jordan's thoughts came to a halt—unless Crawford actually was a lawman, as he had claimed to be at Slaughter's camp. And if that were true, then Walt Woodward, far from being an honest rancher, had been an outlaw in possession of stolen money. The possibility of that struck Ben forcibly, pinning him motionless to his saddle. It could be true, and it would account for Oran Bishop's presence. When he looked back over the past days' incidents, recalled the words spoken by Woodward, Crawford's actions, the way Olivia Woodward, far from a grieving wife, had received the news, a pattern began to fall into place. But if it were so—Woodward an outlaw and Crawford a sheriff or marshal—he was now little better off in the eyes of the lawman than before. Crawford would never believe his story of handing over the saddlebags and the $20,000 to Al Sharpe; he would have to have proof in the form of the deputy himself.

A door slammed somewhere behind Jordan. He half turned, glanced down the narrow lane. Olivia Woodward, carrying a small carpetbag, was coming from her house, walking hurriedly. She was fully dressed with a light coat thrown over her arm. She cut sharply right when she left her yard, headed not for the street and the business section of Langford, but for the dense, wooded area that lay east of the town. As Ben Jordan watched her, his convictions grew. Olivia Woodward was leaving hastily. She was avoiding the settlement. That she had no intention of meeting him at dark was also perfectly clear; such had been only a means for getting rid of him. It all meant something—something that concerned him vitally.

Jordan wheeled the sorrel about. As the gelding swung around, he moved briefly into the street. Ben flung a glance toward the five men and saw they had seen him. Crawford's hand came up swiftly. There was sharp glint of sunlight on metal and then a gunshot echoed along the buildings. Ben felt the warm breath of the bullet and saw the five riders break into a charging run. He drove his spurs into the gelding, sent him plunging down the lane. He swung off to the right of Woodward's place, drove hard for the trees and underbrush beyond it. He did not want to rush on after Olivia Woodward—not yet. He would lead Crawford and his party off to the side, lose them, and double back. She would not go far.

The sorrel thundered along a hedge of wild roses, sailing effortlessly over a low, sagging fence, and gained the thicker growth. At that moment Crawford and his followers rounded the corner. Jordan, low in the saddle, did not look back. He heard Bishop's voice yelling something at him but the words were lost in the pounding of the gelding's hoofs. He expected Crawford to open up again with his pistol, but no more shots came. He raced straight ahead through the welter of rocks, brush, and scrubby trees for several hundred yards. Now there was no need to look over his shoulder; he could tell his pursuers were coming on from the hammering of their horses, and he knew they were not far behind. But they were having difficulty keeping him in sight. As they cleared the fence, he heard Crawford's shout.

"Keep bearin' right! He's headin' that way!"

Jordan grinned and began to curve the sorrel to the left. The brush was dragging at him, tearing at his legs but it was screening his flight effectively. He pressed on, letting the gelding have his head and pick his own way. Through the trees he began to see open ground, realizing they were coming into the open again. He angled the big horse more sharply to the left, and was now riding in the exact opposite direction to that he had taken at the beginning. He listened for sounds of Crawford and the others, but could hear nothing. Evidently they were hanging to the course they had chosen at the start and still believed him to be somewhere ahead.

He broke out onto cleared ground suddenly and saw that he was on the lane that fronted the Woodward house. He pulled the sorrel to a stop and looked about. He was several hundred yards below the house—and below the point where he had last seen the woman. He cut around, sent the gelding up the lane at a trot, his glance searching through the brush for some signs of her. When he came to a fork where a second lane angled off, he halted again. He dropped from the saddle and made a close inspection of the loose dust. The narrow, pointed toe imprints of a woman's foot were unmistakable. Jordan went back onto the gelding and headed him down the side lane. He held the horse to a quiet walk. Olivia Woodward could not have gotten far.

He had no difficulty in following her. Every few yards the print of her small foot was visible, and he knew he had only to use care to catch up eventually with her. Just what it would mean when he did, he had no idea, but that it all tied in with Sharpe and the money, he was certain. Stolen money—and he had aided an outlaw in the furtherance of his crime. That he was an innocent party in the scheme was beside the point; the law would make no allowances for his actions unless, of course, he could recover the money and hand it over to the authorities. Only then might they be inclined to listen. The money—$20,000 in gold coin and currency—where was it? He had last seen it when Al Sharpe, the deputy, had taken it from him, stating that he would take it to Olivia Woodward. The delivery had never been made, and now, here he was, Jordan thought, blindly following the woman for no good reason other than on a hunch that she was more involved than she purported to be, and would lead him to it. If the hunch didn't pan out . . . ? Jordan brushed the possibility from his mind. He would ford that creek when he came to it.

The area was becoming more overgrown, the lane less clearly cut. They were somewhere east of the settlement, he reckoned, in a section that was seldom visited by the residents. A few moments later he caught the first glimpse of Olivia. She was still walking fast, the coat in one hand, the small bag in the other. Jordan halted, allowed her to get well ahead again. He did not want her looking over her shoulder and seeing him on her trail. But she seemed in much too great a hurry for that. She was bent on reaching some particular place—or meeting some person, as quickly as possible.

Ben thought he heard sounds of Crawford and his men shortly after that and he continued to wait and listen in the warm hush. The noise came from the direction where he had last seen the five riders and he wondered if they had discovered their error and had turned back and were now combing through the brush for him. In all likelihood this was the case. The trees and rocks ended a short distance to the south, just as they had to the east. The grove had appeared to be a sort of oasis in the center of which Langford had sprung up. He heard nothing more and put the sorrel into motion once again. He covered a hundred yards, rounded a sharp turn in the lane—and found it empty for a considerable distance. Olivia Woodward had disappeared.

He glanced around hurriedly. She could have done nothing other than turn off. In that next moment he saw her again, a brief flash of color through the trees to his left. She was walking up a narrow path toward a cabin that was set deep in the tangled brush. As Ben watched, she reached the door, lifted the latch, and without hesitation entered. Jordan wheeled off the lane and quietly made his way to a point fifty yards or so from the weathered shack. Tying the sorrel securely to a clump of juniper, he worked in on the rear of the structure. There was but one small window, low off the ground. He dropped to his hands and knees, crept to the opening. Voices, laughter, and conversation reached him. Removing his hat, he raised himself carefully, quietly to where he could look in. The first face he saw was that of Al Sharpe.

XV

Sharpe said: "Always figured I'd make a dang' good lawman! Got that square look."

Everyone laughed. Jordan's body tensed. Sharpe was no deputy—he was an outlaw, too. And so were Tubo Frick and Barney Rosen. He had been wrong all the way. He shifted to where he had a better view of the cabin's interior. Olivia Woodward sat on the edge of a cot upon which the saddlebags had been laid. The pouches were open and the money was partially visible. Sharpe leaned against a crudely built table, a bottle in his hand. Squatted on their heels, backs pressed against a wall, were Rosen and Frick.

"Well, you sure was right," Frick said, fumbling with his cigarette makings. "You kept sayin' if we watched that road long enough, old Walt'd show up. He didn't, but the money sure did."

Sharpe nodded, took a drink from the bottle,

and handed it to Rosen. "When I saw him line out that night after we robbed the bank, I knew he was bad hit. I aimed to follow and then some of that damned posse got on my tail, and I lost him. Didn't worry me none, however. I figured he'd come wagging back to Olivia sooner or later. Or, if he couldn't make it, he'd be sucker enough to send the money to her somehow."

Olivia Woodward turned to Sharpe. "That's why you've been playing the good family friend so much here lately. You were keeping an eye on me."

"Man looks after his own interests," Sharpe said.

She nodded. "I still come in for my share . . . Walt's share, don't I, Al?"

Sharpe grinned. "I got a better idea. Two shares make one big one. Why don't you and me tie up? Won't have to be worrying about Walt now. Could have ourselves quite a time with ten thousand dollars."

Olivia Woodward shrugged. "Sure, why not?"

Sharpe studied her for several moments. "Never could figure what you seen in Walt. He sure wasn't your kind."

"He was good to me," the woman said tiredly. "And he usually had some money."

"We'll have plenty of that from now on," Sharpe said. "And when this runs out, the boys and me'll find us another hick town bank to bust open."

The woman looked down. "And you'll die out

in the brush somewhere, just like Walt did, someday. I had a feeling the night you came over to the house and planned it all out . . . a feeling that something bad was going to happen . . ."

"None of that now!" Sharpe broke in. "You're sounding like a wife already and I won't have it."

Olivia moved her shoulders in a faint gesture of resignation. She extended her hand to Rosen for the whiskey bottle. She took a swallow, shuddered, passed it on to Tubo Frick. "I'll never learn to like that stuff," she murmured. "When do we leave, Al?"

"Soon as it's dark."

"I don't think we ought to wait that long."

"Why not? We sure don't want nobody seeing us leaving the country."

"That cowboy, Jordan, that brought the money. He was pretty upset when he found out you hadn't given it to me. I think I smoothed it over but he still might go to the marshal, and start asking questions."

"Let him," Sharpe said. "And if he comes around again, tell him you've got it . . . the money your loving husband sent you for selling his ranch." Sharpe began to laugh, unable to continue. Frick and Rosen joined in but Olivia Woodward only smiled. "Old Walt sure must've given him a yarn. And making him promise to tote all that money to his poor little wife, come hell or high water. Lord, what a sucker."

Ben Jordan felt his face begin to burn. He had been a sucker, a greenhorn from the word go. Woodward had really taken him in.

"He's an honest man," Olivia said in a quiet voice. "Something we've all forgot how to be."

"No difference," Rosen observed dryly. "A sucker and an honest man is the same thing."

"Maybe Walt wasn't playing him for a sucker so much as he was interested in getting the money to us, so I could have his share," the woman said. "I'd like to think that's the way it was. And it could be."

"Sure, sure," Sharpe said impatiently. "But Walt's dead, gone, buried. He done us a favor, getting the cash to us after he got shot up and knew he wasn't going to make it. That's fine, but forget about it and him. Does no good to keep hashing over the dead."

"I'm for that," Rosen said, wagging his head. "Gives a man the creeps."

Sharpe reached down, picked up a packet of the currency. He rifled the edges thoughtfully. "Maybe you ought to go back to your house," he said, settling his attention on the woman. "Just in case that greenhorn does take Bardett over to see you. We'll swing by when it's time and pick you up."

Distrust was frank on Olivia Woodward's features. "No, I'll stay here. I think we ought to leave now, but if you don't, all right, we'll wait."

Sharpe laughed. "Afraid we might forget to come by?"

Olivia said—"Yes."—in a bold, candid way.

Sharpe roared with laughter. "That's right, girl. Don't trust nobody. Look out for yourself."

"What we goin' to do about eatin'?" Frick asked. "Barney ain't got nothin' here in his shack. You reckon it's safe for one of us to go into town?"

"No," Sharpe answered. "Might run into that Jordan. He's still waiting for me to tell him he can pull out."

"How about Ollie then? Nobody'd pay any mind to her."

"I'm not leaving here," the woman said stubbornly. "If you want some food, one of you run over to my place and help yourself. You're not likely to bump into that cowboy there. He wasn't coming back until dark."

"Coming to your house?" Sharpe asked.

"For supper. Wanted me to sign some papers giving him Walt's horse."

"A horse," Frick said. "We'll be needin' one for Ollie. Where'll we get one?"

Sharpe thought for a moment. "Guess I should have grabbed Walt's sorrel when I had the chance. You know people around here, Barney. Where can we get a nag for her?"

"Rancher about ten miles east of here. Reckon we can get one from him."

"Settles that. Ollie can ride double with me until

we get there. We'll figure to eat and get ourselves some grub from that rancher, too."

Ben pulled back from the window, crouched low in the brush. He had all the answers now, but the problem that faced him was how to recover the money and capture the outlaws. Once accomplished he could turn them and the saddlebags over to Marshal Bardett—or to Bart Crawford—it didn't matter to whom. He considered the advisability of moving in on the men, but the odds were too long. It would be his one gun against three desperate outlaws, plus possibly Olivia Woodward, who showed every sign of being as coolly efficient as they were. And the arrangement of the cabin would double his problem. After a moment he discarded the idea. He could not afford to make a mistake now; already he had allowed himself to be made a fool. This time he must be sure.

Bardett—the town marshal. There was the solution. Sharpe and the others planned to stay in the shack until dark. There would be plenty of time to ride to Langford, locate the lawman, recruit a posse, and return. But why go that far? Why not call on Bart Crawford and his deputies? To allow him and his men to make the capture would undoubtedly ease some of the hard feeling that existed between the lawmen and himself. And they were somewhere close by.

On his hands and knees Ben started back for the

gelding. He could hear Al Sharpe off on another tale of some sort, one that was providing much laughter for Tubo Frick and Barney Rosen. He could not hear Olivia Woodward's voice. Apparently she was not finding Al Sharpe's words amusing. That the widow had little use for the companions of her late husband was evident, but it was also clear that she was determined to have her share of the stolen money. Still low, Jordan reached the stand of thick growth where he had hidden the sorrel. He was on the verge of rising when Bart Crawford's voice, in a hoarse whisper and coming from only a few steps ahead, halted him. "His horse, all right. Means he's around close. Now, I want him . . . any way you can get him . . . dead or alive."

XVI

Bart Crawford's grim words hammered at Jordan's brain—*dead or alive!* They were giving him no chance at all, no opportunity to prove his innocence. Crawford had determined only that the chase would end here. The corners of Ben Jordan's mouth hardened, a whiteness began to show along the edge of his jaw as anger swept through him. Dead or alive—he would have something to say about that. Sure, he had let both Walt Woodward and Al Sharpe make a fool of him, but now he was in a position to rectify his mistakes. And whether Crawford and his men liked it or not, they were going to help him do it.

He raised himself cautiously. Crawford was off his horse, stood only a few paces away. He was facing the opposite way, having his close look at the sorrel's gear, apparently hopeful of finding the stolen money hidden about the saddle. Beyond him, still mounted, were Aaron, Gates, Davis, and Oran Bishop. Jordan drew his pistol. He would have to move fast. The instant he stepped from the brush he would reveal himself to the four riders. Everything depended on his reaching Crawford, jamming his gun into the man's back, and forcing the others to hold their fire.

"What about that cabin over yonder?" Gates said. "Could be he's holed up in there."

"And leave his horse standing out here like this?" Crawford answered, his tone derisive. "No, he won't be doing that. Place don't look much like anybody's been near it for years."

"Still figure we ought to look."

Ben Jordan, like a dark, shifting shadow, moved from the depths of the brush suddenly. In three strides he was crowding in behind Crawford and had his revolver digging into the man's spine.

"Hey . . . look out!" Gates exclaimed, startled. His hand swept downward for the weapon at his hip.

The others stared and then came to life. Jordan's sharp words froze them on their saddles.

"Don't try anything . . . not unless you want me to blow his guts out!" Crawford, swearing in a deep angry voice, slowly raised his hands. Ben reached forward, pulled the lawman's weapon from its holster, and thrust it into his own belt. "Keep looking in that direction," he ordered. "I've got some talking to do."

Crawford only grunted. Oran Bishop, his face red, his eyes snapping, said: "You damned owlhoot! Knew there was something wrong the moment you rode into Ashburn's. You ought to be right pleased with yourself, fooling that old man like you did."

"I didn't try to fool him."

"Hell you didn't! And if I could have found those saddlebags you were so proud of, I . . ."

Then it had been Bishop who searched his quarters. And Colby would have been the rider in the hills who kept watch. "You don't know what it's all about, Oran. Just shut up and listen," Jordan snapped.

"You've got nothing to say I want to hear."

"You'll hear it anyway . . . and I'm warning you all once more . . . make a wrong move and Crawford's a dead man. That clear?"

There was a long moment of silence, and then Crawford said: "Come on, come on, get it over with. What's on your mind?"

"Just this," Ben said, "I never stole that money."

Crawford laughed, a low, forced chuckle. "Don't

give me that. I seen you, watched you ride off on that sorrel. All of us did, except Bishop there."

"Wasn't me you saw. That horse and the jacket I'm wearing belonged to a man named Woodward. Found him in a shack, dying."

"And now you're telling me he handed over a pair of saddlebags loaded with twenty thousand dollars of the bank's money . . . ?"

"He did, but he didn't say it was hold-up money. Claimed he got it from selling some property."

"And was on his way home when some outlaws, meaning us, jumped him. That it?"

"Just what he said. He was shot up pretty bad. Made me promise to deliver the money to his wife here in Langford, personally. That's what I've been trying to do."

"How's it happen you're forking his horse and wearing his brush jacket?" Cleve Aaron asked skeptically.

"Lost mine in a storm. Horse went over a cliff in the Mogollon Mountains with all I owned tied on the saddle. I was afoot when I ran into Woodward."

Again there was silence. Oran Bishop spoke first. "You expect us to swallow a yarn like that?"

Jordan swore impatiently. "I don't give a damn what you think . . . it's the truth. And if I thought it was important enough, I could take you back to where my buckskin is laying dead, halfway down a cañon slope. I can show you where I buried Woodward. But it's not important."

"What's important," Crawford broke in, "is the money. Where is it?"

"I haven't got it."

"Haven't got it!" Gates echoed. "What in the hell did you do . . . ?"

"I was on my way to hand it over to Woodward's widow, like I promised. Three men stopped me at the edge of town. They'd been watching for Woodward, and when they saw his horse, they figured something was wrong. Anyway they stopped me. One of them flashed a deputy marshal badge and said he was the law. He took the money, said he would turn it over to Missus Woodward."

"Did he?" Crawford asked in a low, tight voice.

"No . . . and he's not a lawman. I just found that out."

"Not a deputy?" Crawford said, turning around slowly.

"He's an outlaw, same as the two men with him. They're together now. Woodward's widow is with them. They've got the money."

Crawford's dark, intense face showed interest. "Where?"

"Wait a minute, Marshal," Bishop said. "You ain't falling for this yarn he's handing us, are you? It's ten to one he's cooking up a scheme to get you off his tail so's he can keep going with that money."

"He sure don't have it on him now," Crawford answered. "And I reckon a man could get himself tangled into a mess, like he claims."

"Only thing I'm interested in is clearing my name," Jordan said. "Give me your word there'll be no charges against me, and I'll help you nail the outlaws and get the bank's money back."

At once Crawford said: "Don't see why there'd be any reason to hold you, was you to do that. Far as I'm concerned, it would prove you're telling the truth. Where is that bunch and the money?"

Jordan said: "Then we've got a deal?"

"We have. Now where . . . ?"

"In that shack," Ben said, handing Crawford his pistol. "They're all there, even the woman."

"For hell's sake," Gates muttered in an amazed voice. "That close?"

"How do you know?" Bishop demanded, still far from convinced.

"That's where I've been, listening to them talk. They figure to ride out after dark."

"Only three of them, you said," Cleve Aaron remarked. "Won't be no trouble breakin' in and takin' over."

"Wouldn't be easy," Jordan said. "Couple of us are bound to get killed. And, like I told you, Missus Woodward's in there, too. Be smarter to wait until they come out. Not long now until dark."

"Surround the place," Gates suggested. "Maybe they'd throw out their guns and quit."

"Not them . . . not with twenty thousand dollars at stake. They'd fight and shooting would bring half the town running out here," Crawford said, shaking his head. "Never like outsiders hanging around at a time like this. Always somebody getting shot accidental. I figure Jordan's got the best idea. We'll wait."

XVII

The others dismounted, led their horses into the dense brush, and tied them. Crawford held back until they were again at his side.

"We'll move up, close as we can to the door," he said. "Best we spread out, cover it from all angles. Now, keep low. Don't want them spotting us."

They slipped off into the tangled growth, circling to the east until they were directly opposite the cabin. They paused there briefly, then worked their way up to the edge of the tall weeds, rocks, and scrubby bushes. No more than thirty feet of open yard now separated them from the doorway through which the outlaws would soon come.

Crawford, with whispers and gestures, placed his men at short intervals. Aaron was at the extreme left, then Arlie Davis, and Crawford. Next in the line was Oran Bishop, flanked by Jordan. Gates was at the right end.

"I'll give the word," Crawford said, hunkering on his heels. "Everybody wait for it."

"I'm wonderin'," Gates murmured, "is there a back door?"

Crawford glanced at Ben. "How about it?"

Jordan shook his head, saying: "Only a small window. Could be a door around the side."

"Take a look," Crawford ordered, ducking his head at Gates. "See where they got their horses, too."

Gates made no answer but, on hands and knees, crawled off through the brush. He was back in only a few minutes.

"Ain't no door," he said in a hushed voice. "Just this one here in front. Three horses standin' in a corral behind the shack."

"Supposed to be four," Arlie Davis said.

"The woman walked here from her place," Ben said. "I followed her. She and Sharpe figure to ride double until they get a mount for her."

"Somebody's comin' out," Gates warned softly.

The door opened wide. Tubo Frick blocked the doorway. He glanced at the sky, judging the hour.

Crawford muttered: "Frick . . . that lousy tinhorn."

Jordan looked at the lawman. "Know him?"

Crawford nodded. "A long time. Probably know the others, too. Same as I knew Woodward."

Frick turned about, went into the cabin, and

closed the door. The low rumble of words coming from the dark interior of the shack ceased.

Ben felt Bishop's eyes upon him, twisted about to face the cowpuncher. "You convinced now I'm telling the truth? This proof enough?"

Bishop shrugged. "Could be you figure you've got yourself in a jam. This would be a smart way out."

Impatience sharpened Jordan's words. "You don't make much sense. What would I get out of it? The bank will have its money back and I'll . . ."

"You'll save your own neck."

Jordan spat in disgust. "You're a plain fool, Oran. I wondered why Tom Ashburn didn't turn that job of ramrodding over to you. Now I know."

"Damn' good thing for you I didn't find those saddlebags that night," Bishop retorted. "I'd have had you dead to rights then . . . could have proved to Ashburn what I suspected."

"Or would you have grabbed them and run?" Ben suggested softly, deliberately baiting the man.

"Run . . . with the money? Why, damn you, I . . ."

"Forget it," Bart Crawford snapped. "You talk much louder and they'll be hearing you."

There was silence after that, broken only by the dry clack of insects, the chirping of birds in the trees, and the low cooing of doves. Over in the direction of Langford a dog was barking, and somewhere on a road to the north of the settlement the drum of a hard-running horse could be heard.

The minutes wore on, merged into an hour. As the sun lowered, tension mounted gradually within Ben Jordan. He could see the effects of the long wait putting its mark on Oran Bishop, also. But if it were being noted and felt by Crawford and his three men, there was no indication. They were old hands at it, he guessed. Likely this was far from the first such experience for them. And it was not too different from certain days and nights in the Barranca Negra. There had been times when he, with his father and a few friends, had lain in wait for an expected raid by Mexican bandits. And later, after the death of his father, he had faced such danger without the reassuring presence of his parent. But somehow it was different here. There were only strangers around him, men he did not know and therefore was unaware of their abilities—and reliability, if something went wrong. He wished now he could have some of those who had sided with him during the black nights he had sweated out in the Sonora desert: Felipe Alvarez—Jésus Calderon—Old Manuel—Cristobal Lopez, Mexicans all, he realized suddenly, yet he would have felt more at ease with them than the *gringos*—these men of his own race, crouched near him. But there should be no trouble here. They were six to Sharpe's three, if you didn't count Olivia Woodward. Sharpe would recognize the futility of bucking such odds, and when called upon to throw down his guns, he would be smart enough to comply. And Frick and Rosen would follow his lead.

"Sun's gone," Cleve Aaron said laconically. "They ought to be comin' out."

Crawford said: "Be ready. Have your guns out. You know what to do when I give the word."

"We're just waitin'," Aaron replied.

Ben Jordan fastened his eyes upon the closed door. He wished the outlaws would appear, surrender, and get the affair over with. He was beginning to feel the effect of the long hours, and the urge to get back to the Lazy A and assume his responsibilities was pushing him hard. There would be no trouble explaining it all to Tom Ashburn now. The rancher would listen, but if there were any doubts in his mind, Bart Crawford could clear them up. And that was the way Ben wanted it. No doubts, no shadows. Tom Ashburn, and Sally, must believe in him and trust him, or else there was no future for him on the Lazy A. And they would, he was certain. Only Oran Bishop with his pig-headed stubbornness, might continue to doubt. While it meant little to him, he wished the blond cowpuncher would see matters in their true light, and admit he was wrong. Oran was a man he'd like to call friend.

"Here they come."

Gates's whisper was like a keen-bladed knife slicing through the half darkness. Ben stiffened as tension gripped him. There was a slight rustling

293

sound as the men beside him prepared themselves.

"When I say the word . . . ," Crawford murmured. "Not before."

Olivia Woodward came through the doorway, paused, glanced back into the cabin momentarily, and stepped out into the yard. She turned left, walked slowly toward the far side of the cabin. Frick appeared next. Then Barney Rosen, carrying the nearly empty whiskey bottle by the neck. Both halted in front of the step. Al Sharpe loomed in the doorway. He swung the saddlebags over his shoulder and came on into the open. For a moment the three outlaws made a tight little group against the black rectangle of the cabin door.

Sharpe said—"Let's get moving."—and started to follow Olivia Woodward.

In the next fragment of time Bart Crawford rose to his feet. He said—"Now."—and instantly four guns opened up on the outlaws.

Sharpe, Frick, and Rosen slammed back against the wall, dead from the hail of bullets. Through the boiling smoke and deafening echoes, Olivia Woodward began to scream, a wild, piercing, unnerving sound that sliced to the bone. Ben Jordan stood in horrified silence. Bishop, his mouth gaping, turned to Crawford slowly.

"My God . . . that was pure murder!" he said in a strangled voice. "You never gave them a chance to . . ."

Crawford, calmly reloading his revolver, said: "Didn't plan on it." He glanced at Gates. "Shut that woman up."

Gates brought his gun up, leveled it.

Crawford said: "Not that way. Rap her over the head. That ought to do it."

Arlie Davis and Cleve Aaron moved out of the brush, followed Gates. Olivia Woodward's screams faded before the men reached her. She pulled back against the side of the cabin, her eyes wide with terror as she stared down at the bullet-riddled figures of the slain outlaws.

Jordan brushed aside the revolting sickness that had claimed him suddenly when hard suspicion had sprung to life. He took a half step toward Crawford. He watched the emotionless features of the man for several moments, and then he spoke.

"You're no different from them. You're killers, outlaws. You're not lawmen."

Crawford finished reloading his weapon and brought it up abruptly, covering both Jordan and Bishop.

"You're smart, mister," he said dryly. "Now drop your irons, right where you're standing. Both of you. Then get over alongside the woman until I figure out what I ought to do."

XVIII

Oran Bishop's question was a gasp. "You . . . you're not lawmen?"

"Hell, no," Crawford said. "No more'n them three layin' there on the ground."

"But you said . . . you told us . . ."

Crawford laughed. "You think of a better way to go chasing after a lot of stolen money? It's real easy, long as you ain't around where folks know you." He motioned toward the shack with his gun. "Move."

Jordan gave Bishop a bitter half smile. The blond cowpuncher knew now how simple it was to get fooled. When a man told you he was a lawman and exhibited some simple proof, such as a badge, it never occurred to you to question him. With Bishop, he walked out of the brush, crossed the small yard, and lined up beside Olivia Woodward. Gates was hunched over Sharpe, pulling the saddlebags from beneath the dead outlaw's body. Davis and Cleve Aaron watched closely. Gates laid the pouches across Barney Rosen's back and freed the straps from their buckles.

"It's here," he announced, thrusting his fingers inside and stirring about in the coins and currency.

Crawford said: "Finally run it down. But we got

to be thinking about drifting. That shooting's going to bring half the town out here."

Olivia Woodward, a forced smile on her face, moved toward Crawford. "How about me?" she asked. "Where do I come in? It was my husband who robbed that bank. I'm entitled to a share."

"Like hell," Crawford grunted. "It was him that botched the deal up for us . . . him and them three owlhoots there with him. We were all set to clean out that bank ourselves. They beat us to it by about thirty minutes and got away with a stinking twenty thousand dollars. There was three times that much to be had. Woodward and his bunch didn't know that."

Olivia smiled wider. "Still a lot of money. Either you ought to give me a share, or else . . ."

"Or else what?" Crawford demanded.

Olivia Woodward tilted her head coyly. "Or else take me along with you. I can help you enjoy it."

Arlie Davis said, quick and sudden: "No, sir. We don't want no woman hanging around."

Crawford appraised the woman slowly. He grunted. "I expect you could keep a man mighty busy, sure enough. And spend his money real fast, too, was you given the chance."

"Then you'll take me?"

Crawford shook his head. "Arlie's right. We got no room for a woman tagging along. And there ain't much cash to split anyway."

"What are we doin' with these two jaspers?"

Cleve Aaron asked, coming into the conversation. "Not smart to leave them breathin' so's they can talk."

"We won't," Crawford said. "We're goin' to make it look like a shoot-out between them and the others. But we got to move fast."

Olivia flung a quick glance at Jordan and Bishop. She edged nearer to Crawford. "You're not treating me right," she said protestingly—and threw herself directly into the outlaw leader's arms.

Crawford cursed, tried to step back, stumbled into Gates. In that moment Ben Jordan and Bishop, gambling everything against certain death, lunged forward. Arlie Davis fired as Jordan swept Sharpe's left-hand pistol from its holster. Ben felt the outlaw's bullet burn along his neck. He triggered his weapon as he sprawled flat. Davis jolted as Jordan's slug caught him in the chest, drove him backward. Another gun blasted. Ben heard someone yell—Aaron he thought it was, but he did not turn to look, instead simply rolled. From the tail of his eye he saw Olivia Woodward still clinging to Bart Crawford. The outlaw was staggering about, struggling desperately to dislodge her. Ben saw Gates then, whirling to shoot. He dropped the man with a hasty shot.

Beyond him Oran Bishop was pulling himself to his feet. Blood was streaming down one arm that hung limply at his side. But the blond cowpuncher was grinning, a tight-lipped, hard-cornered grin. Cleve Aaron lay motionlessly beneath him.

Jordan rolled to an upright position, leaped to where Olivia Woodward wrestled with Crawford. He seized the man's hand, wrenched the pistol from his grasp. The woman released her death-like grip and sank to the ground, exhausted and breathless.

Crawford stared down at her, his dark face furious, eyes burning. "A damned woman," he muttered. "Tricked by a damned woman."

Jordan rubbed at the stinging groove along his neck. "You can think about that while they're hanging you for murder," he said. He glanced at Bishop. "Hit bad?"

Oran shook his head. "Not much more than a scratch. You all right?"

"All I did get was a scratch. How about Aaron? He dead?"

"Knocked out. Couldn't get my hands on a gun. Had to use my fist."

"That's two left for the law then," Ben said, adding, "the *real* law this time."

He reached down for Olivia Woodward's hand, helped her rise. She was breathing more normally now, and woman-like she began to pin up her hair, shaken loose by Crawford's frantic attempts to break away from her.

"No need for you to wait here," he said. "Take my horse . . . your husband's . . . and go back to your house before anybody gets here. The town won't ever know you had any part of this."

Ben glanced at Bishop, standing with a gun pressed into Crawford's back. The blond cowpuncher nodded his approval.

Olivia Woodward gave him a grateful smile. "Thank you," she murmured.

"We sure owe you that much," Bishop said.

Off, somewhere along the lane, the beat of oncoming horses sounded.

"You'd better hurry," Jordan said. "You'll find that sorrel over there in the brush. Keep off the road. You won't be noticed."

She nodded, ran across the yard. At the fringe of the brush she paused, looked back. "He's still your horse," she said. "When you get ready to leave, he'll be waiting for you . . . with a bill of sale."

She was gone in the next moment, out of sight in the weeds and brush. Jordan turned and pulled off his belt. Jerking Crawford about, he strapped the outlaw's wrists together. With Bishop helping, they did the same for Cleve Aaron, using a strip of rawhide they found on Barney Rosen's body. They put both men inside the cabin and waited outside the doorway for the riders they could hear coming.

Bishop stuck out his hand. "Reckon I sure made a real prime jackass out of myself," he said. "That Crawford sure fooled me."

"We both weren't very bright," Ben agreed.

Bishop was quiet. Inside the shack Crawford was cursing in a low, furious tone. Aaron, conscious and sitting up, was looking around in a dazed, puzzled way.

Oran Bishop studied the toes of his boots. "I know I don't have much right to say this, but I hope what you said about me staying on the ranch still goes."

Jordan shrugged. "All right with me. Up to you to square yourself with Tom Ashburn, though."

"Won't be no chore. Crawford took him in, same as he did me. But I figure I'd better warn you. I still think I'm the best man for that ramrod job and I aim to keep on working for it. If you don't favor that, you'd better fire me now."

"I'm not afraid of holding it."

"Good enough. Just so you know. And there's one thing more . . . Sally."

"What about Sally?"

"I figure to keep trying there, too."

Jordan grinned. "You just do that, cowboy. She'll pick the best man . . . just like her pa did."

About the Author

Ray Hogan was an author who inspired a loyal following over the years since he published his first Western novel, *Ex-Marshal*, in 1956. Hogan was born in Willow Springs, Missouri, where his father was town marshal. At five the Hogan family moved to Albuquerque where they lived in the foothills of the Sandia and Manzano Mountains. His father was on the Albuquerque police force and, in later years, owned the Overland Hotel. It was while listening to his father and other old-timers tell tales from the past that Ray was inspired to recast these tales in fiction. From the beginning he did exhaustive research into the history and the people of the Old West, and the walls of his study were lined with various firearms, spurs, pictures, books, and memorabilia, about all of which he could talk in dramatic detail. "I've attempted to capture the courage and bravery of those men and women that lived out West and the dangers and problems they had to overcome," Hogan once remarked. If his lawmen protagonists seem sometimes larger than life, it is because they are men of integrity, heroes who through grit of character and common sense are able to overcome the obstacles they encounter despite often over-whelming odds. This same grit of character can also be found in Hogan's heroines, and in *The Vengeance of Fortuna West* (1983) Hogan wrote a gripping and totally believable account of a woman who takes up the badge and tracks the men who killed her lawman husband by ambush. No less intriguing in her way is Nellie Dupray, convicted of rustling in *The Glory Trail* (1978). One of his most popular books, dealing with an earlier period in the West with Kit Carson as its protagonist, is *Soldier in Buckskin* (1996). Above all, what is most impressive about Hogan's Western novels is the consistent quality with which each is crafted, the compelling depth of his characters, and his ability to juxtapose the complexities of human conflict into narratives always as intensely interesting as they are emotionally involving.

Center Point Large Print
600 Brooks Road / PO Box 1
Thorndike, ME 04986-0001 USA

(207) 568-3717

US & Canada:
1 800 929-9108
www.centerpointlargeprint.com